GILT TRIP

A SCRAPBOOKING MYSTERY

GILT TRIP

LAURA CHILDS
WITH DIANA ORGAIN

KENNEBEC LARGE PRINT
A part of Gale, Cengage Learning

GALE
CENGAGE Learning·

Farmington Hills, Mich • San Francisco • New York • Waterville, Maine
Meriden, Conn • Mason, Ohio • Chicago

GALE
CENGAGE Learning·

LIBRARY OF CONGRESS CATALOGING-IN-PUBLICATION DATA

Names: Childs, Laura, author. | Orgain, Diana, author.
Title: Gilt trip / by Laura Childs with Diana Orgain.
Description: Large print edition. | Waterville, Maine : Kennebec Large Print, 2017.
| Series: Kennebec Large Print superior collection | Series: A scrapbooking mystery
Identifiers: LCCN 2016046965| ISBN 9781410496751 (softcover) | ISBN 1410496759 (softcover)
Subjects: LCSH: Women detectives—Fiction. | Murder—Investigation—Fiction. | Large type books. | GSAFD: Mystery fiction.
Classification: LCC PS3603.H56 G55 2017 | DDC 813/.6—dc23
LC record available at https://lccn.loc.gov/2016046965

Published in 2017 by arrangement with The Berkley Publishing Group, an imprint of Penguin Publishing Group, a division of Penguin Random House LLC

Printed in the United States of America
1 2 3 4 5 6 7 21 20 19 18 17

ACKNOWLEDGMENTS

Many thanks to Tom, Diana, Sam, Jennie, Bob, and Dan, as well as all my amazing readers, scrapbooking friends, bloggers, mystery reviewers, scrapbook magazine editors and writers, scrapbook store owners, librarians, and bookshop owners. Thanks for enjoying (and recommending!) the crazy, creative rampages of Carmela and Ava, and please know that there are many more books to come!

CHAPTER 1

It was your typical New Orleans Garden District party. Wealthy, careless men sloshing down too much bourbon, tucked and lifted socialites flaunting their latest fashions, and twenty-something women looking sleek as alley cats as they prowled for rich husbands. And every dang one of them on their best baddest behavior as they shrieked, shimmied, danced, and drank while the Bayou Breezers cranked out a string of raucous zydeco tunes.

"And then there's us," said Carmela Bertrand. She gave a rueful smile as butlers in white tie and tails glided through the crowd serving tiny canapés of duck liver, baked oysters, and beluga caviar.

"Nothing wrong with sniffing the rarified air and seeing how the other half lives," said her friend Ava Gruiex.

"I'd say it's all very posh and predictable," said Carmela. Her tone was flat but her blue eyes danced with mirth as she ruffled a hand through short, choppy blond hair that was, as Ava so delightfully phrased it, chunked and skunked. Blessed with a radiant complexion and relatively calm demeanor (by New Orleans standards, that is), Carmela also possessed a nimble mind and burning curiosity. Which, on more than one occasion, had sent her rushing in where proverbial angels feared to tread.

"Watch this," said Ava, grabbing a champagne glass and tipping it toward an enormous ice sculpture. "Tell me this isn't cool."

A slosh of excellent French champagne gushed down a steep tunnel of ice, foamed slightly as it navigated a quick series of S-turns, and emptied into Ava's crystal flute with a satisfying fizz.

"Isn't that too much!" exclaimed Ava.

"Service with a flourish," said the smiling bartender.

Carmela decided maybe she needed a hit of bubbly, too. "What do you call this ice carving thing?"

"A champagne luge," said the waiter. "Guaranteed to deliver a super-chilled serving of champagne."

Ava, who was Carmela's BFF, shopping cohort, and French Quarter neighbor, gave Carmela a nudge. "C'mon, you do it." She

8

smiled coyly at the bartender. "Ready, baby?"

Nodding, the bartender hefted a magnum of champagne, poured a judicious serving into the delicately carved ice slot at the top of the sculpture, then stood back and smiled.

"Isn't that the coolest dang thing you've ever laid eyes on?" said Ava as she watched the froth of champagne wend its circuitous route to Carmela's glass. The ice luge, carved from a solid block of ice, was almost five feet high and featured, besides the zigzagging slide, a carved Chinese dragon inset with gold coins.

"Only the best for Margo," said Carmela.

"And Jerry Earl," said Ava. She pushed a mass of dark curly hair off her check, angled out one curvaceous hip, and struck a red carpet–worthy pose. "This is some super welcome home party for him."

Margo's husband, Jerry Earl Leland, had just been released from the Dixon Correctional Institute, and Margo was throwing what she called a Get Out of Jail Free Party.

"Jerry Earl's a lucky man," said Carmela. And she meant that in more ways than one. He'd been Margo's ex-husband, then the two had remarried in a red-hot flurry right before Jerry Earl had been carted off to the

9

slammer. And now he'd been released from prison early.

"Champagne, caviar, and a spattering of eligible men," said Ava, glancing about with predatory eyes. "How'd we manage to get invited to this fancy soiree?"

"We're here mostly out of politeness," said Carmela. "I got roped into designing the invitations, and Margo went bonkers when she saw what I came up with. Told me I just had to attend. A *command performance* was how she phrased it." Carmela's scrapbooking shop, Memory Mine, carried all the latest papers and albums and was the go-to spot for having cards, announcements, and invitations designed. Besides being the French Quarter's resident scrapbook maven, Carmela was also a skilled graphic artist.

"I gotta say," said Ava, helping herself to a toast point loaded with glistening caviar, "the lady has style. As well as a pot full of money. I mean, did you get a gander at that gilded fireplace? And all that fancy artwork? And the silk upholstery on her cabriolet sofa? The word *opulent* does come to mind."

Carmela nodded in agreement. Margo's house was a bold statement in conspicuous consumption. But truth be told, she wasn't all that impressed. It hadn't been too many years since she'd resided in this part of town herself. In a white elephant of a house that was currently on the market for two point three million. Of course, her tenure in the Garden District stretched back to the bad old days when she'd been married to Shamus Allan Meechum, heretofore known as The Rat. Shamus, who possessed silky charm, a dazzling smile, and a wandering eye, hailed from the same rich-as-Croesus, crazy-ass family as the Crescent City Bank Meechums. Thus, he'd always felt above it all and not bound by ordinary convention.

Carmela nudged Ava. "There's Margo now."

Margo Leland looked like she'd been hung by her heels and dipped in gold. Her dress was an explosion of gold sequins, her fingernails shimmered, her cantilevered beehive hairdo was spackled with threads of pink and gold, and the chains that clanked around her neck and chubby wrists were real deal twenty-four-karat gold. Though pushing sixty, she still dressed like she was trotting off to Studio 54.

"Holy Coupe deVille," Ava whispered. "Margo's a walking Fort Knox."

Margo immediately noticed them noticing. A wide grin split her flushed face, her eyes lit up, and she immediately tottered over on sky-high gold silk heels to greet them.

"Carmela!" Margo cried exuberantly, throwing her arms wide and losing half of her drink in the process. "You came! *Vous êtes arrivé!*"

"How could we not?" said Carmela. She tried to ratchet up her enthusiasm, feeling a little fake and knowing in her heart that she'd rather be cozied up in her garden apartment, wearing jammies and reading a good mystery. Spending time with her two dogs, Boo and Poobah. She sighed. "And you remember Ava."

"Eva!" Margo shrilled. "You gorgeous thing, you!" Then she turned to Carmela and slurred, "Oh, to be thirty again."

"Twenty-nine," said Ava somewhat crisply.

"And so pretty and model thin," Margo enthused.

"And look at you," Ava drawled back, ever the good sport. "All drippy in gems and jewelry."

Margo wiggled her ample hips, giddy that they'd noticed. Then she fingered a chunky necklace that encircled her neck. "Vintage," she chirped. "Twenty-five carats of Sri Lankan amethyst set in pure gold. Designed and signed by Louis Comfort Tiffany himself."

Carmela, whose jewelry consisted of a gold bangle and small diamond stud earrings, smiled politely. She didn't much care that Margo had decked herself out in the crown jewels. But she was starting to sincerely regret that she and Ava had dropped by this lavish party. It was all a trifle too ostentatious, the gaiety a little too . . . forced.

But the second act was yet to come.

Margo snatched a glass of champagne from a passing waiter's tray and said in a conspiratorial whisper, "I'm going to offer a congratulatory toast to Jerry Earl."

"I guess it isn't every day your hubby gets sprung from the joint," said Ava.

Carmela had to stifle a giggle. Ava didn't have much of a filter.

But Margo wasn't one bit bothered. "Thank *heavens* we were able to apply some judicious pressure to the judicial system," she said, giving an elaborate wink-wink. "And it certainly helps to know the right people."

"I'll bet," said Carmela. While her roots were English, Cajun, and a smattering of French, Margo Leland could trace her ancestry all the way back to the Vicomte François Pierre-Marie. That distant nobleman had fled France for New Orleans in eighteen-fifteen following the exile of Napoleon, and had spawned an entire lineage of prominent New Orleanians. Which Margo never let anyone forget.

Margo took a quick slug of champagne and said, "Time to kick this party into high gear!" She grabbed Carmela's wrist and pulled her over to the band. Standing on tiptoe, she waved airily to the group's front man, a bearded and mulleted redhead. The musicians immediately ceased playing and a microphone was passed to Margo.

There was a momentary high-pitched squeal as Margo shouted out, "Everyone! Everyone! I want to thank you *so* much for coming tonight to celebrate what is truly the most splendid day of my life. And now, I'd like you all to join me in a toast. A toast to the man who puffs me with pride, the husband who still curls my toes!" She hoisted her champagne glass high in the air and paused dramatically. "To Jerry Earl!"

Jerry Earl Leland, who Carmela thought had the rather unfortunate countenance of a Galapagos turtle, was ensconced in a Louis XVI chair and deep in conversation with local businessman Buddy Pelletier. He barely looked up during Margo's heartfelt tribute. And when he finally did, aimed a perfunctory, knowing nod in the direction of the revelers. Then Jerry Earl turned back to resume his conversation.

Fueled by too much champagne, bourbon, and rich food, the tony crowd didn't seem to mind his dismissiveness. "To Jerry Earl!" they roared. Glasses clinked and laughter echoed as one hundred of New Orleans's most prominent socialites poured even more liquor down their gullets.

"You'd think Jerry Earl would be a bit more humbled," observed Ava. "On account of his being incarcerated and all."

"Doubtful," said Carmela. She didn't believe that Jerry Earl was one bit concerned, embarrassed, or mollified. She had no doubt that he'd be back doing whatever he'd been sent to prison for in less than forty-eight hours.

As if reading her mind, Ava asked, "What was he in prison for?"

"That would be your white-collar crime," said Carmela.

Ava cocked her head. "Which means . . ."

"Basically something fraudulent," said Carmela. She wasn't sure if Jerry Earl had engineered a phony land deal or cooked the books on a mythical corporation. And she didn't really want to know, since it was a moot point. Jerry Earl was a free man now and back in business, even though his dealings were probably nefarious.

"And Jerry Earl only did eighteen months?" Surprise colored Ava's voice.

"On a five-year sentence," said Carmela.

"Wow. I guess he got serious time off for good behavior."

"Most likely it was time off because someone was paid off."

"Ohhhh," said Ava, her eyes going wide. "Now I understand. We're talking good old-fashioned Louisiana law, politics, and cronyism."

"Which are all pretty much one and the same," said Carmela. She paused for a few moments and decided the air had gone out of the evening for her. "You know what? It's probably time to go."

"*Go?*" said Ava. "I thought we were just getting warmed up." She swiped a hand across her tummy. "Besides, I'm starving. And I happen to know there's an enormous dessert buffet set up in the solarium. Wouldn't you like a hit of sugar to get your heart a-pumping? Maybe a slice of bread pudding soaked in brandy and dripping with ooey-gooey caramel sauce?"

"Ten more minutes," said Carmela. "Then we call it a night, okay?"

"Got it," said Ava. "Besides, there are some good-looking guys here that I'd like

16

to say how-do to. Beats scouting for a date on craigslist."

"Ten minutes," said Carmela as they pushed through the crowd.

Like everything else in Margo's home, the dessert bar was over the top. Silver chafing dishes overflowed with bananas Foster, bread pudding, and cherries jubilee. There were plates of killer brownies, carrot cake, and pecan pie. Pastel-colored French macaroons were stacked like poker chips.

Carmela and Ava piled up their plates, hooked up with a couple of people they knew, then strolled out to the back patio and sat down. It was a balmy April evening with a light wind that made the humidity more than tolerable. Intoxicating jasmine blossoms and bougainvillea perfumed the air, and a giant green-winged luna moth fluttered leisurely through the dusk.

Just as Ava held a spoonful of cherries jubilee to her mouth, it dribbled down onto her silk blouse. "Oh no!" she cried, making a motion to jump up.

Carmela held out a hand. "No, stay put. If you stand up, it'll only blob down and make things worse. I'll run get a towel or something." She hurried inside and tiptoed down a back hallway, figuring it would lead to a butler's pantry or the kitchen. When she saw a waiter bustling toward her, she made a small helpless gesture and said, "We've had a spill. Is there soda water? A towel?" But the waiter merely hooked a finger over his shoulder and continued on his way.

"Huh," said Carmela, slightly miffed. "I guess I'll have to find it myself."

But the first door she opened led to an office. Carmela poked her head in and glanced around. A cypress-paneled wall held dozens of oil paintings and awards in ornate frames. Another wall was covered in floor-to-ceiling bookshelves and crammed with shimmering geodes, fossils, gold coins set in black velvet, what looked like an Egyptian gold necklace, and glass tubes filled with gold nuggets. An enormous desk sat smack dab in the center of a black-and-persimmon-colored silk Aubusson carpet.

Jerry Earl's office, Carmela decided. She'd stumbled upon it from the back entrance, the servants' entrance.

Curiosity suddenly amped, Carmela took a step in and decided it was quite an amazing place. What had to be a mastodon tusk was mounted on a base of white marble. A large gold mask on a black metal stand, a gold skull of some primitive catlike creature, and sparkling gold coins were displayed on

18

Jerry Earl's desk, making it look for all the world like the office of some museum curator.

Amazing, Carmela thought to herself. An incredible collection of fossils and gold antiquities. Just as she was about to turn and leave, a slight breeze fluttered the curtains.

Carmela hesitated. *Someone there?*

A noise sounded just beyond the green velvet curtains. A kind of scrape, like boot heels on cement. Then a dull clunk, like something metallic.

Was someone outside? Peeking in at her? Or doing . . . what? Had someone been attracted by all this loot?

"Hello?" she called out. "Jerry Earl? Is that you?"

There was nothing save a warm breeze stirring the curtains.

Realizing she shouldn't be in here, feeling guilty and a little discombobulated, Carmela ducked back out and pulled the door closed behind her. She paused for a moment, then took another few steps down the hallway. Placing her hand on a second doorknob, she was about to pull it open when she heard a muffled thump on the other side of the door.

Oh no, what now?

19

A woman's voice, low and urgent, murmured, "Just one more, please? Just one eensy little line?"

A man's voice, husky and slightly taunting, said, "You sure about that, baby?"

Oh great. Carmela moved away quickly. She had a pretty good idea what the woman was asking for. She also had a fairly good idea what her boyfriend, Edgar Babcock, would say about that. And just to be clear, he was *Detective* Edgar Babcock of the New Orleans Police Department. Her own personal Dudley Do-Right snuggle bunny.

"He'd tell me to hustle my sweet patootie out of here," Carmela muttered to herself. "Before I got involved in some kind of drug incident."

And just as she was about to do exactly that, she heard another thump. Only this was the telltale thump thump thump of a clothes dryer tossing its contents to and fro.

Breathing a sigh of relief, for her errand had somehow turned into a mission, Carmela hurried to the end of the hallway and pushed open a louvered door.

A sizzle of bright fluorescents revealed a tidy, compact laundry room. It was warm, steamy, and noisy, as laundry rooms generally are when there's a load in the washer and one in the dryer.

Probably a bunch of bar towels, Carmela surmised. Or the caterer had thrown in a load of dish towels. But that wasn't quite right, was it? Because the top-loading washing machine was standing open and silent. Casting a quick glance at the loudly thumping dryer, Carmela casually wondered what they'd tossed in that was making such an awful racket.

Her eyes had almost pulled away, ready to grab a clean white towel, when she saw what looked like a leather shoe momentarily flash past the dryer's window.

What. On. Earth? Who would toss shoes in a dryer?

Feeling slightly apprehensive, Carmela took two robotic steps forward. And then, like a warning shot fired across the bow of a ship, something deep in the limbic portion of her brain spit out a cautionary note.

Something's wrong here. Something's really wrong.

Don't be silly, she told herself. *There's nothing to be nervous about.*

Except . . . there was that shoe.

Carmela's nose tickled. Her temples throbbed. She was suddenly aware that the air around her was redolent with a strange scent. A sweet, sickening, unnerving scent that was definitely not Downy or Febreze.

Mesmerized, moving as if she were in a trance, Carmela stepped forward, curled her fingers around the handle of the dryer, and yanked open the door.

As the dryer groaned to a sudden halt, Carmela jumped back just in time to see a limp hand flop out. And then watched in horror as the bloody, battered body of Jerry Earl Leland spilled out onto the white-tiled floor.

CHAPTER 2

Horrified and in shock, Carmela inanely spun around the room searching high and low for another witness. On her third, dizzying whirl, the realization finally sank in that she was the only other person in the room. Well, at least the only *living* person.

Swallowing hard, Carmela gaped at the body. Oh dear Lord, could Jerry Earl really have been brutally murdered right in the middle of his own lavish welcome home party? Was that really his limp body sprawled at her feet? Was that the metallic scent of fresh blood stinging her nose?

The angry buzz of fluorescent lights rang in Carmela's ears like a plague of cicadas, and she suddenly found it difficult to breathe in the steamy, claustrophobic room. She spun on her heels, pushed hard on the louvered door, and raced back down the narrow hallway, greedily swallowing great gulps of fresh air and fighting the awful tide

of bile that rose in her throat. Because . . .
I have to get help!

The narrow hallway was eerily deserted now and deathly quiet. No waiters, no caterers, no snuggly couple in the powder room. Then finally, gratefully, Carmela burst out onto the patio, where she'd been sitting just a few minutes earlier.

Ava stood alone in the moonlight, nursing her drink. When she saw Carmela, she raised one shoulder in a casual shrug and said, "Apparently, my witty repartee is no match for the lure of a champagne luge. They've all toddled off for a refill." Then she stared at Carmela, did a double take, and said, "What is it, *cher*? You're shaking like a leaf and . . . good heavens . . . white as a sheet!"

"Jerry Earl is dead!" Carmela blurted out. "Murdered, I think. I went into the laundry room and he . . ." Her right hand made an erratic circling motion. "His body just tumbled out of the clothes dryer!"

Ava's eyes went wide as saucers. She clasped a hand over her mouth, but a soft gasp still escaped. Then she frowned, shook her head, and said in a hoarse voice, "He tumbled out of the *dryer*?"

"Excuse me," said a clipped male voice from directly behind Carmela. "You say

24

there's a problem with the dryer?"

Carmela spun around to face Eric Zane, Jerry Earl's personal assistant, who'd been pointed out to her earlier that night. Zane was a tall, reed-thin fellow of about thirty, with a pale oval face and a proper, almost brittle, manner.

"I've ordered the staff to keep up with the linens," said Zane, radiating a cool annoyance.

"It's not the linens," Carmela rasped out. "It's Jerry Earl. You've got to call the police!"

"Carmela thinks he's been murdered!" Ava added helpfully.

Looking as if he'd just been socked in the gut, Zane took a step backward. "What?" he said in an incredulous tone. "What did you say?"

"Murdered!" said Carmela. "In the laundry room!"

"That can't be!" Zane cried. He seemed to have trouble processing the information. "I just spoke to him." He glanced at his wristwatch, which hung upside down on his narrow wrist. With a trembling hand, he flipped the gold watch over and stared at the face. "Maybe ten minutes ago."

"That was then and this is now," said Carmela. "And now he's lying dead on your

25

laundry room floor!"

Ten minutes later, the party officially over, the guests officially stunned by the grisly news, Detective Bobby Gallant and his team showed up to take charge of the scene.

First order of business was to round up all the guests and keep them in the living room in a kind of holding pattern. The bar was shut down and the musicians silenced as the guests cast worried glances at one another and muttered quietly among themselves.

Margo Leland, who'd practically swooned at the awful news, had forced her way into the laundry room to view Jerry Earl's body for herself. Now, after having a full court press meltdown, she was huddled in her dead husband's office, bleating out a series of heart-wrenching sobs and weeping onto the shoulder of her dear friend Beetsie Bischof.

Carmela and Ava were huddled at the end of the hallway, watching Bobby Gallant bark orders to his fellow officers and crime-scene team.

"Thank goodness Bobby got the call-out," Carmela said to Ava. Bobby Gallant worked as an assistant to her sweetie, Edgar Babcock, who was in Washington DC attending a forensics conference.

"Bobby's a smart guy," agreed Ava. "He'll figure this out."

"Hopefully," said Carmela. She knew he was an experienced homicide detective but she still missed having Babcock's calming presence.

"The guest list!" Gallant shouted to a uniformed officer. "See if there's a guest list! And be sure to ask that personal assistant guy if he thinks there are any valuables missing!"

"Who do you think . . ." Ava said in a dry whisper.

"Is the killer?" said Carmela. She shook her head. "Don't know. I suppose it could be anyone."

"Someone who's still here?" said Ava.

"I guess so. I don't think anyone's left the premises yet." Zane had phoned the police immediately, put the party in lock-down mode, and jumped all over rumor control. So none of the guests had known there'd been a murder until the police arrived. At least that was the theory.

"So the killer's still here?" said Ava, letting loose a small shudder.

"Unless somebody ducked across the patio while I was inside?"

Ava shook her head. "I don't think anyone

did. It was all pretty quiet. I was enjoying my champagne and cherries jubilee . . ." She glanced down sadly at her silk blouse, where the stain had deepened and set.

Carmela bit her lip. "We can get that out later. If not, we'll spill a little more sauce and make a nice pattern."

Ava tried to laugh but it came out as more of a nervous hiccup.

"Carmela!" called a sharp voice. It was Bobby Gallant, staring down the hallway at her. He was relatively young for a detective, with a full head of dark, curly hair and a smooth olive complexion. Tonight, dressed in a leather bomber jacket and khaki slacks, he looked cool, unflappable, and really quite adorable.

"Detective Gallant," Carmela responded.

"You shouldn't be back here," he told her. He looked at one of the uniformed officers and asked, "Why is she here?" But the uniformed officer just shifted nervously.

"But I was the one who . . ." Carmela began. She was shocked by the murder, but certainly intrigued, too. Who would murder a man who'd just been released from prison? And in his own house!

"I know, I know," said Gallant. "Still . . ." He hooked a thumb and jabbed it in the air, indicating for them to both move away.

"Come on, *cher,*" said Ava. "Let's go wait in that big office."

They trooped past Gallant, trying to peer into the laundry room as they did, but he carefully blocked their view with his shoulders. "I'll talk to you two later," he told them.

Margo Leland turned her tearstained face toward Carmela and said, "Why? Why?"

Carmela crossed the room quickly, knelt down next to Margo on the whisper-soft Chinese carpet, and said, "I don't know, honey. But I promise you, the police are going to figure all of this out."

Beetsie gazed at Carmela, a look of despair on her narrow face. "You seem like you know some of those officers."

Carmela nodded. "I do. And please believe me when I say that they're really good at what they do. They *will* find out who killed Jerry Earl."

"Just when I finally got him back!" wailed Margo. "My poor sweetie!"

Beetsie patted her friend's shoulder. "I know, dear, I know."

Margo twisted a hanky in her hands. "So . . . Carmela. They tell me that you were the one who . . . found him? In the laundry room?"

Carmela nodded. "I'm afraid so."

"Did you think . . . did it look like he suffered?" Margo asked hopefully.

Carmela thought about all the blood and the horrible bumping around that Jerry Earl's body had sustained, but said without hesitation, "No. I'm pretty sure he didn't suffer."

"That's a huge relief," said Margo.

"A blessing," agreed Beetsie.

A lie, thought Carmela. But certainly one told out of kindness.

Bobby Gallant suddenly pulled open the door and stepped into the room, causing everyone to immediately stop talking and stare at him. He wiggled his fingers at Carmela and Ava and said, "Okay, now we can have our little confab."

Carmela gave Margo's hand a final, reassuring pat, then she and Ava joined Bobby Gallant in the hallway.

Gallant pulled the office door closed behind them and said, "Okay, I want the straight poop."

"Sweet talk will get you everywhere," said Ava, batting her eyelashes. She'd gone from scared to flirtatious in about ten seconds flat. A new land speed record.

"I'm serious," said Gallant. He looked at Carmela with hooded brown eyes and said, "Walk me through it."

So they all went out to the patio and Carmela started from the very beginning.

"We were all right here," said Carmela.

"Who's we?" said Gallant.

Carmela and Ava started to run through their story. And all the while, Carmela kept wishing she'd never gone looking for a towel. Why didn't she carry one of those detergent sticks in her purse? That would have neatly solved the problem of a stain on Ava's blouse. More important, she and Ava could have finished their cherries jubilee and been long gone before Jerry Earl finished the dewrinkle cycle. Instead, she'd encountered a gruesome laundry room scene that was sure to haunt her nightmares forever!

"So then you went inside to get a towel?" Gallant prompted.

"That's right," said Carmela. She had to force herself to focus.

"And you were the only one around?" Gallant asked.

"No," said Carmela. "I saw a waiter in the hallway."

"Do you remember which one?"

"Are they all still here?" she asked.

Gallant nodded.

"If you line 'em up, I'm pretty sure I can point him out." Carmela started to say something else, then hesitated.

"What?" said Gallant. "Spit it out. This is no time to be coy."

"There were also two people in the powder room."

Gallant cocked an inquisitive eye. "How do you know that?"

"Hey," said Ava. "If Carmela says there were two people, then there were two people."

"I'm not questioning her honesty," said Gallant. "I'm just trying to get the story straight." He nodded at Carmela. "Go on."

"I heard voices anyway," said Carmela. "They were sort of giggling and thumping up against the door. I think . . . well, I think they were doing drugs."

"You know that for a fact?"

"Kind of. The woman was asking the man if she could do another line."

"And you think she was referring to a line of cocaine?" asked Gallant.

"I don't think it was a dance line," said Carmela.

Gallant nodded. "Okay. Where did you go from there?"

Carmela crooked a finger, indicating the laundry room. "In there. But I'd rather not go back."

Gallant shook his head. "No, no. We can't

go in right now. The crime-scene guys are still at work."

As if on cue, there was a loud clunk, then a metal gurney poked its nose out of the door. It rammed into the opposite wall, then was pulled back inside again.

"Oh my," said Ava.

There was another clunk and this time the gurney burst through the doorway and halfway out into the hallway. On top of it lay a shiny black body bag that obviously contained the dead body of Jerry Earl Leland.

"Is that him?" asked Ava. "Is that Jerry Earl?" Her tone was hushed but filled with curiosity.

The young man who was pushing the gurney finally muscled it all the way out into the hallway.

"Charlie," said Gallant. "Are you guys about finished in there?"

"I want to run a few more spatter pattern tests," said the young man. He was nerdy looking in a pair of oversize blue scrubs with floppy blond hair and serious-looking horn-rimmed glasses that made him look like a young, learned owl.

"Carmela, Ava," said Gallant. "This is Charlie Preston. He's kind of our crime-scene whiz kid."

"Nice to meet you," said Carmela. "Considering the circumstances."

But Ava was assessing him carefully. "You don't look old enough to run a crime scene," she told him.

Charlie grinned happily. "That's what everybody says."

"That means you must be good," said Ava.

"What was your name again?" asked Charlie, his grin stretching even wider.

"Ava Gruiex," said Ava.

"Is that your married name?" said Charlie.

"I'm not married," said Ava, dimpling prettily.

"Good to know," said Charlie. If he'd been a puppy dog, he'd have wagged his little tail.

"Do either of you know," said Carmela, her eyes now riveted on the body bag, "how Jerry Earl was really killed? I mean, it wasn't just death by clothes dryer, was it?"

"From preliminary examination, it appears he was stabbed," said Gallant.

"You mean with a knife?" said Carmela.

"Nooo," said Charlie, jumping in. "It's actually . . . a little strange. And rather interesting. It appears that the deceased may have been stabbed with a weapon that was long and possibly serrated."

"Like some kind of butcher knife?" said Carmela

"More like a knife used to cut sugarcane or stick hogs," said Charlie.

"Eeyuh!" said Ava. "That sounds awful."

"It does," said Charlie happily. "Of course, that's just a guess on my part. Any final determination will have to be made by the medical examiner."

"Murdering someone with a serrated knife is grisly enough," said Carmela. "So why the *coup de grâce*? If Jerry Earl was already dead, why stuff his body in a clothes dryer?"

Gallant thought for a moment. "Dumped in postmortem, yes. Maybe because the killer wanted to throw us off on time of death?"

"That would do it," agreed Charlie. "That would alter the lividity factor big time."

Carmela's eyes wandered back to the metal gurney that was parked in the hallway. Jerry Earl's body was lying in that black plastic bag, stiffening and getting cooler. "That doesn't seem . . ." she mumbled to herself.

"What?" said Gallant. "Why do you think he was stuffed in the clothes dryer?"

Carmela hesitated for a moment, then gazed directly at Gallant and said with great earnestness: "I think it was done out of hatred. Pure, unabashed hatred."

CHAPTER 3

"Whew," said Ava. "What a night." They were crossing the flagstone courtyard that separated Carmela's garden apartment from Ava's Juju Voodoo shop and her tiny, funky upstairs apartment.

Carmela paused next to a large pot of candy pink bougainvilleas. "Come on over," she said. "I'll make us a cup of tea."

Ava nodded. "I need something to warm me up. I feel out of sorts and chilled to the bone by all of this."

"And you didn't even get to see the grisly part!" Carmela said. She inserted her key into the lock and let them both into her French Quarter apartment.

"I didn't need to," said Ava. "Or want to. Your description alone scared the bejeebers out of me." She was about to say something else when two furry bodies came hurtling toward her.

"Boo, Poobah," Carmela warned. "Be

37

careful of your Aunt Ava."

But Carmela's words fell on deaf doggy ears. Boo, Carmela's wrinkly, fawn-colored Shar-Pei, basically rushed in and knocked Ava for a loop. And Poobah, a spotted mongrel that Carmela's ex-husband had rescued from the streets, had also closed in for the kill. Or in this case, killer kisses.

"Uncle! Uncle!" Ava cried while the dogs pranced, danced, and swirled about her as she tried to hobble her way to the leather chaise. Finally, she flopped down, but not before she was overwhelmed with more kisses and coerced into stroking Boo's tiny triangle ears.

"Are they bothering you?" Carmela called. She was standing in her small galley kitchen, filling a red tea kettle with fresh water.

"I'm okay," said Ava. "I'm just enduring a little canine lovefest."

"Are you hungry?" Carmela asked. "Because if you are, I've got banana nut bars and peanut butter cookies."

"Home baked? By you?"

"Yes, of course," said Carmela. She was pretty good in the cooking department; now she was trying to fine-tune her baking skills.

"Then let's have at 'em. You know I've got a serious sweet tooth issue." Ava picked up the remote control, aimed it at the TV, and snapped it on. "Think there'll be anything on about the murder?"

"I sincerely doubt it," said Carmela. "Jerry Earl's body isn't even cold yet."

"That's never stopped the relentless 24/7 news cycle before," commented Ava.

The tea kettle let loose a piercing shriek, and Carmela measured out tea, then poured hot water into a floral bisque teapot she'd found in one of the scratch-and-dent rooms of the French Quarter antique shops that she liked to haunt. Placing the teapot onto a wicker tray with cups, saucers, and a small plate of cookies and bars, she squeezed past her dining room table and over to Ava. She settled the tray onto her marble coffee table and plunked herself down on her brocade fainting couch.

There, she thought. Better. Better than a champagne luge. More comforting than a room full of crazy people, and infinitely cozier than a mansion in the Garden District. Home was where you could relax, let down your hair, and let down your guard. And feel safe, too.

Ava took a sip of tea. "Mmn, this is tasty. What kind?"

"Chamomile," said Carmela. "I ordered it from the Indigo Tea Shop in Charleston. It's not really caffeinated, so it's supposed to be highly conducive to relaxation and pleasant dreams."

"I always have pleasant dreams," said Ava.

You wouldn't if you saw what I did tonight, Carmela thought to herself. *You'd be tossing and turning and having bad dreams.*

Ava aimed the remote control at the screen and switched over to KBEZ-TV. Instantly, bright blue lights swirled around the station's logo and a graphic that said *NEWS BULLETIN* lit up the screen.

"Uh-oh," said Carmela.

"And you said it was too soon," said Ava. "But look!" A photo of Jerry Earl Leland suddenly appeared in a framed box that was superimposed behind the TV anchorman's head.

"Turn it up," said Carmela. "Let's see how bad it is."

It was bad. Real bad.

"Murder in the Garden District!" proclaimed the anchorman. He had perfectly blow-combed hair, what appeared to be a spray tan, and impossibly white Chiclet teeth.

"What are they sayin'?" asked Ava, leaning forward.

"Details are sketchy so far," intoned the anchorman in a voice that promised to deliver vivid details as soon as they were available. "But what we know for sure is that prominent New Orleans business tycoon Jerry Earl Leland was brutally murdered at his Garden District home earlier this evening. In a strange chain of events, Leland had just been released from Dixon Correctional Institute, where he'd been serving a three-to-five-year prison sentence for fraud. Though police officials were reluctant to comment on the exact details of tonight's violent crime, it has been learned through an unnamed source that a welcome home party had been in progress at the time."

"I wonder who the unnamed source was," said Carmela.

"Not me," said Ava.

The anchorman continued: "Standing by to comment, we have our own Zoe Carmichael talking to Conrad Falcon, the businessman and whistle blower who helped put Leland in prison."

There was a quick shot of a distinguished-looking man with dark eyes and gray hair gazing directly into the camera's lens. "Jerry Earl Leland made a lot of enemies," said Falcon. "It was probably only a matter of time."

"Ouch," said Ava.

The camera pulled back to reveal a two-shot. "So you think it was a kind of justice?" Zoe asked. She was petite and pretty with reddish-blond hair and a cherubic smile.

Falcon drew breath and shook his head. "A very sad justice."

"I understand," said Zoe, "that you had been vehemently opposed to Mr. Leland's early release?"

"Yes, I was," continued Falcon. "I was on the phone with several legislators, cautioning them against his release. In fact, had the justice system not been so severely tampered with and Mr. Leland remained incarcerated, this murder might have easily been averted."

Zoe dimpled prettily and said, "And now back to you, Guy."

"Look at that," said Ava, still studying the screen. "That guy Conrad Falcon was pretending to be all serious and concerned, all on-the-fence politically correct. But you can tell he's really jumping with joy."

Carmela was skeptical. "You think so?"

"Oh yeah. I read this article about body language in *Star Watch* magazine. It said that if somebody looks up to the left when they're talking, it means they're lying. And if they look right, it means they're telling the truth."

"No kidding."

"It was all very scientific," said Ava. "A lot

like astrology or tarot cards."

"Shhh," said Carmela, "I want to hear what else they have to say."

The camera moved in tight on the news anchor and he said, "As our viewers may recall, Leland's construction company, Leland Enterprises, was found guilty of overbilling the federal government for twelve million dollars' worth of highway and bridge work in and around the New Orleans area."

"I guess that explains why Margo's got such fancy jewelry," said Ava. "And why Conrad Falcon wasn't a guest at tonight's party."

"If Falcon had been there," said Carmela, still studying the screen, "he'd probably be the number one suspect."

"But he wasn't there," said Ava. "So it had to be somebody at the party, don't you think?"

"Maybe," said Carmela. She nibbled at one of the cookies.

"The weird thing is, we were all having such a great time! At least it sure felt that way."

"I guess we'll just have to wait and see who pops up on Detective Gallant's radar screen," said Carmela. "Although he's got a ton of interviews to get through."

"Some of those people aren't gonna want to talk to him," said Ava. "You know, the wealthy ones, the people who jealously guard their privacy."

"There's a lot of that going around," agreed Carmela. The wealthy of New Orleans, especially those who resided in the Garden District, were especially careful of their privacy. Many of the homes had security systems worthy of Fort Knox, and many families even employed private security forces.

Ava took a final sip of tea and stood up. "Well, time to shove off, I guess. Big day tomorrow. I've got a busload of tourists coming in for tarot readings and voodoo doll demonstrations."

"Take a cookie for the road," said Carmela.

Ava grabbed two cookies. "Don't mind if I do, *cher.*"

Carmela walked Ava to the door, then watched as her friend hurried across the courtyard and let herself into her shop. From there it was a crooked flight upstairs to an apartment that had been painted a rather amazing Pepto pink.

Because Carmela's head was still in a whirl, because she was a little too keyed up for bed, she fussed about her own apartment for a few minutes. Packing up the leftover cookies, rinsing out teacups, thinking about poor old Jerry Earl.

Why had he been murdered? What was the motive? Did it have something to do with all the glittering gold and antiquities that were strewn so casually about his office? Was it related to his construction business? To the people he'd bilked out of money? Or was it something else entirely?

Carmela frowned and let loose a deep sigh. Had it been an inside job? Someone who'd been at the party?

Had to be.

She spun around, her back to the sink now, and gazed about her apartment. At the cozy brick walls, leather furniture, and plush Oriental carpet that gave it such a warm, lived-in feeling. Happy to be here, she thought to herself. Happy to be safe and comfortable. And yet Margo Leland had probably felt that exact same way, too. But someone had come to her party, invaded her inner sanctum, and murdered her husband.

Like Plague in the *Masque of the Red Death,* Carmela thought. Stealing quietly among the unsuspecting revelers with ice-cold death in his heart.

A sudden noise outside startled Carmela

from her reverie.

Someone crossing the patio?

That didn't happen very often, since the only street access was a narrow porte co-chere. But no, there was Boo, the perennial watchdog, her ears laid flat against her head, nose pointed toward the door, a low growl rising in her throat.

Carmela hastened to the window to peer out cautiously. And saw . . . absolutely nothing. Just the low branches of a live oak tree swaying in the evening breeze, the small fountain pattering away.

But she had heard something.

Just like I heard something outside Jerry Earl's office window.

For some reason that incident had completely slipped her mind! But now Carmela knew she had to tell Detective Gallant. It could have been nothing, or it could be a detail that was critical to his investigation!

Should she call Gallant right now? She started across the room to grab her phone, then stopped. Walked back over instead and double-checked the lock on her window.

Tomorrow, Carmela decided. She'd definitely tell him tomorrow.

CHAPTER 4

After spending a fitful night, Carmela was excited to get back to the Monday morning normalcy and routine of her scrapbook shop. She lifted a knee, angled her hip, and bumped open the front door of Memory Mine — all the while juggling two cups of chicory coffee that she'd picked up at the nearby Café du Monde.

She also carried a ubiquitous green-striped cardboard container that held the richest, sweetest treats known to man or beast. Because after what she'd been through the night before, Carmela had decided she needed a delicious and sugary kick-start to her morning. And then there was Gabby to contend with.

Gabby Mercer-Morris, her very capable assistant, saw her struggling to get through the door and quickly lunged to help. Grabbing the cardboard box, she said, "Let me help you with that."

Carmela had to laugh. Gabby had gone for the good stuff right away. "It's the Pavlov dog effect, isn't it?" she said. "This box could be empty, but you'd still start salivating."

"If I know you," said Gabby, brushing back blondish-brown shoulder-length hair, "it's not empty." She raised delicate eyebrows as she eagerly pried open the box to reveal three powdered sugar–covered beignets. "Wow. Talk about loot."

"There's more," said Carmela. She carefully placed a small jar of raspberry jam and a container of vanilla dipping sauce on the counter.

Gabby took in the sweet treats and raised her eyes to Carmela. "Okay, what's wrong? What happened?"

Carmela handed one of the coffees to Gabby and said, "What do you mean?" What she was really thinking was: *Doggone it! After working together for five years, Gabby knows me a little too well!*

"Raspberry jam? And dipping sauce?" said Gabby. "These are heavy-duty stress busters. What's going on? Did you break up with Babcock?"

Carmela shook her head. "No. Thank goodness."

"Well, *something* happened," said Gabby.

48

She plucked a beignet from the carton and held it daintily to her nose. "Ah, the delicate essence of powdered sugar, oil, and . . . what? Is it butterfat that smells so divine?"

"Has to be," said Carmela.

Gabby took a bite and waggled her fingers. "So c'mon. What gives?"

Carmela knew she had to spill the beans eventually. "Okay, do you remember the lady I did the party invitations for last week? The Get Out of Jail Free Party?"

"Sure," said Gabby, chewing. "Margo somebody."

Carmela nodded. "That's right. Margo Leland. Well, Ava and I went to her party last night and there was an incident. Really an accident."

Gabby took another bite of beignet. "Yeah?"

"Basically," said Carmela, trying to back her way into an explanation, "Margo's husband was murdered."

Gabby's eyes suddenly bulged as roundly as her cheeks, which were stuffed with half a beignet. "What!" she cried out in surprise. Only it came out "Whuh?"

"Margo's husband, Jerry Earl?" continued Carmela. "I found him dead and stuffed inside a clothes dryer."

"What?" Gabby said again.

Carmela handed Gabby a paper napkin and indicated her chin. "*Un petit peu* of cleanup."

Gabby swiped at her chin a couple of times while she fought to find her voice. "That's terrible!" she finally cried. "It's awful!" She took a step backward, as if to distance herself from the bad news. Her chin quivered and she looked as if she was about to burst into tears.

Oh dear, Carmela thought. She knew Gabby possessed a fairly delicate constitution. And she really hadn't meant to ruin her day like this. Or her coming week.

Gabby waved a hand rapidly in front of her eyes in an attempt to ward off possible waterworks. "So what did you . . ."

"We called the police," said Carmela. "What else could we do?"

"And when you found him, he was . . ."

"Dead," said Carmela. *Dead as a doornail.*

"Oh dear," said Gabby. "Oh my." She wiped her hands on a paper napkin, then pulled her mint green cardigan closer around her as she gazed at Carmela with limpid brown eyes. "So . . . then what? Did Detective Babcock show up?" She was well aware that Edgar Babcock was Carmela's boyfriend, sweetie, and snuggle bunny du jour. In fact, Carmela and Babcock had met

50

on a case a few years earlier when Carmela's ex-husband, Shamus Meechum, had been kidnapped. They'd managed to get Shamus back in one piece, but their marriage had been left in disarray.

"Not Babcock," said Carmela. "He's out of town. Remember I told you he was attending that seminar on forensics up in DC?"

"Okay," said Gabby. "I guess." She still didn't look happy.

"But Detective Bobby Gallant got the call-out," said Carmela.

"And you have faith in him?"

"Oh, absolutely," said Carmela. She paused. "Besides . . ."

"Besides what?"

"I'm really hoping this will be an open-and-shut case."

Gabby tilted her head to one side. She seemed to be getting over her initial shock. "How so?"

Carmela took a sip of coffee. "I'm betting that Jerry Earl's murder was business related. All Gallant really needs to do is figure out who hated him the most."

"Can Gallant do that? He's that good of an investigator?"

"Probably." Carmela helped herself to one of the beignets. "Of course, now that I think about it, there were probably quite a few people who disliked Jerry Earl."

"Really?" said Gabby. "That's so sad."

"You didn't know Jerry Earl," said Carmela. "Margo may have loved the man enough to marry him twice, but he was mean as a cottonmouth and tough as a hunk of old shoe leather. I've also heard that when it came to business he was a hard-nosed jerk."

"But he paid the price," said Gabby.

"That's right," said Carmela. "He went to jail."

"No," said Gabby. "I mean the ultimate price. His life."

They got busy then, readying the shop for the coming week. This was the time, early morning, that Carmela liked best. When she could straighten the colored pens and glue sticks, arrange packages of beads and embellishments, add new rubber stamps to their huge wall display, and create a fun little still life in the front window using their new albums, spools of ribbon, and special scissors. Since Memory Mine was located in the French Quarter on Governor Nicholls Street, the shop itself pretty much oozed old world charm. Longer than it was wide, the shop featured high ceilings, wide wood-planked floors, a lovely arched bay window in front, and yellow brick walls.

It was along this longest wall that Carmela had placed her wire paper racks. They held thousands of sheets of paper in every color, style, and texture — and brought her an immense amount of joy. Because Carmela was (and she made no secret of this) a bit of a paper addict. She adored mulberry paper with its infusion of fibers, as well as Egyptian papyrus, which was linen-like and gorgeous. Both papers really got her creative juices flowing when it came to creating dimensional bags, boxes, and invitations. Of course, the botanical vellums imbedded with real flower petals and the fibery Nepal lokta paper were pretty darn fabulous, too.

Recently, Carmela had received a shipment of Indian batik paper. Infused with rich, dark colors that hinted at the Orient and a slightly puckered, accordion effect, she was looking forward to using this paper in one of her many projects.

And though business wasn't always as brisk as Carmela would like it to be, she had lots of loyal customers who gladly supported her. Which made her more grateful than ever to have built this little business and kept it going, even when Hurricane Katrina and Hurricane Isaac had swept through town and caused their respective hiccups.

Carmela was sitting in her small office in back, sketching out a design for a triptych, when the phone rang.

"Carmela," Gabby called from the front counter. "Your sweetie's on the line."

Grinning from ear to ear, Carmela snatched up the phone. "Hey there!"

"How are you doing, Carmela?" came a rich, warm, baritone voice. Carmela felt her heart give a little flutter. She could just picture Babcock in her mind's eye. Tall, lanky, and handsome. Ginger-colored hair cropped short and neat. His blue eyes constant pinpricks of intensity. And, of course, he was always well dressed. A cop with a curious taste for Armani and Hugo Boss.

"I'm great," she told him. "Now that *you've* called."

"I heard there was a rather unexpected turn of events at Margo Leland's party last night."

Uh-oh, he knew. "You talked to Bobby Gallant?" Obviously he had.

"Yes, I did," said Babcock. "It's funny how the phone lines stretch all the way up here to DC."

"What exactly did he tell you?" She wondered if Babcock was upset that she hadn't called him.

"That information is strictly confidential," said Babcock. "Nothing to concern your head over."

"But I —" began Carmela.

"Yes, I'm well aware that you were there, Carmela. But there's still no reason for you to get involved. No reason to try to insinuate yourself into police business or this particular investigation."

"I wouldn't do that," said Carmela.

"Yes, you would," said Babcock. "You would do that in a heartbeat." He hesitated. "You realize, my dear, and I'm quite positive we've had this conversation before, that when someone gets killed in New Orleans, it isn't up to you to solve the crime."

"I know that." Carmela swung her chair in a circle, studying the walls of her office, looking at paper swatches she'd tacked up, bits of ribbon, and sketches she'd made of future projects. Wishing Babcock wasn't so darned prickly about this. "I'll keep my distance. I promise."

Babcock made a strangled sound, somewhere between a cough and a chuckle.

"I miss you, too," Carmela said.

This time Babcock laughed out loud. "Stay out of trouble and I'll be sure to bring you something nice back from DC."

"Thanks," she said. "But *you're* the only thing I want back from DC!"

Carmela was standing at the front counter, adding a snippet of ribbon to a newly created memory box, when the door flew open. *Our first customer,* she thought. *About time.*

But it wasn't a customer at all. It was Margo Leland, her hostess from last night. Dressed in a tomato red outfit, she clung forcefully to the arm of a distinguished, white-haired gentleman that Carmela estimated to be in his early seventies.

"Margo!" said Carmela. She hadn't expected to see her again quite so soon. And why oh why was the poor soul toddling into her shop this morning? Somehow this looked like a disaster in the making.

Margo lifted sad eyes that were as red as her outfit and said in a gravelly voice, "Carmela, darling."

Margo's tight red sweater jacket was rife with frills and ruffles that accentuated her every curve. She wore a short matching red skirt and stiletto heels so high that Carmela feared she might topple over. Margo's wrists were festooned with thick gold bangles that jingled and jangled with every movement, and she clawed pathetically at her companion, wringing the sleeve of his suit jacket until it looked worn and crumpled.

Carmela and Gabby exchanged worried looks.

"Shall I make tea?" Gabby asked.

"Please," said Carmela. She figured she'd need something to soothe Margo's obvious distress. Then she reached under the front counter for a box of tissues and placed them within Margo's reach, all the while wondering what this unexpected visit was really about.

Margo released her viselike grip on her companion and gave a small wave. "This is my friend, Duncan Merriweather," she explained. "I don't know if you met him last night."

"No, I didn't," said Carmela. She smiled politely at Merriweather and said, "Pleased to meet you."

"Likewise," Merriweather said. He gave Margo's arm a solicitous squeeze and said, "Would you like me to stay close, sweetheart?"

Margo steeled her shoulders and shook her head. "No. Perhaps you could amble around the French Quarter? While Carmela and I have a little chat."

"As you wish," said the very solicitous Merriweather.

As he exited the shop, Gabby returned with a cup of tea for Margo.

"Here you are," said Gabby. "And please do accept my sincere condolences."

"Thank you," said Margo, accepting the cup of tea with hands that visibly shook. "You're very kind. You're both very kind."

Gabby moved discreetly away, leaving Carmela to face Margo.

Margo was a woman who was used to wielding her considerable power and influence and generally getting her way. Thus she got right to the point.

"Carmela," Margo said in a dry, brittle voice. "I need your help."

"My help," Carmela repeated. What exactly was Margo asking? Help with the funeral? With some sort of invitation? Perhaps a memorial card?

"You have to help me find Jerry Earl's killer!" Margo suddenly cried.

"Um . . . excuse me?" said Carmela. This request had come out of left field and tapped her on the noggin hard.

But Margo seemed to have her mind made up. She took a sip of tea and said, "Yes, you."

Carmela touched a finger to her chest. "I couldn't. Really. I'm . . ." Words seemed to fail her.

But Margo had found a modicum of composure and was suddenly insistent. "I warn you, I'm not a woman who is used to taking no for an answer."

"Just because I was there," Carmela stammered, "as a sort of witness. That doesn't make me any kind of investigator."

"That's not what I hear," said Margo. She gritted her teeth and forced out a kind of mirthless grin. "I understand that you're extremely smart and clever. That you're basically an amateur investigator who's not afraid to pursue angles that the police sometimes deem improbable."

Carmela bristled a bit. Who'd been talking behind her back?

"Who on earth told you that?" she asked Margo.

Margo drained the rest of her tea in one gulp. "If you really must know, it was Jekyl Hardy."

"Ah," said Carmela. That explained it.

Jekyl Hardy was an antique appraiser, premier Mardi Gras float builder, and one of Carmela's bestest, closest friends. But when it came to spreading gossip and the rumor du jour, Jekyl was worse than a runaway train. He yapped to the Pluvius krewe as well as confided in the Rex krewe. Then he confabbed with his friends at the

New Orleans Museum of Art as well as every antique dealer up and down Royal Street. If a yellow dog happened to wander across his path, Jekyl would probably talk to him, too.

"I'm flattered that Jekyl thinks so highly of me," said Carmela. "But there's absolutely no way I can get involved. You see, I promised Detective Babcock —"

Margo's perfectly waxed brows rose in twin arcs. "Babcock?" she hooted. "Who's this Babcock person? I thought Detective Gallant was in charge!"

Carmela cringed inwardly. No way did she want to share the details of her love life with this much-married Garden District doyenne.

"He's . . . um . . ." She wasn't about to tell Margo that Babcock was her honey, so she said, "Detective Babcock is Detective Gallant's superior officer."

"And you're well acquainted with this Babcock person?"

"Ah . . . yes, I am," said Carmela. She noticed that Gabby had moved a few steps closer to them. Gabby was obviously caught up in Margo's plight and seemed distraught that Carmela was reluctant to help.

"He's Carmela's boyfriend," Gabby said suddenly in a small, squeaky voice.

Margo's eyes lit up and she smacked her fist against the counter, jangling her armload of bangles. "That's absolutely perfect!" The jangling seemed to please Margo because she repeated her gesture again saying, "Now I really must insist! It would appear you're privy to all sorts of information!"

"No," said Carmela, backpedaling. "I'm not privy to anything at all."

Gabby crept forward some more. "Couldn't you just help her a little?" she asked.

Carmela threw a horrified look at Gabby, who was gazing at her with pleading eyes. Unfortunately, the balance of power in the room had just subtly shifted. Now it was two against one.

Carmela pressed her lips closed as the silence grew deafening. She wished for a customer, a delivery person, anyone, to come galloping in and interrupt this bizarre standoff.

"Please?" Margo said in a cajoling voice.

"Please?" said Gabby. "You know you're good at this."

Carmela released the sigh she'd had bottled up inside her. "I'll *think* about it," she said, reluctance heavy in her voice.

Margo was suddenly jubilant. "I *knew* you wouldn't let me down!" she cried. She clasped her hands together and smiled at Gabby. Tears leaked from her eyes.

"Mmn," said Carmela. *What did I just get myself into?*

"Come to my house tomorrow morning," said Margo. "And I'll pull together a list of names for you."

"You mean names from the party or names of people who hated Jerry Earl?" Carmela asked.

Margo weighed her question for a few moments. "Both, I suppose."

"Sure," said Carmela. "Whatever." Anything to extricate herself from this unnerving conversation.

But Margo was thrilled beyond belief that Carmela had climbed on board to fight her cause. She smiled, sniffled, snuffled, and wiped her eyes with a tissue. Then her gaze fell upon the shadow box that Carmela had been working on. She poked a bejeweled finger at it and said, "What is this sweet little thing?"

The wooden frame box, which had been artfully spackled with blue and cream paint, was about two inches deep and held bits of torn paper, a bouquet of dried flowers, a tiny bird's nest, and a small blue and pink feathered bird.

Carmela picked up the shadow box carefully. "It's just one of the many crafts we do here. Scrapbooking isn't just about photos and albums, you know. You can create memories or celebrate a person or event with all sorts of things — shadow boxes, miniature albums, collages, scrapped jewelry, you name it."

Margo reached out a finger and gently stroked the box. "It's lovely."

"Thank you," said Carmela.

"No, thank *you,*" said Margo. She turned a relieved smile on Gabby again. "And thank you, my dear, for being so helpful. For being on my side."

"No problem," said Gabby.

"So tomorrow," said Margo, turning back to Carmela.

"Tomorrow," said Carmela.

"Bless you," said Margo. She gave a shy wave then pushed and jangled her way out the front door.

When they were finally alone, Carmela pointed a finger at Gabby. "You were *not* helpful."

"Carmela, please," said Gabby. "You're good at what you do. The investigating part, I mean. So why not put it to good use?"

"Maybe because it always gets me in a heap of trouble?"

"Not always," said Gabby.

Carmela turned the shadow box over and studied it absently. "And just how am I supposed to figure out this murder anyway? I don't have a clue in the world about where to start!"

"I know you'll think of something," said Gabby. "Besides, your meeting with Margo tomorrow should be helpful. Especially if she puts together a kind of hit list."

"Or in her case, a shit list," Carmela mumbled to herself.

CHAPTER 5

Luckily, they got busy. Customers trickled into the shop looking for paper, charms, albums, and rubber stamps.

While Gabby rang up sales at the front counter, Carmela helped one of their regular customers, a woman named Mindy, find some rubber stamps and ephemera for her travel scrapbook project.

"You see," said Mindy, "I've got all these great photos of Rome and Venice and I'm just not sure how to organize them."

"You want an entire album devoted to your trip?" asked Carmela.

Mindy nodded as she fingered a small album. "I think so, yes."

"Well, that album you have in your hand would work beautifully," Carmela pointed out. The album had a pebbled brown cover and was eight-and-one-half inches by ten inches in size. "You could mount one of your photos on the front cover using a sheet of GlueFilm."

"I've got a great photo of some Roman statuary," said Mindy.

"Perfect," said Carmela. "You mount the photo under GlueFilm to protect it and make it semi-permanent, then color the edges with bronze or gold paint to simulate the look of a frame. Then you simply glue it to the cover."

"So that sets the tone for the interior, too?"

"It can," said Carmela. "In fact, I've got some sheets of scrapbook paper with neat travel images on them. And I know we've got a packet of ephemera here that contains some Italian postage stamps."

"Perfect!" said Mindy.

Carmela hummed to herself as she unpacked a box of rubber stamps. She was happy she could help inspire her customers. It was always gratifying to get them pointed in the right direction on a fun creative project.

On the other hand, some projects were not fun. Case in point, helping Margo Leland. If Babcock found out . . . well, he *couldn't* find out! It was as simple as that. If he found out she was pussyfooting around the investigation, he'd blow a gasket. And that was never pretty.

"Carmela?" Gabby had tiptoed up behind her.

"Hmm?" She was still a little miffed at Gabby for insinuating herself in the Margo Leland conversation.

"Want me to run down to Pirate's Alley Deli and get you a po-boy for lunch? One with fried oysters?"

Carmela gazed at Gabby. "That's not really playing fair."

"Whatever do you mean?" Gabby was suddenly all smiles and innocence.

"You know that's my all-time fave."

"Then that's what I better pick up." Gabby gestured toward the front of the shop. "You can keep an eye on things?"

"Natch," said Carmela. It was hard staying mad at Gabby. She really was a terrific assistant. With good intentions and a heart as big as all outdoors.

By the time Carmela located a fleur-de-lis rubber stamp for a customer, cut a swath of purple velvet ribbon for another, and gave tips to two more women on how to create a fiber art collage, Gabby was back.

She thrust a brown paper bag into Carmela's hands and dashed back up to the front counter.

Feeling a rumble in her stomach, knowing what juicy goodness was dripping away inside her paper sack, Carmela retreated to her office for a quick lunch. As she unwrapped the po-boy sandwich, she mulled over the events of the morning. Exactly how was she going to investigate Jerry Earl's murder without alerting Babcock and throwing him into a tizzy? Her sandwich, dripping cole slaw and mayonnaise from beneath the toasted bun, was certainly a delicious mess. Just like poking her nose into the investigation would likely be.

Hmm.

Delicately lifting the top bun, Carmela popped a fried oyster into her mouth. And licked her fingers. Oh well, some things were just meant to be messy. Case in point, po-boys and murder investigations.

Nibbling at her sandwich, Carmela eyed the shaker box that sat on her desk. She hoped her class, which kicked off in just a few minutes, would intrigue her customers. She'd never done this kind of project before. Most of her previous classes had focused on paper, lettering, stitching, using brads and beads, or Paperclay. But this was new and different. So . . . fingers crossed.

Just as Carmela was enjoying the last bite of her sandwich, a loud voice cut through the normal clatter of the shop.

"Where is she?" came a cry.

"Probably huddled in her office," said another voice, this one a little more strident and piercing.

Baby and Tandy? Carmela wondered. *Here already?* She glanced at her watch and realized that they weren't early. Rather she was late. She swept the sandwich debris off her desk and into the wastebasket, then hurried out to greet her friends.

"You poor dear!" Baby Fontaine cried out when she saw Carmela. Her flawlessly coiffed pixie blond hair swung from side to side. Baby was fifty-something and luminous, gorgeously sporting designer jeans and a perfectly pressed pin-striped blouse with an Hermès scarf tied carelessly at the neck.

Tandy Bliss, who was short and skinnier than a cat left out in the rain, shrieked, "Poor dear nothing! Carmela loves getting caught up in these crazy investigations!"

"I do not!" Carmela said, more than a little offended.

"It must have been awful!" said Baby. "Finding that poor man stuffed inside a clothes dryer!"

"Was his tuxedo wet?" Tandy asked. "Or was it already perma-pressed by the time you found him? Then she snickered at the shocked expression on Baby's face.

"Murder is no laughing matter!" Baby admonished.

Tandy ran a hand across her tight crop of curled and hennaed hair, as if this gesture might mask her amusement.

"Does everybody know about Jerry Earl's murder?" asked Carmela.

"Oh honey," said Baby, "it's been all over the TV. And tongues are definitely wagging all over town."

"And you were there!" said Tandy. "It must have been a pretty gruesome scene, huh? Got any gory details you'd like to share with friends?"

"Tandy!" said Baby. "I never!"

"That's right, you never like to hear the good stuff," chuckled Tandy. She poked an index finger at Carmela and said, "So . . . you're up to your eyeballs in this thing, huh?"

"Not exactly," said Carmela. She was reluctant to spill too many details about the murder. It just seemed like . . . bad karma. To say nothing of bad manners.

"Ah," said Tandy, "we already know what happened. The stabbing, the clothes dryer. Talk about a bad heat cycle."

"Poor Margo," said Baby. She pulled out a chair and sat down at the large back table they'd all dubbed Craft Central. "Just when

70

she'd finally gotten Jerry Earl back home again."

"Yeah," said Tandy, "I'll bet she's really crazed and dazed."

Baby nodded. "Margo likes to be . . . how shall I say it? In control at all times. But in a situation like this, a murder investigation, Margo's not going to have much say at all."

"Which is probably why she asked me to help," said Carmela. *Why not just throw it out there on the table?* she decided.

"Whoa," said Tandy. "Seriously? She asked for your help?"

Carmela nodded. "She was just here."

"Well, why shouldn't Carmela help?" piped up Baby. "She's good at piecing things together. Remember when poor Byrle was killed? Over at the church?"

"Terrible," muttered Tandy.

Baby continued. "Carmela pretty much figured out that whole scenario. Helped bring the killer to justice and everything."

"Yes, she did," said Tandy. "And God bless her for that."

"Margo Leland is lucky to have Carmela looking into things," said Baby. She swiveled her gaze to Carmela. "Do you have any leads yet, honey?"

Before Carmela could reply, Tandy said, "You gotta follow the money. There's always something there. Greed always wins out. Oh, and I saw that guy Conrad Falcon on the news? He didn't seem one bit sorry about Jerry Earl Leland. Of course, they were arch rivals when it came to business."

"Falcon had no love for Jerry Earl," agreed Baby. "He probably figured that, with Jerry Earl released from jail, he'd be faced with more competition again. And his business would suffer."

"Not anymore it won't," said Carmela.

"Here's the card stock and vellum you asked for," said Gabby. She dropped an armload of supplies in the center of the table.

"And here's something else you might like," said Tandy. She dug into her scrap-book tote bag and pulled out a paper sack. Just like that, the fragrant smell of chocolate brownies wafted through the air.

"Treats!" said Baby as Tandy passed the brownies around.

"I can't believe that Tandy can eat constantly and still be skinnier than a stick bug!" said Gabby.

"Tandy's been blessed with a metabolism more powerful than a nuclear reactor," said Carmela.

Tandy chuckled as several more ladies came in and joined them at the table. "It's always been that way." She reached out and rapped her bony knuckles against the table. "Knock on wood."

Carmela stood at the head of the table and waited for chairs to be pulled out, customers to be seated, and tote bags to be stowed.

"Okay," she said finally, calling her class to order. "We're talking shaker boxes today."

"This is so exciting," one of the newcomers whispered. "I've never taken a class here before."

"What I'm going to show you is just a quick example," Carmela continued. She held up a sample of a finished shaker box. It was a semi-flat wedding bell shape made with a backing of silver card stock and a front piece of clear acetate.

"Why is it called a shaker box?" asked Tandy.

Carmela shook it and hundreds of small cream-colored beads made a whooshing sound.

"Ah," everyone breathed. They got the idea.

"Shaker boxes are similar to flattened-out snow globes," Carmela explained. "Basically see-through envelopes that have small bits of paper or beads inside. You start by cutting a piece of card stock into the shape of a circle, heart, or whatever, for the back. Then you cut a piece of clear acetate in the same shape to use as your front. The two sides are attached — stitched, glued, fastened with brads, or whatever your want — and then filled with punchies, beads, or seeds."

"And we use them how?" asked Baby.

"It's just a fun little craft item that adds a bit of motion to a scrapbook page or the inside of one of your homemade greeting cards," said Carmela. "Plus you can make one in any shape or theme that you want."

Gabby indicated the dozen or so stencils that sat in the middle of the table. "We have an umbrella-shaped stencil if you're working on a scrapbook page about a rainy day. Or a heart-shaped stencil if you're doing a Valentine's Day. Wedding bell shapes if you're doing a wedding or anniversary." She riffled through the stencils and held one up in the shape of a turtle.

"Oh!" one of the ladies squealed. "That's perfect for me. I'm putting together my snaps from a trip to Cabo San Lucas and we got to observe sea turtles at night. It was beautiful!"

Carmela grabbed a basket that was filled with tiny bags of seeds and crystals. She grabbed one of the bags and set it down in front of her turtle-loving customer. "These are tiny seashells. They'd be perfect to use as your filling."

The woman's hand snaked out to grab the shells. "Thank you!"

All the crafters selected their supplies and got to work then. Carmela watched one woman cut heart shapes from hot pink cardstock and clear acetate. Then she selected red beads for the inside.

"Want to try the white beads?" Carmela asked. "It'd be more of a contrast to the paper."

"No," the woman said. "I want red."

Carmela handed her the red beads, then watched as the woman quickly glued the sides of her shaker box. When she poured the red beads inside, Carmela turned away. The bright red was too reminiscent of blood. Of Jerry Earl being stabbed and flopping out of the dryer.

The killer must have been strong, Carmela thought to herself. And smart. Smart to have lured Jerry Earl away from that big crowd. Strong enough to kill him, manhandle him, and lift him into a machine. Unless there'd been more than one killer? Was that possible?

There had been that couple in the restroom nearby.

And where exactly had Jerry Earl been killed? Had it happened in the laundry room? Or in his office? She hadn't seen any blood anywhere, though the killer could have easily concealed the mess.

Clearly, she needed a lot more information if she was going to help Margo in any way.

As Carmela mulled over the murder, a thought struck her. She eased into her office and quickly called Ava at her voodoo shop.

"Juju Voodoo," said Ava. "In harm's way? We got charms today."

"Hey," said Carmela. "You remember that crime-scene tech from last night? The one who was following you around like a lovesick puppy?"

"You mean Charlie?" said Ava.

"Was that his name? Okay, good. Could you please call him and work your prodigious female wiles on him? Flirt with him, then see if there's anything more on the murder weapon?"

"I can do that," said Ava. "But just so you know, that might make me beholden to him. I might have to go out with him. On an actual dress-up date."

"And that's a bad thing?" Ava was basically a serial dater anyway.

"It's just that I've been on so many blind dates lately, I'm probably entitled to a free dog."

"But this would be for a very good cause," said Carmela. "And just so you know, Margo stopped by the shop this morning and asked if I'd kind of look into things for her."

"Of course she did," said Ava, as if it were a purely logical thing. "Because you were the one who discovered Jerry Earl's poor mangled little body."

"That and because Jekyl's been flapping his mouth all over town. Telling people what a clever little crime solver I am."

"You *are* a clever little crime solver," said Ava. "You're the Nancy Drew of the Big Easy."

"Well, it isn't so easy these days," said Carmela. "With Babcock out of town, we're going to be privy to a lot less information. You know as well as I do that Bobby Gallant is playing this fairly close to the vest."

"Eh, I'll make the call," said Ava.

"Good girl," said Carmela. "Then come on over for dinner tonight, okay?"

"I was hoping you'd say that," said Ava. "Whatcha gonna whip up, *cher*?"

"I hadn't thought about it. What would you like?"

77

"I wouldn't mind some of your shrimp *étouffée*. But anything's great."

"You got it," said Carmela. She hung up, thought for a few moments, and dialed the phone again. It took a good five minutes to talk her way through all the gatekeepers, but finally she had Bobby Gallant on the phone.

"What?" he said, sounding brusque and none too friendly. "I'm busy."

"I forgot to tell you something," said Carmela.

"What?"

"I said I —"

"I heard you," said Gallant. "I meant what did you forget to tell me?"

"Oh," said Carmela. "The thing is, I kind of peeked inside Jerry Earl's office last night."

"What!"

"I said I —"

"Cut to the chase, Carmela."

"I got turned around in the hallway," said Carmela, "when I was looking for the laundry room. And I sort of stumbled into Jerry Earl's office."

"Okay," said Gallant. "Is there a point to this? Is it leading somewhere?"

"The point is," said Carmela, "I might have *heard* someone outside. At the window.

Well, really, the French doors."

"You *did* hear someone or you *might* have heard someone?" asked Gallant.

"It's hard to say," said Carmela. "But I had the strangest feeling that there was someone out there."

"You're sure it wasn't just the wind? Or noise from guests?"

"Yes. No." She hesitated. "I'm not sure."

Gallant sighed.

"There's something I need to ask you," said Carmela. "I noticed there were an awful lot of antiquities on display in Jerry Earl's office. Do you know if any of them are missing?"

"We don't have any idea on that yet."

"When you do know, can you let me know?" asked Carmela.

"No!" said Gallant.

Stunned by his vehemence, Carmela hung on the phone for a few more moments. Until finally, she realized he'd hung up on her.

CHAPTER 6

As Carmela stirred butter, flour, salt, and pepper into a rich golden brown roux, her front door bell rang. Boo and Poobah let out anxious yips, rushed over to the door, and staged a brilliant flanking maneuver worthy of the Napoleonic Wars.

"Down, doggies," Carmela said as she wiped her hands on her apron and pulled open the door.

Ava immediately held out a bottle of Syrah. *"Laissez les bons temps rouler.* Let the good times roll, *cher."*

"Immediately!" Carmela said, pointing Ava toward her dining room table, where two red wine glasses and a bottle opener waited.

Ava clicked over to the table in her lime green heels and plunked herself down. Along with her trademark skintight jeans, she wore a low-cut blouse that perfectly matched her shoes.

"You're wearing your Jimmy Choos," Carmela remarked. "The ones you found at The Latest Wrinkle." The Latest Wrinkle was their favorite resale shop on Magazine Street. They pretty much haunted the place looking for designer duds, especially jackets that hinted at Chanel.

"Some fancy lady must have got sick of the color," said Ava, sticking out a shapely leg and pointing her pink-lacquered toes. "But I think it's punchy. I can't tell you how many lovely comments I've gotten from men!"

"Ava, honey," said Carmela, retreating to the kitchen, "you'd get comments from men if you wore a potato sack and two-dollar flip-flops."

"I certainly hope so," said Ava. She pulled the cork with a flourish and carefully poured out two glasses of wine.

In a pan sizzling with butter, Carmela sautéed onion and bell pepper. Then she added paprika, salt, black and red pepper, and finally fresh shrimp. She added water, covered the pot, and checked a separate pan of rice. Called to Ava, "Dinner in about fifteen minutes."

"Smells delish already," said Ava.

Carmela joined Ava at the dining room table and accepted the glass of Syrah from her. "So tell me. Did you reach Charlie?"

"I talked to him," said Ava.

"I hope you did more than that."

"Okay, I flirted with him," said Ava. "And then I asked my questions. He answered them okay, but swore me to total secrecy."

"Of course he did," said Carmela. She took a hit of wine, waggled her fingers, and said, "So what'd he say? Anything about the murder weapon?"

"This is gonna sound totally whacky," said Ava. "But do you know what a trocar is?"

Carmela shook her head. "Nope." She had no idea what it was, but it didn't sound good.

"It's some kind of unpleasant implement used by funeral directors." Ava wrinkled her nose. "A tool that's used during the embalming process."

Carmela leaned back in her chair. "Oh man. That sounds positively . . . hideous."

Ava grimaced. "It does, doesn't it?"

"Wait a minute, are you telling me that's how Jerry Earl was stabbed?"

"I'm afraid the word Charlie used was *eviscerated*," said Ava.

"But Gallant was so sure it was a knife," said Carmela. She was having trouble wrapping her brain around this information. Stabbed was one thing, eviscerated sounded . . . totally maniacal and crazy!

"The medical examiner definitely said trocar," said Ava. "And judging from what Charlie told me, that's the guy who has the final word."

"Wow." Carmela wondered why Gallant hadn't mentioned it to her on the phone. Then decided she knew why. Because the less information she had, the less apt she was to meddle. Yes, it was going to be more than a little tricky walking this investigatory tightrope.

"And now I have to go out with him," said Ava. "Charlie, I mean." But she didn't sound one bit upset.

"I've been thinking about the whole murder scenario," said Carmela. "And it seems to me the killer had to be pretty strong to overpower Jerry Earl, stab him, and then lift him into the dryer, right? So maybe there was more than one killer. Remember I told you about the couple doing drugs in the bathroom?"

"But you didn't actually see them, did you?" asked Ava.

Carmela shook her head slowly. "No, I didn't."

"Too bad." Ava took another sip of wine and said, "I have to say, that was a pretty crazy party. I've attended my share of wild warehouse raves, but Margo's party topped out majorly on my wack-o-meter."

"You think?" said Carmela. "What about the Mardi Gras party you threw at Juju Voodoo?" Juju Voodoo was Ava's pride and joy, her cozy little shop just across the courtyard that was stuffed to the rafters with magic charms, evil eye jewelry, voodoo dolls, and saint candles. "One of your guests swore to me that he was an honest-to-goodness werewolf."

"I think he was just off his meds," said Ava.

Carmela laughed and stood up. "I better go check my shrimp."

"Wait." Ava picked up the bottle and topped off Carmela's wine. "It's good to keep the cook happy."

Carmela swirled the inky Syrah in her glass and smiled. "If you really want to keep me happy, you can set the table."

"I'm on it," said Ava.

While Carmela pulled together the final stages of the meal, Ava set out yellow Fiesta ware plates and bowls for each of them.

"What about flatware?" Ava asked.

"Over there in that mahogany cabinet."

Ava pulled open the top drawer and said, "Hey, girlfriend. You got new knives and forks and stuff?"

"Not really," said Carmela.

Ava held up a spoon to the light. "And it's embellished with the letter *M.* Wait a minute . . . don't tell me. You didn't!"

"M for Meechum," said Carmela. "That's right, I finally talked Shamus out of the good silver."

"How on earth did you manage that?"

"Told him he needed to polish it. And since Shamus abhors menial labor of any sort, he gladly traded the stainless steel for the sterling silver."

"You literally pried the silver spoon out of Shamus's mouth," said Ava, clearly impressed. "Good for you!"

Ten minutes later, the table set, two white candles flickering, they sat down to eat. Two drooling dogs sat nearby, watching with beady eyes.

"Perfection," said Ava. "Hot, creamy shrimp *étouffée* on rice and creamy cole slaw. You know the way to my heart."

"Or an early grave," joked Carmela.

"Please," said Ava. "Who cares if New Orleans is infamous for our slightly unhealthy food? We're *happy.* That's what really counts! I mean, do you really want to live in hippy-dippy land and eat tofu burgers and baked kale?"

"Not me," said Carmela. "In fact, everything turned out so smashingly well tonight, I'm probably going to repeat this same menu for Babcock. To make up with him."

Ava frowned. "Are you two lovebirds in a peck fest?"

"More like a duel of wills. He called this morning and told me to basically mind my own business. So I'm sure he'll go absolutely postal if he finds out I'm meeting with Margo tomorrow."

"That's easily solved," said Ava. "Just don't tell him." She frowned and suddenly pointed a finger at Carmela. "Wait a minute. I just had a very nasty thought. What if Margo did it? What if *she* killed Jerry Earl?"

"Why on earth would you think that?"

"For one thing, Margo could have easily lured him into the laundry room and stabbed him. And then cleaned everything up." Ava snapped her fingers. "Yeah. I forgot to tell you. Charlie told me they found bloody towels stuffed in the washing machine."

Carmela shuddered. "Oh man. It just gets worse and worse."

"See?" said Ava. "It could have been Margo."

"What possible reason could Margo have?"

"How about pure embarrassment?" said

Ava. "What if, besides putting on the dog, Margo was putting on a brave face at her party? What if she was really furious with Jerry Earl because he disgraced her in front of all those Garden District swells?"

"Then why wouldn't she have just divorced him?" said Carmela. "Yet again. Instead of staging an elaborate party and acting like she was all gaga over him."

"That could be part of her ruse," said Ava. "With Jerry Earl out of the way, Margo doesn't have to settle for inheriting half of his money. She seizes what is literally a golden opportunity and inherits the whole enchilada."

"Versus just a smaller chile relleno," said Carmela. She took a sip of wine and rolled it around inside her mouth. "I hear you. I hear where you're coming from. But if Margo is truly guilty, why on earth would she ask me to look into things?"

"I don't know," said Ava. "Maybe she thinks you can function as a kind of smoke screen. Maybe she's trying to get as many people as possible to stick their fingers into the pie and mess things up. Maybe she's trying to manipulate this thing from both ends." She took a sip of wine. "I don't know, maybe you should just come right out and ask Margo if she did it."

"I don't think so," said Carmela. "I'm thinking I should just have a low-key meeting with her and let this thing play out. Sometimes people let slip a lot more information when you don't pry or ask questions."

They cleared the dinner dishes together, gave a few judicious scraps to Boo and Poobah, then settled in the living room with the remaining Syrah.

"You bought a new print," said Ava. She pointed to a framed etching of Andrew Jackson addressing his troops.

"It's just something Toby White had hanging in his antique shop. It finally went on sale."

"It's nice," said Ava. "Conservative but nice. But you gotta admit, Jackson's certainly no George Clooney." She grinned wickedly as her cell phone burped from inside her purse. She pulled it out and glanced at the Caller ID. "Oh! It's Sully!"

Carmela raised one quivering eyebrow at her.

"Don't make the lemon face," Ava said.

"What?" said Carmela. *Am I that obvious?*

"That face you make every time he calls, like you just sucked on a sour lemon!" Ava hit a button on her phone and purred, "Hey there, sugar."

Carmela was not a big fan of Sullivan Finch. He was an artist they'd met recently at a charity art show at the Click! Gallery. The fact that he painted what he called "death portraits" creeped her out. And his smart-ass, erudite Ivy League posturing bugged her like crazy. But Ava was a woman smitten, and when Ava was smitten, there was no stopping her.

As Ava cooed into the phone, Boo and Poobah crowded around her. Obviously they thought the cooing was intended for them.

"Hey, guys," Carmela murmured softly. She grabbed Boo's collar and pulled her away. As she was reaching for Poobah, trying to get a grip as he wiggled around, she heard Ava say, "Seriously? Margo Leland?"

Now what? Carmela thought to herself. *Does everyone and his brother-in-law know what's going on?* Was this going to turn into one of those high-profile society murder mystery cases? If that was the case, she was going to be crowded out and squished like the proverbial bug.

Ava shook her head as she set down her phone.

"What?" said Carmela. "Something about Margo?"

Ava put a hand to her heart and drew a

89

deep breath. "*Cher,* I think we might have a problem."

"What problem? What's wrong?"

"Margo Leland," said Ava.

"I get that," said Carmela. "What about Margo Leland?"

"Sully just told me that Margo commissioned him to paint a portrait of Jerry Earl." Ava raised her right hand and made a spinning motion. "You know, one of his infamous death portraits."

Something pinged deep within Carmela's brain. Something felt not right. "When?" she demanded. "When did Margo call him? Like . . . today?"

"That's the really cuckoo thing," said Ava. "Sully said she called him last week!"

Carmela sucked in a sharp breath. Why on earth would Margo Leland commission a death portrait when Jerry Earl was still alive? Unless she had the ability to see into the future. Or worse yet, had manipulated the future!

CHAPTER 7

Running more than a little late this Tuesday morning, Carmela skipped across Decatur Street, dodged past a yellow and red horse-drawn jitney on Bourbon Street, and headed down Governor Nicholls Street. The sun was lasering down, bathing the brick storefronts with a creamy light, making all the little cottages that were painted Caribbean pink and blue and green look as if they'd been air-lifted in from Jamaica. So pretty — she could almost forget that a brutal murder had cast its pall over the city.

The first thing Carmela saw when she sailed through the door of Memory Mine was Gabby being her usual helpful self with a customer.

"Hey there," Carmela called out as the bell *da-dinged* overhead.

Gabby gave a decorous nod and smiled.

Their lone customer, a young woman in a snappy silver-gray dress with knee-high black boots, grinned expectantly at Carmela. She was flipping through one of the sample scrapbooks Carmela had put together and was obviously impressed.

"I had no idea that scrapbooks could be so pretty," the woman told her. "Each page is like its own individual work of art."

Carmela gave a distracted smile and said, "Scrapbooking is all about preserving your memories in a personal way." Was that what Margo had intended when she hired Sullivan Fisk to paint a death portrait of Jerry Earl? she wondered. Preserving a memory of his death?

There was nothing wrong with having a portrait of your dead husband, of course. The only catch, the big trip wire in all of this, was that Margo had hired Sullivan *before* Jerry Earl had died. Which seemed to make no sense at all. Or perfect sense if Margo Leland was the nasty, scheming sort of wife.

Part of Carmela dreaded going to her meeting with Margo Leland today. The other part craved answers. Would Margo really ask her to help snoop out Jerry Earl's killer if she was the one who was guilty? That didn't seem to make any sense at all. Therefore, there had to be a lot more to this story.

"Do you think you could help me get started?" the customer asked Carmela.

Carmela snapped back to attention and realized she had no idea what the woman had just said.

Luckily, Gabby stepped in. "Why don't you let me assist you? We'll select an album and look at some of the fun papers. Also, in case you're interested, we're having a Paper Moon class tomorrow afternoon. Perhaps you might like to join us?"

"I might like to!" the woman said.

Carmela left Gabby and the woman at the counter and hustled back to her office. There were orders to be placed, catalogs to be perused, and bills to be paid. It was paperwork, just not the creative hands-on kind that she really enjoyed. But Carmela worked doggedly at her tasks, and by mid-morning, she was able to slip out the door for her meeting with Margo.

The Lavish Garden District Mansion looked oddly sad and neglected to Carmela in the wake of Jerry Earl's death. The camellias drooped, the grass was uncut, even the windows seemed to reflect a lifelessness.

Nevertheless, Carmela trudged up the front walk and rang the doorbell. She waited, heard a deep metallic *bong* resonate

93

from inside the house, then peered through the wrought-iron security door as the impressive wooden door slowly creaked open.

A woman peered out at her. Not Margo. This woman, whom Carmela was pretty sure she remembered from two nights ago, had black, cropped hair and a narrow, angular face that could only be described as severe. She wore slim black slacks and a black turtleneck.

"You're right on time," said the woman. She extended a bony hand to Carmela. "I'm afraid we haven't been formally introduced. I'm Beetsie Bischof, Margo's dearest friend."

Carmela shook her hand. "Carmela Bertrand." She offered a faint smile. "You were the one comforting Margo Sunday night." Actually, Beetsie had been wailing piteously right alongside Margo.

"That's right," said Beetsie. She had the low, throaty voice of a lifelong smoker. And probably the metabolism of one, too, Carmela decided, since Beetsie appeared to be just skin and bones as she led her through the parlor and down a long hallway. Carmela noted that the home's interior was significantly more somber than it had been Sunday night.

Beetsie threw open the door to Jerry Earl's

office and announced in a deadpan voice, "She's here."

Margo was seated at Jerry Earl's desk. Next to her was Duncan Merriweather. Their heads were bent close together, nearly touching, as they sifted through a number of important-looking documents.

Startled by Beetsie's introduction, Margo looked up expectantly. Then a smile bloomed on her pink face. "Carmela! You came!" She sprang to her feet and lurched toward Carmela, grabbing her and embracing her so tightly that Carmela couldn't draw breath for a moment. "Thank goodness!"

Carmela gently disengaged herself from Margo, noting that this morning she was decked out in a flouncy pink skirt suit with a dozen gold bangles once again encircling her chubby wrists.

"Duncan?" said Margo, practically batting her eyes. "Could you make those calls now?"

"Of course," said Duncan. He surreptitiously slipped the papers he and Margo had been discussing into a folder and quietly gathered it up. Nodded solemnly to Carmela as he exited the room. Held the folder protectively to his side.

"Obviously you've met Beetsie," said Margo, shifting gears. "She happens to be my oldest and dearest friend. You might say I trust her implicitly."

Carmela just smiled.

Margo flapped a hand, motioning for Carmela to sit in the chair that Merriweather had just vacated. "Sadly, we were just planning Jerry Earl's funeral. It's going to be Thursday at St. Louis Cathedral. Internment will be in our family tomb at Lafayette Cemetery Number 1." She paused, her face downcast. "You'll come, won't you?"

Carmela nodded as she sat down next to Margo. "If you wish." She thought about how Margo and Merriweather had been whispering so conspiratorially. How he'd carefully removed the folder.

What else could Margo and Merriweather have planned together? Possibly a murder?

"So," said Carmela, eager to start things off, anxious to ask a few questions. "Have you put together that list for me?"

With an erratic change in mood, Margo cocked her head playfully. "What list?"

Carmela leveled her gaze at Margo. "The list of Jerry Earl's potential enemies."

Margo shook her head. "Everybody loved Jerry Earl," she said emphatically.

"Clearly not everyone," said Carmela. After all, the man had been murdered.

Margo's hands flew to her face and she suddenly seemed distressed. "I never in my wildest dreams imagined that . . ." She paused and sucked in a great gulp of air.

Carmela decided that Margo was good at turning on her emotions at will. And stonewalling, too.

"Yes," Margo said finally. "I suppose there were a few people — mostly workers — that Jerry Earl had cause to fire over the years."

"Were any of them present Sunday night?" asked Carmela.

From across the room Beetsie gave a delicate snort.

"No workers were guests at our party," said Margo. She said the word *workers* as if she were referring to manure.

"Okay," said Carmela. "What about the people Jerry Earl did business with? Construction clients. Any of them present?"

Margo's nod was imperceptible. "Yes. A few."

"Any strained relationships among those people?"

"None that I know of."

Carmela tapped a finger against the top of the desk. This was like pulling teeth. "What about Conrad Falcon?" Aka The Whistle Blower.

Margo reared back as if she'd been struck

97

in the face. "That thieving rat! Do you seriously think I'd have him in my home?"

"I'm guessing he's not one of your favorite people," Carmela said mildly.

Margo was practically foaming at the mouth now. "Conrad Falcon *hated* Jerry Earl. Falcon was always jealous of Jerry Earl because he was smarter and more successful."

"You're telling me they were fierce rivals," said Carmela. "Because they both owned construction companies."

"They were in rival Mardi Gras krewes, too," put in Beetsie. "Jerry Earl was in the Rex krewe, while Falcon was in the Pluvius krewe."

Conrad Falcon was in the same as Shamus, Carmela thought. Interesting.

"It seems to me," said Carmela, "that you're pretty much pointing a finger at Falcon."

Margo frowned. "Yes, I suppose I am highly suspicious of the man. Obviously I am."

"And there's no way Falcon was at your party Sunday night?"

"Never!" said Margo.

"Absolutely not!" echoed Beetsie. "He may live in our neighborhood, but we always make it a point to snub him."

"Tell me," Carmela said to Margo, "did you share your suspicions about Conrad Falcon with Detective Gallant?"

"I might have mentioned it," said Margo.

Carmela gazed at Margo, who was toying idly with a gold coin in a Lucite frame. "Why do you think Jerry Earl slipped away from the party?" Privately, Carmela figured the man had tucked into his office because he'd developed a burning desire for a few nips of a real drink, a man's drink like bourbon or whiskey.

"I don't know," said Margo. "Perhaps he received a phone call?"

"How would Jerry Earl know that?" Carmela asked. "The musicians were playing, the crowd was noisy and exuberant, and your husband was being lauded by well-wishers and mingling with guests."

"I suppose Eric would have told him," said Margo.

Carmela stared at her. "Eric . . ."

"Eric Zane," said Margo. "Jerry Earl's personal assistant."

"Ah, yes, he was at the party," said Carmela. Of course, he was. She remembered Zane as the brittle young man who'd been questioned at length by Gallant.

"But he wasn't an invited guest," said Margo. "Zane is on our personal staff."

"Is Zane here now?"

"He should be."

"Then let's get him in here," said Carmela.

Beetsie crossed the rug, her soft-sole no-nonsense shoes barely making a whisper. Carmela looked down at the carpet on which she'd just trod.

Where exactly had Jerry Earl been killed?

Surely the delicate carpet would still be a bloody mess if Jerry Earl had been stabbed in his own office — and it didn't appear as if the Rug Doctor had made a recent house call. Could the killer have lured Jerry Earl into the laundry room and done the deed there? That had a nice hard tile floor. Easy to spritz a little 409 and tidy up the blood once you were all done committing bloody blue murder.

And who had access to the laundry room? Well, she supposed pretty much anyone and everyone who wandered down that back hallway.

As Carmela mulled this over, Beetsie returned with an unhappy-looking Eric Zane. But Zane wasn't just here to answer questions; he'd been pressed into service as a sort of temporary butler. He carried a silver tray that held a teapot and matching bone china cups and saucers. Tea for three.

But not for four.

Zane poured a cup of tea for Carmela and handed it to her with a slightly trembling hand. Then he did the same for Margo and Beetsie.

"Eric, please tell Carmela what you remember about Sunday night," Margo instructed.

Zane's spine straightened as if Margo had prodded him with a hot poker. "Sunday night?" he said, his voice cracking.

Beetsie took a sip of tea and stared at Zane with hooded eyes. "Carmela is very clever. She's going to help us find Jerry Earl's killer."

"Excuse me," said Zane. He seemed to muster a bit of courage. "Are you asking what I remember about the party? Such as which guests were in attendance?" He frowned. "Because if you recall, I gave the detective our guest list —"

"It's not so much what you remember," said Carmela, "but rather the chain of events. For instance, I was wondering if you knew why Jerry Earl left the party. The last time I saw him — probably the last time any of us saw him — he was sitting in an easy chair talking to Buddy Pelletier. But shortly after his body was discovered and the police arrived, you mentioned that you'd spoken to Jerry Earl not ten minutes earlier."

Zane blinked at her.

"Can you explain that?" asked Carmela.

"Well," Margo demanded. "Answer her question."

Eric shook his head as if he'd drifted off for a moment. "Oh. I . . . was there a question?"

Carmela set her teacup down with a *clink*. "It seems you were the last person to see Jerry Earl alive. So I'm just wondering about your interaction with him." She knew Zane had related his story to Detective Gallant; now she wanted to hear it.

"There *wasn't* an interaction," Zane said crisply.

"You realize," said Carmela, "we're not accusing you of anything."

"This isn't a tribunal," said Margo.

"All we're trying to figure out," said Carmela, "is what you were doing around the same time Jerry Earl was killed."

"If you must know," said Zane, "I was in and out of the kitchen and butler's pantry looking for a bartender and waitress who'd skipped out on their posts."

The couple in the bathroom? Carmela wondered.

"You also mentioned that you were tending to the linens," said Carmela.

"Yes, ma'am," said Zane. "When there's a high-caliber event going on, you have to ride herd on everything. The catering and wait staff needs to be supervised, the bar towels have to be laundered, every detail has to be perfect." He carefully enunciated his final words to Carmela as if he were talking to a very small child.

"But you were aware that Jerry Earl had retired to his office?" said Carmela. This time she was fishing a bit. She didn't know if he really had.

"Oh yes," said Zane. "I saw the lights on in Mr. Leland's office and I peeked in."

"And what did you see?" asked Margo.

Zane shrugged. "Just that he was on the phone."

"Any idea who he was talking to?" asked Beetsie.

"I would never presume to eavesdrop," said Zane. He squared his shoulders and stared at Margo. "I hope you're not suggesting that I had a hand in Mr. Leland's death."

Margo waved her hands wildly, spilling a big splotch of tea in her lap. "No, no, Eric. We're not suggesting that at all!"

"Because," said Zane, "I didn't talk to him, I didn't quarrel with him, and I certainly didn't kill him!"

Carmela noted the anger that seethed below the surface with Zane. Zane certainly had access to Jerry Earl, and lots of employees entertain murderous thoughts about their boss. But most of the time they were just . . . thoughts. If Zane really had murder on his mind, would he kill Jerry Earl smack dab in the middle of a fancy party? With a hundred guests milling around? Or would that be the *ideal* time to kill someone? When people were tipsy and raucous and there was a houseful of potential suspects?

"I can assure you," said Zane, "I did everything humanly possible to ensure the success of Mr. Leland's party — not disrupt it. I helped select the highest-caliber caterer, bartending staff, florist . . ."

"Your taste is to be commended," said Beetsie.

Before Zane could respond, the phone on the desk started to ring. Margo reached out and grabbed it.

"Hello?" Margo squawked into the line. Then she smiled and nodded. "Oh yes, Detective, one moment." She put a hand over the receiver and said to Zane, "I'm going to take this in the other room. Please hang up when I pick up the extension."

Zane nodded. "Of course, ma'am."

Margo set the phone down next to a large gold mask that rested on a black metal stand and hurried out of the room. Carmela, Beetsie, and Zane waited in silence until they heard Margo call out. Then Zane replaced the phone on the hook.

"Where were we?" Beetsie asked.

"Florist," said Carmela.

Zane rolled his eyes. "That vendor proved to be slightly problematic. Mrs. Leland wasn't one bit happy with the zinnias. We ordered lavender and pink and the florist delivered yellow and white. Ghastly. Not a bit of pop. And the dahlias were wilted."

"First thing I noticed," said Beetsie. "The poor things were losing petals by the minute. Reminded me of a Pomeranian I once had, shedding hair constantly until all that was left was his poor dimpled pink skin."

With the conversation taking a sudden jog, Carmela wondered if she'd gotten as much information as she could. The answer was probably yes. Both Margo and Beetsie seemed prone to theatrics and veering off course.

Carmela aimed a smile at Zane. "Thank you for answering my questions. I'm sure this hasn't been easy for you."

Zane scrunched up his face and said, "I want Mr. Leland's killer brought to justice

105

as much as anyone. So if there's anything else I can do, any way I can help, please let me know." He reached down, picked up the teacups, and set them on the tray.

"Thank you," said Carmela. "We'll be sure to keep you in the loop."

Zane scurried out of the office. By the way the teacups clinked and clattered against each other, Carmela guessed he was happy to escape.

Margo's footsteps sounded in the hallway.

"Margo, dear," said Beetsie. "Did the Detective . . ."

Margo staggered into the room, looking white-faced and stricken.

Now what? Carmela wondered.

"What's wrong?" Beetsie gasped. "More bad news?"

"Strange news," said Margo. "That was Detective Gallant on the phone."

"What did he want?" asked Beetsie.

"He asked about tattoos," said Margo. She managed to walk another couple of feet then sat down heavily behind the desk, looking more than a little upset.

"Tattoos?" said Beetsie.

"Why was he asking about tattoos?" said Carmela.

"I can't quite believe this," Margo gasped, "but apparently the medical examiner found two tattoos on Jerry Earl's body! Jerry Earl didn't have any tattoos when he went off to prison!" She shook her head in total disbelief. "What on earth do you think it means?"

CHAPTER 8

Carmela, ever the practical one, said, "I think it probably means somebody tattooed Jerry Earl with a ballpoint pen while he was in prison."

Beetsie bought into Carmela's explanation immediately. "Prisoners do that, you know. Take ink pens and gouge all sorts of crazy designs into their skin." She nodded emphatically. "Crosses, eagles, even skulls."

Beetsie seemed so knowledgeable, Carmela figured she must be a closet fan of *Miami Ink.*

"Do you think a gang of prisoners tattooed Jerry Earl against his will?" asked a horrified Margo. "I hate to think that they held him down and forced him!"

"I don't know," said Carmela. She could think of worse things. "I suppose it depends on where the tattoos are."

Margo reached over with her right hand and absently touched her left shoulder.

"The medical examiner said one was here. On his shoulder."

"Did they say what kind of tattoos they were?" Carmela asked.

"No."

"He must have joined a gang," said Beetsie. "A prison gang."

Margo shook her head. "Jerry Earl wasn't a big joincr. Just thc Springhill Country Club. And the Republican Party, of course."

"Maybe he joined some sort of gang for preservation reasons," said Carmela. "If he *was* part of a gang, maybe it meant the other members would offer protection." Carmela hesitated. "When you spokc to Detective Gallant, was he able to tell you any more about the murder weapon?"

Margo's hands fluttered to her chest and she covered her heart, clearly in distress. "No, he didn't mention it. Should I have asked him?"

"Probably not," Carmela said. Knowing the grisly details of her husband's murder wasn't going to help Margo sleep any. There was no reason to distress the woman more than she already was.

Beetsie leaned close to Margo and patted her hand. "You're being so brave and strong about this when anyone else would have fallen to pieces."

Carmela nodded in agreement.

Beetsie directed her gaze at Carmela. "Do you know, Margo's even going ahead with her donation to the Cakewalk Ball on Saturday night."

"I have to," said Margo. "Everyone's counting on me big-time. I'm co-chair of the event."

The Cakewalk Ball was an annual charity event held at the New Orleans Museum of Art. Individual big-buck donors as well as major corporations commissioned lavish cakes from the finest bakeries in town. Then each cake was decorated with an expensive piece of jewelry. After the dining and dancing and schmoozing were done, all the cakes and jewels were grandly auctioned off, with the proceeds going to charity.

"Still," said Beetsie, "it's amazing how you manage to carry on in the face of adversity."

"I just couldn't let Angela down," said Margo.

"You're talking about Angela Boynton, the curator?" said Carmela. "She's honchoing this event?"

"Yes," said Margo. "Do you know her?"

"She's a good friend of mine," said Carmela. "And I've worked with Angela on the Children's Art Association, too."

"Then you simply *must* come to the ball,"

Margo urged. "In fact, I'll send over a couple of tickets for you and Eva."

Carmela would have preferred to spend Saturday night at home, awaiting the arrival of Detective Edgar Babcock, who was due back that evening. But Margo looked so miserable and forlorn that Carmela couldn't refuse. "That would be nice, I've always wanted to attend the Cakewalk Ball. I think Ava has, too."

"Carmela?" Margo was casually studying one of her ginormous diamond rings. "There's something else I want to ask you."

"What's that?" said Carmela.

"Could you possibly arrange a private tarot reading for me? At your friend Eva's shop?"

"Ava's shop," said Carmela. A tarot card reading? Margo was just full of surprises.

"That's a very good idea," chimed in Beetsie.

But Carmela wasn't so sure. "Are you sure you want to do that?" she asked. What if, through the luck — or bad luck — of the draw, Margo got the death card or some other card that freaked her out?

"I'm positive," Margo said. "You see, I want to try very hard to *communicate* with Jerry Earl. Since he . . . um . . . left us so abruptly, I know there's a passel of unfin-

111

ished business. I'm sure there's *something* he wants to tell me."

"If only that he loves you," Beetsie murmured.

"And another thing," said Margo.

"Yes?" said Carmela.

"When I was at your scrapbook shop yesterday, I fell in love with that adorable shadow box that you created."

Carmela smiled. "With the bird's nest?"

"That's the one," said Margo. "Anyway, I was wondering if you'd create something like that for me. As a kind of artistic commission."

Artistic commission. Just like the death portrait.

"I'd be happy to," said Carmela. "Did you have a particular theme in mind?"

"Oh, I'd want it to be dedicated completely to Jerry Earl," responded Margo. "A kind of mini memorial to celebrate his memory."

I think that's a lovely idea," said Carmela. "Do you know what sorts of paper or photos or objects you'd like to include?"

"I have a few ideas." Margo stood up, walked over to a shelf, and pulled down a red and blue paisley photo box. "For starters, I'm sure we can find plenty of material in here," she said as she handed the box to

Carmela.

Carmela opened the box and flipped through a stack of photos while Beetsie looked over her shoulder.

"Look at that one!" Beetsie giggled. "Back when Jerry Earl still had a full head of hair. What a charmer he was. And look at his shirt with the pineapples all over it! Isn't that precious?"

Carmela fingered another photo. One of a smiling Jerry Earl in a more decorous-looking business suit holding some sort of plaque.

"Now that one," said Margo, "was taken when the mayor gave Jerry Earl the Keystone Award for his many civic contributions."

"Maybe this is the perfect photo for your shadow box," said Carmela. Remembering Jerry Earl in his glory days.

Margo thought for a moment. "Maybe not, since that award was rescinded when Jerry Earl was sent to prison."

"Next!" cried Beetsie.

Carmela's eyes wandered across the top of Jerry Earl's desk, taking in the scatter of geodes, gold coins, and fossils. "How about if we include something like this?" she said, fingering one of the geodes. "It's a great little eye-catcher."

"It's certainly apropos," Margo declared. "Fossils and geology were one of Jerry Earl's passions."

"We'll also need some sort of background," said Carmela. "I have some lovely handmade papers at my shop . . ."

Margo grabbed a small leather book from Jerry Earl's desk. "Why not take a page from his notebook?" She handed it to Carmela.

Carmela turned the leather-bound book over in her hands and examined the worn leather. Then she flipped the metal hasp and opened the book. "Wow." She ran the tips of her fingers over thin sheets of vintage parchment paper that were covered with scribbles, drawings, and notations. "This looks quite old."

"It is," said Margo. "Jerry Earl discovered that notebook in an antique shop many years ago. Best we could determine, it belonged to a man who was an amateur paleontologist. Anyway, my dear husband decided it was good luck and always used it for jotting down notes or ideas for his fossil hunting."

"So just use a page?" said Carmela.

"Tear out any page you want," said Margo, sniffling. "Jerry Earl won't be needing it now."

"Margo?" Duncan Merriweather stood in

the doorway, looking large and imposing with his hangdog face. "We have to leave now." He tapped an index finger against the face of his gold Rolex watch. "The people at Baum and Bierman will be waiting."

Margo's face crumpled like a paper bag. "The funeral home," she said in a hoarse whisper. "We have to go select . . . you know."

Carmela gazed at Merriweather. "Can you give us a moment?"

He nodded and withdrew.

"Beetsie?" Carmela said. "I'd like to speak with Margo in private."

Beetsie clenched her teeth so tightly she looked like she was going to pop a filling. But she rose from her chair stiffly and rather ungraciously stomped out of the room.

"What?" said Margo, staring at Carmela. She looked worried and a little perplexed.

"I hate to bring this up," said Carmela. "But I have to ask . . ."

"Ask me anything," said Margo.

"I understand you commissioned a death portrait of Jerry Earl."

Carmela had barely uttered her words when Margo's lower lip began to quiver and tears shone in her eyes. Then her chest heaved and she let loose a stuttering moan.

"Margo?" said Carmela. She couldn't tell if the woman was stonewalling again or completely overcome with emotion.

Margo pulled a tissue from the pocket of her jacket and dabbed at her eyes. "Yes," she said. "I'm afraid I did."

"Why. On. Earth?" said Carmela.

Margo gazed upward as if searching for an answer in the heavens. Or at least in the cove ceiling. "Because . . . at the time I did it . . . it seemed . . . fun."

"Fun," Carmela repeated.

"You know . . . trendy," said Margo. "A few weeks ago, Beetsie and I saw some of Sullivan Finch's work at the Click! Gallery. And I thought . . . why not?"

"You just decided it might be a wild and crazy thing to do?" said Carmela. She glanced at the cypress-paneled walls that were hung with dozens of staid-looking landscape paintings. And tried to imagine a death portrait hanging among them. Just the notion of the incongruity sent a shiver down her spine.

Margo snuffled into her tissue. "Beetsie was all gung-ho cheerleadery about having a portrait done. She was the one who really pushed for it. So I just . . . well . . ." Tears streamed down her face. "Oh, Carmela," she sobbed. "Do you think I brought it on?"

Carmela shook her head. "Brought what on?"

"Jerry Earl's death. His . . . murder!" she said in a loud stage whisper.

"You're asking me if commissioning the portrait was some kind of talisman or bad magic?"

"Yes!" Margo breathed.

"No," said Carmela. "I don't think it works that way. I don't believe in — what would you call something like that? A psychic inducement?"

"So it wasn't my fault?" Margo asked tearfully.

No, Carmela thought. But why on earth had Beetsie goaded her into it? Why on earth would Beetsie be all rah-rah over a crappy death portrait? Was Beetsie not what she appeared to be?

Margo, Beetsie, and Merriweather took off then, leaving Carmela waving good-bye from the front door. They'd urged her to stay as long as she needed. To peruse the rest of the photos and objects in Jerry Earl's office and select whichever ones she thought would work best.

But now the house felt strange and deserted. Down the hallway a clock ticked loudly. Upstairs, Carmela could hear the whisper of footsteps. A maid perhaps? Or cleaning woman? And there was a far-off low rumble of something else, too. Carmela prayed it wasn't the clothes dryer.

They'd already selected a half dozen photos, and Carmela decided she'd better scoot back to Jerry Earl's office and grab that small, sparkling pink geode, too. It would be a perfect addition to the memory box.

But when she got to the office, Eric Zane was standing at the desk. And he seemed to be studying a sheaf of papers.

"Hello," said Carmela.

Zane practically came out of his loafers. "You! I didn't know you were still here!" He was startled and discombobulated, but not enough so that he wasn't able to cover up the papers he'd been peering at.

This is a house filled with secrets, Carmela thought to herself.

Carmela approached the desk and saw what looked like some kind of geological map.

Interesting.

"I'm just tidying up some business," Zane told her primly.

"So you functioned as Jerry Earl's personal assistant?" Carmela asked. She knew that he knew she'd glimpsed the map.

"That's right."

"What kinds of things did you do for him?"

Zane held her gaze. "Whatever needed doing."

"I suppose you handled business matters as well as personal matters?"

"You might say that," said Zane.

Carmela picked up the small geode. "It appears that your employer was quite the antiquities buff, what with all the fossils and *maps* and things."

"He was an antiquities freak," said Zane. "Always trying to add more and more to his collection." He indicated a bone mounted on a metal stand. "You see this? It's the jawbone from a mastodon. Part of one that was dug up back in nineteen eighty-two in West Feliciana Parish, just northwest of here."

"So it's not just fossils Jerry Earl was crazy about," said Carmela. "It was dinosaurs, too."

"Technically, mastodons weren't dinosaurs," said Zane. He gave a self-satisfied smile. A know-it-all smile. "They went extinct at the end of the Pleistocene era, about ten thousand years ago. Dinosaurs preceded them by some one hundred and fifty million years."

"So no dinosaurs were ever discovered in Louisiana?"

Zane shrugged. "It was always Jerry Earl's hope to find one."

"And he liked gold," said Carmela. "Judging from all the gold coins and nuggets and trinkets that he collected."

"That's another thing," said Zane. "Mr. Leland was a real gold bug."

"Precious metals," said Carmela. "Always a tricky thing."

"Given this economy," said Zane, "Mr. Leland thought it was the *only* thing."

Her head spinning with more questions than answers, Carmela decided to make a quick detour to Ava's voodoo shop.

With its wooden shake roof, multipaned front window, and glossy red front door, Juju Voodoo always reminded Carmela of a quaint little Hansel and Gretel cottage. Of course, that's where the fairy-tale image ended. Because when you looked closer in the window, you saw purple bottles filled with potions, Day of the Dead characters with snarky grins, and a bright blue neon sign in the shape of an outstretched palm — complete with head, heart, and life lines.

Carmela pushed open the heavy front door and stepped into the dark, cool interior. Candles flickered; flute music wafted in the air. While she waited for her eyes to adjust, her nose was greeted by the mingled aromas of sandalwood oil, sweet patchouli, and burned coffee.

"Ava?" she called out.

Ava, dressed in a leopard print corset top with skintight leather pants and strappy high-heel sandals, came scurrying from the back reading room. Her mass of dark hair fanned out about her fine-boned face, and her heels clicked like castanets. She looked, Carmela thought, like a cross between a Vegas showgirl and a bondage queen.

"*Cher?*" said Ava, clearly surprised. "I wasn't expecting you!"

"Some psychic you are," Carmela quipped.

Ava shrugged. "I'm just having a weird day. For some reason Tuesday morning feels like Monday morning." She touched a hand to her forehead. "Also, I'm nursing a Reese's Peanut Butter Cup hangover."

"It's that late-night snacking that does it every time," said Carmela.

"Miss Gruiex?" a voice called. Then a diminutive Japanese man emerged from the back reading room. He wore big round glasses, a brown sport coat, and tan slacks, and clutched a black messenger bag.

Ava winked at Carmela. "Give me a minute." She quickly rang up a saint candle (Saint Peter, patron saint of longevity), a small wax voodoo doll with a packet of red pins, and a shrunken head. "That all comes to thirty-nine fifty, darlin'."

The man seemed pathetically grateful as he cheerfully handed over his Visa card to Ava, and Carmela wondered if he was happy with his bizarre souvenirs or just thrilled to be waited on by a bombshell like Ava. All dolled up in leather to boot.

"Don't forget," Ava told him, "that special on love potion runs until Saturday. And it comes with a thirty-day guarantee!"

When her customer had finally put his tongue back in his mouth and departed, Ava turned her attention to Carmela. "So how'd it go with Margo?"

"Eh, Margo seems to run hot and cold. One minute she's sniffling about Jerry Earl, the next she's giggling with her buddy Beetsie."

"You mean that dreary-looking skinny gal who talks without moving her jaw?"

"That's the one," said Carmela. "In fact, Margo says Beetsie was the one who urged her to commission a death portrait. Said they did it on a lark."

"Do you believe her?"

"I think so," said Carmela. "I mean, what crazy woman would get all excited over a death portrait and then murder her husband?"

"Crazy like a fox?" said Ava. "A rich woman who'd like to be even richer?"

Carmela shrugged. "Maybe." She fingered one of the evil eye necklaces hanging on a rack on the counter. "The big news is that Detective Gallant called while I was there and freaked Margo out in a major way."

"How so?"

"Apparently the ME discovered prison tattoos on Jerry Earl's body."

Ava let loose a low whistle. "Tats on old Jerry Earl? Maybe underneath those stuffy Brooks Brothers suits, he was a biker boy at heart."

"More like somebody worked him over with a ballpoint pen," said Carmela.

"What were the tats? A skull and crossbones? Screaming eagle?" Ava smirked. "A cupid heart?"

"No idea."

"Better call up Bobby Gallant and pump him for information, girlfriend. This could be a serious clue!"

"Oh," said Carmela. "And I ended up hustling some business for you, too. Margo's all worked up about having a tarot reading."

"We can arrange that. I'm sure Madame Blavatsky will be happy to accommodate us." Madame Blavatsky was really Ellie Black, a tarot and *I Ching* reader that Ava had found working the tourist crowds over in Jackson Square.

"Great," said Carmela as she turned to leave. "I'll set it up."

"And be sure to call Gallant," said Ava. "Get the scoop and tell me all about it tonight!"

Carmela stopped in her tracks. "Tonight?"

Ava stared at her. "Please don't tell me you forgot!"

"I didn't," said Carmela. Of course she'd forgotten.

"You know darned well the Star of the South Cat Show is tonight!" cried Ava. "It's Isis's big opportunity to shine!" Isis was Ava's elegant black Persian cat that she'd inherited a couple of years back after the death of a friend.

"I've been looking forward to it," Carmela lied.

"Me, too!" said Ava, practically delirious with excitement. "In fact, Isis is at the groomer right now."

Carmela nodded, trying to rally a little inner excitement. "Getting all prettied up."

"Getting a pet-icure!" said Ava.

CHAPTER 9

As soon as Carmela got back to Memory Mine, she made a beeline for her office.

"Hello to you, too," Gabby said as Carmela sailed past.

"Hi. Hi. Sorry I'm in such a crazy rush. I gotta make a quick phone call to Bobby Gallant."

"What's in the envelope?" Gabby asked as she snipped a length of lavender velvet ribbon for an invitation she was working on.

"Shadow box project for Margo Leland," Carmela called over her shoulder.

Gabby nodded. "You'll have to fill me in."

Carmela plunked herself down in her chair and spun around. Because, honestly, that was how she felt. As if her world was spinning out of control and she was able to glimpse only the briefest hints of truth. Then she took a deep breath, picked up the phone, and dialed Gallant. While she waited, she studied a book of paper swatches from

Kingston Paper, one of her premier paper vendors. Though they offered several varieties of parchment and parchment look-alikes, there was nothing of the same high quality as was found in Jerry Earl's little notebook.

When Gallant came on the phone, the first thing he said was, "Babcock warned me this might happen."

"Nothing's happening," said Carmela. "I just want to confirm some information I got from Margo."

"She didn't ask you to call me?"

"Nope. I'm just a private citizen making a simple inquiry."

"Not so simple," Gallant grumbled.

"Sure it is," said Carmela. "Just tell me about the tattoos."

"You know I can't do that."

"Sure you can. Look I already *know* about them. It's not like they're a deep, dark secret."

"I'll tell you one thing and one thing only," said Gallant. "The tats were crude drawings of a sailboat, a tiny map, and a constellation of stars. Possibly done by a group of prisoners that belonged to something called the End of the World Gang."

"A gang?" said Carmela. "What do you make of that?"

"Not a whole lot," said Gallant. "There are gangs that call themselves the Hell Whompers, the Walking Zombies, the Bounty Hunters, the Killer Boyz, you name it."

"But End of the World," said Carmela. "That sounds kind of . . . fatalistic."

"Yes it does. It sounds like crazies who'd drink strychnine-laced Kool-Aid or believe in doomsday predictions by Nostradamus."

"Your kind of customer," said Carmela.

Gallant sighed deeply. "Unfortunately, the New Orleans PD has way too many customers like that!"

"What?" said Gabby, once Carmela was off the phone. She'd managed to hang in the doorway and listen in on part of the conversation. "What's going on? What's this about a gang? Please don't tell me Ava's hanging out with those motorcycle guys again!"

"It's nothing like that," said Carmela. "But here's the thing — the medical examiner found prison tattoos on Jerry Earl's body. And they were apparently done by some group called the End of the World Gang."

"That sounds awfully creepy," said Gabby.

"Gallant thought so, too," said Carmela. "Do you think it means, like, the *real* end of the world? Like the Rapture or something?"

"Somehow I'm guessing these guys aren't exactly into religion." She'd been turning that particular phrase over and over when, suddenly, in the back of her mind, something blipped quietly on her radar.

"What do *you* think End of the World Gang means?" asked Gabby, just as the front door opened and two customers rushed in.

"Not sure," said Carmela. "Until I check on something."

While Gabby waited on their customers, Carmela sat at her desk mulling things over. And came to a number of conclusions: Margo was crazy as a hoot owl, Beetsie had a nasty, sinister side, and Eric Zane was either a dedicated employee or a scheming traitor. She spun around in her chair again and gazed at some of the scrapbook ideas she had pinned to her wall. A torn tissue paper heart, some recycled fabric, and some vintage photos with buttons sewn around the border.

But all the while, she was thinking, *I gotta call Shamus. I gotta ask him about this.*

It was just after three, so she figured he'd probably still be at the bank. Unless he'd ducked over to Galatoire's for an afternoon bump at the bar. Shamus, so tall and good-looking, with his languid smile and casual arrogance, could undoubtedly pick up a sexy blonde in about two seconds flat.

Carmela hit her speed dial, figuring she'd probably get Shamus's voice mail. Instead, she got the real deal Shamus.

He came on the line all hearty and upbeat. "Babe! I was just thinking about you."

"Favorably, I hope."

"Always good times, babe."

Carmela snorted. "Except for our marriage."

"We had our moments," said Shamus, trying hard to sound philosophical. "But look at the bright side — we're in a good place now."

"That's right, we're divorced."

"I'm just happy we're still in each other's lives."

Carmela smiled to herself. Such a sweet thought. And just when her heart seemed to thaw a tiny bit, Shamus asked, "What's going on with my Garden District house?"

Which helped Carmela remember why she'd divorced the rat fink in the first place. "It's my house now, remember? I got it as part of the settlement."

"Settlement? I'd call it highway robbery."

"No, I wangled it fair and square," said Carmela. *Or at least my smart-as-a-whip lawyer did.* "Besides, if you and Glory had gotten your way, I would have ended up with fifty bucks and a used Ping-Pong table." Glory was Shamus's older sister, a parsimonious crab who'd always despised Carmela. She'd made no bones about the fact that Carmela was too blue collar to be part of their family.

"I hear you put the house on the market for two point three million," said Shamus. He may have been an indolent, do-nothing member of the Meechum banking family, but he somehow managed to get his facts and figures straight.

"Something like that," said Carmela.

"Big number."

"I didn't price it, Shamus, my Realtor did. Anyway, I wasn't calling for real estate advice. I wanted to ask you a question."

"Is it about that little incident at Pappy's Brewhouse last weekend?" said Shamus. "Because the manager dropped the charges and I already paid to replace the ceiling fan."

"No," said Carmela. "It's not about that because I don't even *know* about that."

"Then what?" said Shamus.

"I wanted to know what *end of the world*

means to you?"

Shamus was instantly on alert. "Is this a trick question?"

"No, it's just a standard Q and A question."

"Because if this is some kind of stupid pet trick, don't think I'll be amused."

"You're rarely amused, Shamus. Now, please, just answer the question. In fact, just give me the first thing that pops into your head."

"End of the world . . . end of the world," said Shamus. "Okay, let me get this straight. If I'm not mistaken, it's how the people in Venice refer to their unincorporated town." Venice, Louisiana, was the last stop on the Great River Road and located in Plaquemines Parish right on the edge of the Baptiste Collette Bayou. It had been almost completely destroyed by Hurricane Katrina in 2005 and hadn't fared well with Hurricane Isaac in 2012.

"You're sure about that?" said Carmela.

"Sure I'm sure. They call it that because it's kind of the last bit of civilization. Yeah," Shamus rhapsodized, "I had me some excellent fishing trips down that way. Good game fish: wahoo, marlin, snapper, you name it. I don't think there's a prettier place on earth."

"Yes," Carmela said softly. The memory

of all the nights they'd spent together at Shamus's little camp house in the nearby Baritaria Bayou came flooding back to her. The rain pattering gently on the corrugated tin roof, a crackling fire, fresh grilled snapper. Those were good times, better times. "Thank you, Shamus," she murmured.

"Hey, did I get it right?"

"This time, Shamus, I think you might have."

Carmela hung up the phone and thought about that isolated little spit of land south of New Orleans. What would Venice, Louisiana, have to do with Jerry Earl's murder? It was all bayous and bars and swamp rats. How on earth would the little down-on-its-heels town of Venice intersect with the gilded life of Jerry Earl and Margo Leland?

Is this where the prison gang hailed from?

If so, why would they be after Jerry Earl? Could things have gone terribly wrong in prison? Had Jerry Earl violated some sort of prison code?

On the other hand, maybe she was coming at this the wrong way. What if, instead of looking at people, she viewed the murder from a completely different angle entirely? Such as . . . trying to find out more about the grisly murder weapon?

The trocar.

Even the name sounded alien to her. Spooky and threatening and old-fashioned. Still, Ava had called Charlie the crime-scene guy and that's what he'd confided to her. Murder via trocar.

How could she find out more about a trocar? Whom could she call? Who might know?

Like the proverbial lightbulb popping on above her head, Carmela suddenly remembered Oddities, the little shop next door.

Little Shop of Horrors is what Gabby calls it.

Still, talking to Marcus Joubert, the owner of Oddities, might give her a smattering of insight.

"I'm running next door for a second." Carmela told Gabby as she breezed past her yet again.

"Ugh." Gabby made the appropriate face to accompany her remark.

"Don't worry, I'll be back in two shakes."

"I *do* worry," Gabby called after her.

But Carmela was already out the door. From there it was a quick ten steps to the front door of Oddities. She pushed her way in and was instantly struck by the extremely bizarre inventory. There were Victorian-era top hats, stuffed bats, leather riding crops, animal skulls, butterfly and beetle collections, tribal masks, a real-life sarcophagus, and so much more. The narrow brick walls and strange objects seemed to close in on her as she walked through the store.

"Carmela!" Marcus Joubert looked up from a glass case and smiled his toothy grin. He was tall and slightly stooped with a bold lantern jaw. If he were a few years younger, he could have been mistaken for Lurch in the Addams Family. "What can I do for you?" he asked, wiggling bushy gray eyebrows at her.

Carmela glanced around at the knick-knacks in his shop. "Something's different."

Joubert waved a thin, bony hand. "Aren't you the observant one. Yes, I've changed up the merchandise somewhat. The stuffed monkeys and toads weren't selling all that well. Now steam punk is the hot new thing!"

"What's steam punk?" Carmela asked. She'd heard the term, but wasn't sure what it meant.

"It's a sci-fi or fantasy subgenre," Joubert explained. "A sort of mash-up of nineteenth-century industrialized looks with Victorian flourishes." He held up a black leather fitted top with multiple lacings and studs. "See?"

"OMG," said Carmela. "Do *not* show that to Ava!"

Joubert peered expectantly at Carmela, one bushy eyebrow arched up, the other slanted downward. "Would she like it?"

"Like it? She's a pushover for Goth and Victorian. It's got sexy vamp written all over it. Of course she'd love it."

"Bring her by!"

Carmela groaned inwardly. The last thing she needed was Ava prancing around town looking like an extra in the movie *Edward Scissorhands.* No, she'd come here for information and she was going to get it. Even if she had to wiggle into that top herself.

"This is going to sound a little strange," Carmela said. She dropped her voice and leaned toward Joubert, as if pulling him into her confidence. "But do you know anything about trocars? I mean, some of your inventory here includes old medical instruments, correct?"

"Ah, trocars," said Joubert, his face lighting up. "The mortician's trusty friend."

Carmela made her lemon face.

"I might even have some photos here," said Joubert. "Hold on." He rummaged around behind a counter and pulled out a handful of dog-eared catalogs. After leafing through several, he smiled and spread the pages out for Carmela to see. "Here are some fairly good illustrations for a number of antique medical instruments. And this particular one . . ." He pointed a bony finger to a drawing of a long, serrated tube with a wooden handle. "This one is a turn-of-the century trocar."

Carmela swallowed hard. "Dare I ask what it was used for?"

"Oh my," said Joubert. "You really don't know?"

Carmela shook her head. *Do I really want to know?*

"In the embalming process," said Joubert, "it is quite necessary to remove most of the internal organs. The trocar merely facilities this."

"So it . . ." Carmela was grasping for words.

"Macerates them for easy removal," Joubert supplied helpfully. "Of course, that basic design is still in use today for laparoscopic surgeries. But now the modern ones come with an autolock mechanism and ergonomic grip."

Carmela raised a hand to stop Joubert. If she listened to any more grisly details, she'd probably want to forget the entire investigation.

"Interesting, no?" said Joubert.

No, thought Carmela. Because now she

understood that someone had sliced into Jerry Earl as if he were undergoing open-heart surgery. Only he hadn't had the benefit of anesthesia. Or a doctor for that matter.

Carmela swallowed past a dry patch in her throat. "Have you ever had a trocar in your inventory?"

"Actually, I had one several months ago," said Joubert. "I picked up a set of old embalming tools at an auction in Shreveport."

"But the trocar's no longer here?"

"It's been sold."

Carmela thought for a moment. She wondered who would buy something like that. A collector of weird items? A killer?

"Do you remember who the lucky buyer was?"

"Sadly, no."

Carmela met his gaze. "You know why I'm asking about this, don't you?"

Joubert nodded. His eyes were dark and intense. "Because of the murder."

"That's right," said Carmela. "I was at that party. I discovered Jerry Earl Leland's body."

"I read all the details in the paper," said Joubert. He glanced at the medical illustration again. "All except one, apparently."

Carmela followed his gaze. "That's right," she said. "Jerry Earl was stabbed with a trocar."

"How very odd," said Joubert. "And grim."

Gabby was deep in conversation when Carmela returned to Memory Mine. She'd pulled out a couple of examples of wedding scrapbooks, and she and a fresh-faced young woman were eagerly paging through them.

"I love this!" squealed the woman. "Look at that adorable wedding bell design. Ooh, and those are my exact colors, champagne and dusty pink!"

Obviously a bride, Carmela decided. Here to get some ideas for invitations, place cards, and wedding scrapbooks. She found that more and more brides were creating their own invitations these days. Maybe it was a reaction to the tough economy; maybe it was because they wanted to make their invitations more personal. Whatever the reason, Memory Mine seemed to be doing a land office business with brides.

Tossing her bag on her desk, Carmela snatched up the phone. And was lucky enough to catch Bobby Gallant just as he was leaving.

"Carmela, I'm just out the door." He sounded tired and crabby. "What do you want now?"

"I have a couple of things for you to noodle over," she told him.

"This isn't going to work," said Gallant.

"What's not going to work?"

"You running some sort of parallel investigation."

"It's not really," said Carmela, "so just hear me out. You know that shop next door to me? Oddities?"

"Yes," came Gallant's bored answer.

"Well, I was just over there, doing a little research into trocars."

"How did you know about the trocar?" Gallant thundered.

"Never mind about that," said Carmela. "Suffice it to say that I do know."

"Now you're being perverse," said Gallant. "Is there a point to all this?"

"Yes, there is. I was talking to Marcus Joubert, the shop's owner, and he mentioned that he'd recently sold an antique trocar."

"Okay, I'll bite," said Gallant. "Who bought it?"

"That's the unfortunate part. He doesn't know."

"And you thought this was helpful how?"

"Just a sort of an FYI thing," said Carmela.

"And that's it? That's what you wanted to tell me?"

"There's more," said Carmela. "I may have figured out what End of the World means."

"Seriously?" Now there was wariness in his voice.

"You said Jerry Earl had a gang tattoo, right? Well, is it possible the gang hails from somewhere around Venice, Louisiana?"

The silence on the other end of the line told Carmela she'd just struck investigative gold.

"Well?" she said. "What do you think?"

"You put two and two together?" he asked. "Just like that?"

"That's right."

"Why? How?"

"Because I'm smart," said Carmela. "And I'm right, aren't I?"

"There's a remote possibility," said Gallant. "I did some checking with the prison officials where Jerry Earl was incarcerated, and there *was* a gang that hailed from around Venice."

"Do you think Jerry Earl hung out with them?"

"That's still being investigated," said Gallant.

The notion of old Jerry Earl chumming with a bunch of redneck Cajun swamp rats somehow tickled Carmela. "Are those guys still in prison? Can you talk to them? Maybe Jerry Earl knew his life was in danger and that's why he joined up with them."

"Most of them have already been released," said Gallant.

"At the same time as Jerry Earl?"

"No, no, some maybe a month earlier. Some three or four months earlier. They weren't there because of any major crimes. It was mostly junk stuff — poaching, bootlegging, that sort of thing."

"Do you think Jerry Earl might have done something to anger them? That *they* might be the killers?"

"Anything's possible," said Gallant.

"Well, are you going to talk to these guys?"

"If and when we locate them, yes. Venice barely exists anymore, and most of these former prison guys live way off the grid." He hesitated for a moment and then said, "But don't *you* try and find them."

"I wouldn't," said Carmela. "I wouldn't do that." But all the while she was thinking, *Maybe I* should *take a little trip down there.*

CHAPTER 10

The courtyard of the Trillium Hotel was paved with red brick cobblestones and surrounded by impressive stone masonry that included a mash-up of Greek columns and Roman statues. A grove of potted palm trees bobbed their shaggy heads next to a sparkling azure pool. At the outside bar, which was one umbrella short of a tiki bar, a couple was toasting each other, tipping their giant hurricane cocktails together with a resounding *clink*. A hotel worker in a black Chinese-style jacket mopped a spill nearby.

Ava gripped Isis's carrying cage as she and Carmela headed for the hotel's ballroom. She was decked out to the nines in hot pink Capri pants, a clingy off-the-shoulder white blouse, and sky-high gold sandals. Carmela followed in jeans, a blazer, and more sensible shoes. She was trying to tell Ava about her conversation with Bobby Gallant, about how he'd pretty much tap-danced around everything she'd brought up. But it wasn't working.

"Oh, *cher,*" Ava complained as she lurched and wobbled for about the fiftieth time. "My heels keep getting stuck between these cobblestones." She held out the carrier to Carmela. "Do you think you can take Isis?"

Carmela grabbed the cat carrier as the hotel worker hurriedly dropped his mop and rushed over to assist. Predictably, his eyes roved over Ava and his tongue practically wagged out of his mouth.

"Can I help you, miss?" asked the young fellow. He offered his arm to assist her. "I'd hate to see a pretty lady take a tumble."

Ava dimpled prettily. "Aren't you just a perfectly darling Southern gentleman!" she squealed. Then she clutched his arm tightly and began a running commentary on how *fabulous* it was for him to offer such *welcome* assistance as she marched on ahead of Carmela.

Carmela raised the carrier to eye level and gazed at Isis. "What am I," she asked the cat, "chopped liver?"

Isis meowed, her pink tongue flashing between sparkling white teeth.

"I don't actually *have* liver for you, my dear. I'm asking if . . . oh, never mind. But I must say, you look exceedingly lovely tonight. In fact, you're almost as spiffed up as Ava."

The star of the South Cat Show was big. In fact, as they entered the Millennium Ballroom, where the show was being held, Carmela saw that it was humongous. Basically Cat Central.

There were fifteen rings with judging all going on at once. Categories ranged from bench judging to feline agility, as well as specialty contests for themed cat costumes and even cage decorating. And, oh my goodness, what an amazing array of cats and kittens! There were Persians, Maine Coons, Norwegian Forest Cats, Savannahs, Siamese, Oriental Shorthairs, Bengals, Ragdolls, and even tabby kittens. In one corner of the ballroom, Animal Rescue New Orleans had even set up a booth where cats and kittens were being offered for adoption.

As Ava took Isis and hastened to the registration desk, Carmela wandered between the show rings, enjoying the scene. Pausing at one ring, where three elegant Siamese finalists were awaiting the judge's final verdict, she spotted the face of her friend Jekyl Hardy bobbing through the crowd. He was pale, tall, rail-thin, and wore his dark hair pulled back in a ponytail.

145

Dressed in his trademark black silk shirt, black slacks, and black high-gloss shoes, he was a dead ringer for Anne Rice's Vampire Lestat. Although, to Carmela's knowledge, Jekyl had never shown any aversion to the sun.

Jekyl saw her and gave a wave. He was as excited as Carmela and Ava to watch Isis compete in her first show.

"Car-*mel*-a!" Jekyl called as he approached. "Looking gorg as always. And where's my other divine diva?"

Carmela nodded toward the registration desk, where Ava seemed mired in paperwork.

"Ava!" Jekyl called. "Hey, baby!" He waved madly at Ava, who winked and blew kisses back to him.

"Let's find a seat," Carmela said.

She and Jekyl pushed their way past cats, cat lovers, stacks of cat carriers, and various food vendors, heading for a stand of audience bleachers that had been set up. The smell of freshly shampooed cats, fried crab cakes, and spicy andouille sausage filled the air around them.

Jekyl raised a sharp eyebrow at Carmela. "Can I tempt m'lady with a crab cake?"

Carmela shook her head. "I think I've already exceeded my caloric allotment for today." She'd for sure hit her quota at lunch, not to mention dinner.

Jekyl snorted. "Poor dear, you are missing out." He put up one slender finger and motioned to the crab cake vendor.

After receiving his fried treat in its little red and white striped cardboard container, he dripped on enough aioli sauce to induce a medium-sized coronary. Then they climbed the bleachers and, from their vantage point, enjoyed a clear view of Ava holding her cat while she preened for the judges.

"So," said Carmela, "thanks to you, Margo Leland has pressured me to look into the circumstances surrounding Jerry Earl's murder."

Jekyl gave her a sideways glance and then proceeded to stuff half a crab cake into his mouth.

Carmela rolled her eyes. "Oh, I see you can't talk about it now. But you certainly didn't have any trouble yapping to Margo that good old Carmela happens to be a cracker-jack amateur investigator."

Jekyl's eyes danced with amusement as he continued to chew.

"Anyway," said Carmela, "I had a very interesting meeting with Margo and her friend Beetsie this morning."

"Tell me," said Jekyl finally.

So Carmela told him about Margo, weird old Beetsie, and weirder old Duncan Merriweather. Then, because her story sounded like a crazy, jumbled mess, she threw in the part about Eric Zane, too.

"Don't you love the gall of Garden District swells?" Jekyl chortled. "They think just because they have money, they can snap their fingers and make all their problems go away."

"Not in this case," said Carmela. "There's been no snapping of fingers or exchanging of money as far as I can see."

Instead of one of his usual sharp retorts, Jekyl proceeded to wipe his fingers with a paper napkin.

"What?" said Carmela.

"Nothing," said Jekyl.

"Something," said Carmela. "You *know* something."

"Just a rumor that's been flying around the ozone."

Carmela waggled her fingers. "Concerning . . ."

"Beetsie Bischoff."

"Margo's self-proclaimed BFF? What's going on? You better tell me."

Jekyl shrugged. "I shouldn't really."

"How about I twist your arm and pinch

148

your nose closed until you turn blue and can't breathe?" Carmela knew it wouldn't come to that. She knew Jekyl was positively *dying* to tell her.

"Mind you," said Jekyl, talking in a low, conspiratorial voice now, "I got this information secondhand." He thought for a moment. "Well, maybe thirdhand. I talked to Devon Dowling, who heard it from Stefan Purdy at the Estate Gems and Jewels Gallery."

Carmela waggled her fingers again. "And?"

"And what I heard," said Jekyl, "was that Beetsie and Jerry Earl were *involved.*"

Carmela frowned. "You mean . . . involved in a compromising situation?"

"Bingo. Give that lady a plush pink panda."

Carmela let this information percolate for a few moments. *Beetsie and Jerry Earl?* How could Beetsie and Jerry Earl be having an affair and Margo not tumble to it?

Then she remembered the death portrait. That little bit of mischief had been Beetsie's brilliant idea. A chill zipped up Carmela's spine. Had Beetsie wanted Jerry Earl dead? If so, why? He certainly wouldn't be leaving his fortune to "the other woman"!

"I'm just saying," said Jekyl. "Mind you,

149

this is just a rumor."

"Still," said Carmela, "if there's any truth behind it, then . . ." She hesitated. Then what? Then Beetsie was definitely a suspect? Or Margo was a suspect because she'd deprived Beetsie of her husband's ardor? None of it felt right. And yet . . . there it was. Sitting there like a big fat meatball of information.

"Well, I'll be darned," Jekyl chuckled.

Carmela looked up and suddenly saw Ava hopping up and down like crazy. And wonder of wonders, the silver-haired judge was smiling brightly at her and handing her a white ribbon!

"Oh my gosh!" Carmela exclaimed. "Isis won?"

"Correction," Jekyl said in a droll voice. "I'd say *Ava* won. Judging by the look on that judge's face."

"Still," said Carmela. "It counts, right?"

"Why wouldn't it?" Jekyl grabbed her arm. "C'mon, let's go congratulate the winning team."

They clambered down the bleachers and shouldered their way through a crowd of people who all seemed to be cradling furry white cats.

"What possessed me to wear black?" Jekyl mumbled out of the corner of his mouth.

"I'm going to need three lint rollers to get all this —"

"We won!" Ava shrilled as she ran to greet them. She thrust Isis into Jekyl's arms, grabbed Carmela, and pulled her into a hippity-hop victory dance. "We did it!"

"*You* did it," said Carmela. "What is that ribbon anyway?"

Ava dangled her white ribbon before Carmela's eyes. "Third place!"

"How many contestants?" asked Jekyl.

"Four," said Ava. "So we really did it — we won!"

"Of course, you did," said Carmela. "It's a major award."

Ava suddenly stopped her little dance. "I need a drink. My face is numb from smiling at that judge and my throat is absolutely parched."

"Maybe a frozen daiquiri?" suggested Jekyl.

"Fantastic!" said Ava. She glanced at Carmela. "You want one?"

But Carmela had just spied someone in the crowd who looked vaguely familiar to her. Could it be . . . She shook her head as if to clear it, then held up a hand. "Pass. I think I'm just going to look around for a bit."

"Okay," said Ava, skipping off with Jekyl.

151

"See ya in a few minutes."

Carmela edged closer to the man she'd spotted in the crowd.

That gray hair . . . and rigid, uptight posture. I feel like I know him. But . . . who is he?

Carmela drew breath sharply. Oh, wait just a hard minute! Because now she really did recognize him. Now she could put a name to the face.

It was Conrad Falcon! The overbearing jerk that she'd seen on TV two nights ago. The man who was Jerry Earl Leland's business rival, neighbor, and overall foe.

Falcon, obviously a successful breeder and cat fancier, was smiling magnanimously as he posed for a photo. In his arms he cradled a gorgeous Siamese cat that had an enormous purple rosette pinned to its collar.

Carmela edged closer to him. The photographer, who had probably been hired by the producers of the Star of the South Cat Show, was shooting him from different angles. Taking two-shots of Falcon and his cat, then moving in closer to frame just the cat. And all the while, Conrad Falcon was keeping up a running patter with a man who stood just a little to his left. A man with a tough, flat face, brush-cut gray hair, and cheap navy blue suit. From the looks of things, they were having what must be a very serious conversation. But about . . . what?

Curious now, Carmela moved in closer.

The man in the bad suit was nodding vigorously, as yes-men often do.

Am I rushing in where angels fear to tread? Carmela wondered. *Yeah, maybe. Probably.*

But that didn't stop her. She edged even closer, trying to hear what Falcon was saying. He was talking in a low monotone that was difficult to catch, so she heard only part of it . . .

". . . now that he's not around anymore to make a stink," snarled Falcon as his henchman nodded again.

What on earth? Could they be talking about Jerry Earl? Is that what Falcon means by not around anymore?

The photographer, done with snapping photos of the Siamese, abruptly straightened up and moved off. Which left Carmela standing there, staring directly at Falcon and his cat.

Trying to make a fast recovery, Carmela said, "Congratulations on your win. Such a beautiful cat."

Falcon stared at her. "Thank you."

Keep him talking, Carmela told herself.

"What's your cat's name?" Carmela asked.

"Lady Devonshire of Chatsworth," said Falcon.

"That's a pretty big name for such a dainty little cat," Carmela replied.

Falcon grunted and was about to turn away, when Carmela took a step closer.

"If I'm not mistaken," she said, "I saw you on the news the other night."

Falcon glanced up at her. Now she had his attention.

"You were speaking about Jerry Earl Leland and his tragic demise," Carmela continued.

Falcon's lips twisted and his brows bunched together. "I *was* on the news, yes."

"You made a few rather pointed remarks about Jerry Earl Leland because he was your neighbor and business rival."

Falcon squinted at Carmela. "Leland was my *neighbor* before he screwed up and landed himself in prison. And you, miss. Who may I ask are you?"

"Carmela Bertrand." She extended a hand.

Falcon ignored her. He inclined his head toward his henchman. And the man, picking up on his cue, immediately held up a cage. Falcon turned and quickly deposited Lady Devonshire inside it.

"I'm a friend of Margo's," Carmela said.

154

Falcon stood rigidly, his back to Carmela. He took extreme and slow care to secure the hasp on the tiny gate of the cat's carrier cage. After a moment, he turned to address Carmela.

"Margo, yes. This string of unfortunate events must certainly be trying for her."

"She was pained by your words as well," said Carmela.

Falcon gazed at Carmela with the intensity of a cobra sizing up a mongoose. "Perhaps she's better off without him." Then he shrugged. "And if the justice system hadn't been so rudely tampered with, Jerry Earl Leland might still be alive. He'd be behind bars, mind you, but I doubt he would've been murdered there."

"I understand you two were business rivals."

Falcon twisted his mouth into a harsh sneer. "When it comes to business, young lady, *everyone* is my rival."

Carmela was about to let loose a sharp retort, but stopped herself short. After all, this was a man who ran a huge company and had an army of people at his command. When a man wielded that much power, she surely didn't need to make an enemy of him!

Ava tapped Carmela on the shoulder.

"Who was that unhappy-looking man you were just yucking it up with?"

"Remember the guy we say on TV the other night? Conrad Falcon?"

Ava's eyes grew large. "Whoa. That was Falcon? The whistle-blower? What'd he say? What'd you ask him?"

"I tried to talk to him about Jerry Earl," said Carmela. "But he clearly wasn't having it."

"He was rude to you?"

"More like hateful. It pretty much oozed out of every pore!"

Ava clutched the white ribbon to her chest as if to protect herself from hatred contamination. "Ooh, that means he's negative juju, *cher.* Let's get out of here."

"Good idea," said Carmela. "Where's Isis?"

"Jekyl's got her. He's showing her off to some of his friends. You'd think *he* entered her in the darned contest."

"Let's get her and go," said Carmela.

They found Jekyl cooing over Isis and chatting with a bunch of fellow antique dealers. Once they pried Isis away from him, they cut a direct path through the crowded room, heading for the exit. As they passed the booth sponsored by Animal Rescue of New Orleans, a woman in tan pants and a pink blazer held a tiny tabby kitten out toward Carmela.

"Are you interested in adopting a kitten, dear?" asked the woman.

Carmela shook her head, but Ava nearly exploded.

"Oooh! Look at the itty-bitty baby!" Ava reached a finger out to gently stroke the adorable little kitten. The kitten let out a sound that was somewhere between a purr and a pleading squeak. "He's saying, pleeease love me! Now you have to adopt him!" Ava pleaded to Carmela.

"No, no," said Carmela. "Not with two dogs."

"They'd love a baby kitty to play with," Ava said.

Carmela laughed. "Somehow I can't fathom that working out."

Ava took the kitten into her hands and pressed her cheek against the kitten's fur. "But he's so soft and cuddly!"

"I know, now give him back." Carmela took the kitten from Ava and handed him back to the Animal Rescue lady, who in turn raised an eyebrow.

"Are you sure?" she asked.

Carmela nodded. "Afraid so." She made a note to herself to send a donation to the Animal Rescue people. They did fantastic work and she knew they could use all the help they could get. Of course, if the world were a perfect place, there wouldn't be any hapless little creatures who needed homes.

Carmela gunned her engine as she turned from Decatur onto St. Louis, heading for home. The night was cool and the colorful neon lights from the nearby clubs and bars spattered prisms of red, blue, and green across her windshield — a French Quarter light show.

"So what did Conrad Falcon say when you mentioned Jerry Earl?" Ava asked. She was holding Isis in her lap, looking happy and relaxed, beginning to come down a little from her triumphant win.

"He said maybe Margo was happy to be rid of him."

"Yeah?" said Ava. "Do you think she is?"

Carmela drove for another block, thinking. Then she said, "I'm not sure. She vacillates between being weepy and a kind of manic high."

"What do you think that means? That she should be popping Prozac? Or that she really should be considered a suspect?"

"You know," said Carmela, "in a case like this, the spouse is *always* a suspect."

"What would be her motive?"

"Money, I suppose," said Carmela.

"And Conrad Falcon? What motive would he have?"

"Pure hatred."

"Okay," said Ava. "And suspect number three, Eric Zane. What's in it for him?"

"I don't know," said Carmela. "Freedom?"

"Couldn't Zane have just quit his job if he hated it so much?"

"Easier said than done," said Carmela. "Sometimes it's trickier than just kicking the dust off your shoes and walking out the front door. Sometimes people are physically and emotionally stuck, so they're unable to make any kind of move."

"Huh," said Ava. "Like being Velcroed to the wall." She wiggled her shoulders. "Awful."

"I found out something else, too," said Carmela.

"What's that?"

"Jerry Earl was carrying on with Beetsie Bishoff. At least that's the latest scuttlebutt according to our good friend Jekyl."

"No!" said Ava. "That scrawny old bird and Jerry Earl?"

Carmela nodded.

"What a betrayal!" Ava dropped her head and planted a little kiss on the top of Isis's furry head. "Do you think Margo knows?

Or that she suspected?"

"I don't think Margo has a clue. She wouldn't still be all buddy-buddy with Beetsie if she knew Beetsie had been canoodling with Jerry Earl. And I have no idea if the affair was carried on while he was in prison."

"How do you even have an affair with a guy who's in prison?" Ava asked. She sounded interested.

"You're asking me?" Carmela said as she zigzagged around a slow-moving vehicle. "You're the relationship expert. You've dated in just about every crazy situation —"

Ava held up a hand. "Excuse me! I don't do jailbirds or married men. A lady has to draw the line somewhere!"

Carmela laughed. "You don't think men in orange are cute?"

"It's not the orange that I object to, it's the baggy jumpsuits," Ava said, smiling wickedly.

"Speaking of jailbirds and jumpsuits," said Carmela. "Remember those tattoos I told you about? The ones the ME discovered on Jerry Earl's body?"

"Yeah," said Ava. "So you found out more?"

"Well, I talked to Bobby Gallant — it was like pulling teeth, but I finally got some inside information — and he told me about this crazy group of guys down in Venice who were in prison the same time Jerry Earl was."

"What are you saying?" asked Ava.

"There's a possibility they might be involved."

"That they murdered Jerry Earl?" said Ava.

"Maybe."

"There are a lot of maybes in this case," said Ava. "Too many."

Carmela shrugged. "I know." She hesitated. "But one more maybe?"

"What's that?" said Ava.

"Maybe we should drive down to Venice and check out those guys for ourselves."

"We could do a road trip!" squealed Ava. "Just like *Thelma and Louise!*"

"As long as you don't shoot anyone," said Carmela.

"And you don't drive us off a cliff!" said Ava.

CHAPTER 11

Carmela was scrutinizing her racks of paper this Wednesday morning, trying to figure out what might tickle the fancy of her crafters for her afternoon Paper Moon class. Maybe her Japanese rice papers with the kimono designs? She pulled a few sheets out. And how about the suede papers? Sure, why not. The suede paper was gorgeous. She also grabbed a few sheets of vellum and foil paper and was debating over the cork paper when the bell over the front door did its high-pitched *da-ding.*

Carmela glanced up at the same time Gabby did. Gabby was standing at the front counter, creating a display with seals and rubber stamps, when a man in a blue uniform charged in.

"Carmela?" he said, looking at her.

"Gabby," she said.

"Got a delivery here for a Carmela," the man said.

"That's me," said Carmela. She set her stack of paper down and walked the few steps to the front. "Whatcha got?"

The man shrugged, then handed her a long white envelope. "Don't know, ma'am, I just make the deliveries."

"Thanks anyway," said Carmela as he charged back out the door.

"That looks awfully small to be the foam core I ordered," said Gabby.

"I don't know what it is," said Carmela. She hooked a fingernail under the envelope's flap and flipped it open. "Oh. Tickets." She glanced at Gabby. "For Saturday's Cakewalk Ball. You know, from Margo."

"I thought you weren't interested in going to things like that," said Gabby. "After Shamus dragged you to every charity and society event in town."

"Eh," said Carmela, "I kind of got pressured by Margo. She's co-chair or something like that."

"Well, I'm glad you're going. Now I'll have someone to hang out with."

Carmela raised a single eyebrow. "What about Stuart?" Stuart Mercer-Morris, Gabby's husband, owned eight Toyota dealerships and was known as the Toyota King of New Orleans. He dressed like a preppy, voted conservative, was a bit of a control freak, and lived and dreamed car deals. He got particularly excited when it came to fleet leasing.

"Stuart will be busy yucking it up with his friends as usual," said Gabby. "And probably bragging about his cake."

"What's he planning to donate? I hope he didn't pinch something from your jewelry box."

"No," said Gabby. "One of his managers has a wife who's an amateur baker and cake decorator. She's going to do a four-layer cake and incorporate a long strand of opera-length pearls and a diamond-studded key pendant."

"Classy."

Gabby wrinkled her nose. "You think?"

"It is for a car dealer."

Twenty minutes later they were up to their ears in customers. A trio of women came tripping in and started grabbing packs of beads, colored brads, and stickers.

Another woman, a semi-regular named Amanda who'd just acquired a stash of antique paper dolls, cornered Carmela and inquired about the best way to display them.

"Display them?" asked Carmela. "Or showcase them in an album?"

"Hmm," said Amanda. "Maybe I would

164

rather put them in an album. If I did go that route, what would you recommend?"

Carmela reached up and grabbed an album off the shelf. It had a pebbly black leather finish that made it look old, like a vintage ledger or banker's book. "This might work." She carried it to the craft table in back. "How many paper dolls do you have?"

Amanda opened her portfolio and showed her. "A dozen."

"So maybe give each paper doll her own page?"

"That's a lot of pages," said Amanda. "I don't know if I can manage that many." Her finger touched one of the dolls. "What I'm saying is, I don't know that I'm that creative."

"The thing is, we have a lot of antique-looking paper. So if you use that for background, you're already halfway there."

Amanda remained doubtful. "Can you show me? Just one example?"

"Sure." Carmela spun around and grabbed a sheet of paper that was printed with a wonderful collage that included old newspapers, antique flower seed packets, and vintage postcards. "You see, this sets the vintage tone right away."

"Neat. But what else?"

"You could also add a snippet of vintage fabric or lace, add some buttons, and even pressed flower petals."

"I love it," said Amanda. "What other papers do you have that would work?"

Carmela grabbed a handful of twelve-by-twelve-inch sheets of paper that featured designs of old sheet music, vintage wallpaper, Audubon prints, and butterfly designs.

"I get it," said Amanda. "And I think I can figure out the rest."

"I knew you could," said Carmela.

Gabby seemed to have everything in the shop under control, so Carmela retreated to her office. She plopped down in her chair and studied the items she'd brought back yesterday from Margo's house.

She leafed through some of the photos, then picked up Jerry Earl's antique leather journal. As she carefully turned the pages, she was quickly mesmerized by all the notes and scrawls and diagrams. She could understand why Jerry Earl had found this little journal so fascinating. She wondered if he had regarded it as a sort of good luck talisman in his own search for treasure.

A discreet knock on the doorframe caused Carmela to lift her head and turn around. Gabby was standing there, a crooked smile on her face.

"What on earth are you reading?"

"A very fascinating little notebook," said Carmela. "Did you know that all sorts of fossils and bones have been discovered in Louisiana?"

"No, I did not," said Gabby.

"Well, according to Jerry Earl's notes, this state is a hotbed for them."

The phone suddenly rang, as if to punctuate her sentence. And Gabby, ever the good and mindful shopkeeper's assistant, reached across the desk and grabbed it. She listened for a moment, then covered the receiver with her hand.

"Speaking of hot beds," said Gabby, "your ex is on the phone."

Carmela made a face.

"Now, now," said Gabby, chiding her.

Carmela took the phone. "What?" she said.

"Babe," said Shamus, "is that any way to say hello?"

"Hello," said Carmela. "What?"

"I have a favor to ask," said Shamus.

"No," said Carmela.

"You don't even know what it is!"

"The answer is still no," said Carmela.

"Pleeease," said Shamus. "I need your help. I need to tap that spark of creative

167

genius that burns inside your pretty little head."

"What are you talking about, Shamus? Spit it out."

"I can't. Not over the phone. Meet me for a drink after work, okay?"

"I don't like this, Shamus, you're being very mysterious."

"Does that mean you'll meet me?"

"Is this about money?" Carmela asked. "Because I have no intention of rehashing old —"

"It's not," said Shamus. "It's just a teensy, tiny personal favor that's right up your alley."

Carmela sighed. "Okay, but this is against my better judgment . . ."

"Across the street from your shop," said Shamus. "Glisande's Courtyard Restaurant. See you at five."

"This better be good, Shamus!"

Two seconds after she hung up, the phone rang again. This time Carmela snatched it up. "Memory Mine," she said in a pleasant tone. "How can we help?"

"You can start by explaining a few things," said a rich, baritone voice.

Babcock! Carmela felt a warm flutter of butterflies deep within her stomach. "How are things going?" she asked. "How's your seminar? Are you learning lots of exciting new investigative techniques?"

"Never mind my seminar," said Babcock. "What I want to know is why are you interfering so much in Gallant's case?"

The butterflies stopped fluttering and took a nosedive. "I'm not."

"That's not what I hear."

"Um . . . he called you?"

"Yes, he called me. He works for me, remember?"

"I maybe asked him just a couple of little things, that's all," said Carmela.

"Are you being truthful?"

Carmela crossed her fingers to help mitigate her little white lie. "Sure."

"Well, just take it easy on Gallant, okay? He's tearing his hair out over this Jerry Earl Leland case."

"It's a tough nut to crack," admitted Carmela.

"Just don't *you* try to crack it," said Babcock.

"Um," said Carmela.

"Listen, Carmela. Margo Leland is really, really rich. And her husband, like it or not, has been a major political contributor in the past."

"So what are you saying?" said Carmela.

"There's some serious pressure to solve this thing," said Babcock. "From the mayor's office on up."

"Got it," said Carmela. She didn't want to get into another big go-round with him, so she hastily changed the subject. "When will you be home?"

"Probably late Saturday."

"Any chance you can make it to the Cakewalk Ball at NOMA? Um, the New Orleans Museum of Art?"

There was a pause and then Babcock said, "Cakewalk Ball? You never mentioned that before. What on earth is it?"

"Just your basic annual charity event. Big-buck donors, lavish cakes, dinner, dancing, schmoozing, and a *de rigueur* auction."

"So it's fancy. Does that mean I have to wear a monkey suit?"

"It would be quite appropriate if you did, yes." This was a man who favored Hugo Boss, Zegna, and Armani, but was unhappy about wearing a tux? Gimme a break.

"I'm not sure I'll be able to make it in time."

Carmela heard indecision in his voice. "I'd love it if you'd try," she said. "I promise to wear something cute!" Nothing like trying to up the ante.

"You mean like a party dress?" Now

170

Babcock sounded interested.

"Something like that, yes."

"Well . . . I can try to make it, but don't hold your breath."

After lunch, with one eye on the clock, Carmela got busy and pulled several more sheets of paper for her Paper Moon class. Since she was so intrigued by the little journal, she pulled a bunch of parchment paper, too.

"Parchment," said Gabby, studying her choices. "That's unusual. Usually you're all gung-ho over sheets of handmade paper and Japanese rice paper."

"Oh, we'll have that, too," said Carmela. Then the front door chimed, and Baby and Tandy came flying in. Baby, as usual, was dressed impeccably in a tailored black and white houndstooth jacket with slim-fitting designer jeans. Tandy looked snazzy in a fire red and orange top that matched her mop of hennaed hair.

They caromed through the shop and slung their scrapbook totes onto the table in back.

"Well," said Baby, picking an invisible piece of lint from her blazer. "What's new on the investigative front? Have you figured out who killed Jerry Earl?"

Carmela squinted at her. "I haven't solved

the case yet, if that's what you're asking. Then again, neither have the New Orleans Police. But there are more and more seedy details that keep coming to the surface."

"Tell us!" Tandy squawked. She was always up for a choice tidbit of gossip. "What scandalous information did you find out?"

"Just the usual — betrayal, backstabbing, and shameful affairs," Carmela said. She dropped her armload of craft supplies in the middle of the table, where it landed with a *thunk*.

"Since it's a murder investigation," Gabby chimed in, "there's got to be betrayal." She paused and poked a hank of blond hair behind her ear. "But what's this about affairs?"

Baby inhaled sharply. "Was Margo having an affair?"

Tandy slammed a hand down on the table. "Holy buckets, that's it, isn't it! Margo murdered Jerry Earl so she could run off with her lover! So . . . who is he? Some nasty social climber who's interested in her money or some misguided young swain?"

Carmela gave a Cheshire cat smile. "You've got half the equation right."

Baby edged closer. "Which half?"

Carmela glanced around to make sure it was just the four of them who were in earshot. "It was Jerry Earl who was having the affair."

Tandy whistled. "Hound doggin' around. Can't say I'm surprised."

"That rat," said Baby.

"A total louse," put in Gabby.

"So who was he carrying on with?" Tandy asked.

Carmela was about to clue them all in when the front door slammed open and two women pushed their way in.

"We're here for the Paper Moon class," a woman in an elegant feather hat called out. She had long curly blond hair that peeked out from beneath her hat and was dressed in a flouncy pink blouse and black skirt. Her friend shared similar facial features and the same honey-colored hair.

Carmela decided they had to be sisters. "Welcome," she said and gave a friendly wave. "Come on back and meet the rest of the gang."

"Fill us in later, okay?" whispered Tandy as two more women burst through the front door, eager to join their class.

Carmela kicked things off with a quick introduction on the different types of papers that were available, passing around sheets of vellum, crinkle paper, linen paper, batik papers, and others that she'd pulled earlier.

"Remember," she told her class, "these types of paper aren't just for scrapbooking. They're perfect for journaling, card making, tags, booklets, shadow boxes, labels, and wherever else your creativity leads you."

"But what are we going to work on today?" asked Tandy. She was a scrapper of the first magnitude, always eager to dig in and work on a new project.

"Who knows what gold leaf is?" Carmela asked.

Baby held up a hand. "You mean like the gold leaf you see on statues or fancy picture frames?"

"That's right," said Carmela. "But I'm going to let you in on a little secret."

The ladies seemed to strain forward en masse, in anticipation of Carmela's words.

"Gold leaf is a snap to do," said Carmela. She picked up a small package and pulled out a single, flimsy, glittering sheet. "It comes in these micro-thin sheets and can be easily applied over a simple adhesive."

"Show us," said one of the women.

Carmela grabbed a small picture frame that she'd already covered with a rich paisley paper. "You simply apply some adhesive . . ." She brushed on a coat of clear liquid. "Then you lay down a small piece of

174

gold leaf . . ." She tore off a small piece and laid it down. "And then you brush it with a special brush."

There were oohs and aahs as the gold leaf began to adhere.

"As you can see," Carmela continued, "a few pieces flake off. But that's okay, because then you achieve a slightly distressed look." She showed her frame around for all to see.

"It looks gorgeous," said Baby. "Antiqued but even better."

"Gilded," said Tandy.

"You can add gold leaf to just about anything," said Carmela. "Invitations, greeting cards, papier-mâché boxes, notebook covers, even candles and beads. And if you're nervous about handling this type of thin gold foil, there are also gold leaf paints and gold leaf pens."

"Could you make your own gift wrap using that technique?" asked one of the women.

"Of course," said Carmela. "Or your own stationery. Really, ladies, you can finally have gold on anything and everything your little heart desires!"

The class enjoyed a good laugh, then got to work gilding everything in sight — a small hexagonal-shaped kraft paper box, album covers, even some red lacquered beads that, when partially gilded, looked like something straight from the Ming Dynasty!

An hour into the class, Gabby cleared a space on the table and set out a tray of bars that she'd purchased from the Merci Beaucoup Bakery.

"Mmn," said the lady with the feather hat. "What have we got here?"

"Coconut bars and marbled brownies," said Gabby. "Help yourself."

"Can you gild food?" asked Tandy, a twinkle dancing in her eye.

"Of course you can," responded Baby. "Haven't you ever had one of the desserts at Marvel's Bistro? Their pastry chef creates delicately sculpted chocolate leaves and covers them with edible gold leaf!"

"Yum," said Tandy.

With her class focused on their projects, Carmela decided to work on her own small commission — namely, the shadow box commemorating Jerry Earl. She gathered up the photos, notebook, and the rest of the items and carried them out to the craft table.

"Mmn," said Tandy, suddenly noticing the geode. "What's that pretty little rock?"

"It's a geode," said Carmela.

"What are you going to do with it, pray tell?" asked Baby.

"Margo Leland asked me to create a shadow box. To sort of commemorate Jerry Earl's passing."

One of the blond ladies perked up. "Jerry Earl Leland? The tycoon who was murdered at his own party?"

The table went silent as a tomb and all eyes turned toward Carmela.

"I'm doing it as a kind of favor," she explained. "For his widow."

One of the crafters, who went by the unfortunate name of Tootsie, said, "If he was a really rich guy who got murdered, then probably the butler did it."

"I don't think he had a butler," said Carmela. "But he did have an assistant." *One who seems a little snarky and was definitely hiding something from me.*

Tootsie winked at her. "It was the assistant then. Guilty as charged."

"You know what," said Tandy. "I wouldn't mind making one of those shadow boxes, too."

"Me, too," said the feathered hat lady. "Those look kind of cool."

"Are we done gilding, ladies?" Gabby asked.

"Mine for sure needs to dry now," said Baby.

"So a second class?" said Carmela. To which they all gave enthusiastic nods.

To best explain how to create a shadow box, Carmela pulled out one of her finished projects. It was a shadow box with sheet music as the background, bouquets of dried flowers, a white ceramic angel statue, and a few silver stars suspended on nearly invisible nylon thread.

Then Gabby pulled out a stack of unfinished wooden shadow boxes and passed them around, and the women wandered through the shop, picking out paper, ribbon, and decorative items. The blond sister decided on a Parisian theme, while another of the women chose an African safari theme.

As her customers worked at painting and gluing paper to background their little shadow boxes, Carmela leafed through Jerry Earl's notebook and tore out the page that intrigued her the most. It was a page that had a sketch of what looked to be a map of western Louisiana. The paper was a lovely, yellowed, aged parchment and the map was surrounded by a myriad of cryptic little notes in cramped handwriting. All in all, a perfect backdrop.

To add more interest, Carmela glued a

piece of purple velvet ribbon around the edges of a photo of Jerry Earl. Then she brushed gilt paint around the edges of an old black-and-white image of the Garden District that had been taken at the turn of the century, and placed that inside. From there she only had to add two gold coins, a fossil, and the geode.

As she was positioning the geode, Carmela was suddenly aware of Baby looking over her shoulder.

"That's just lovely," Baby murmured. "You should take it over to Margo as soon as you can. I'm sure it will be a great comfort to her."

"Let me see," said Tandy, crowding in, too. "Oh yeah, that really is nice."

"No matter what you think of Margo," said Baby, "she doesn't deserve all the bad luck she's had of late."

Unless Margo's the killer, Carmela thought to herself.

Tandy was still studying Carmela's little creation. "There's something kind of familiar about that map in the background."

"You think?" said Carmela.

"Yes, but I just can't put my finger on it."

"I think it's some area around here," said Carmela.

Tandy shrugged. "Yeah, probably." Then,

in a whisper the others couldn't hear, she said, "Carmela, who was having the affair?"

Baby leaned in closer, the better to hear, as Carmela whispered, "Jerry Earl and Beetsie."

"Oh!" said Baby.

CHAPTER 12

Her guests long gone, all craft supplies cleaned up and put back in their rightful places, Carmela scurried across Governor Nicholls Street to meet Shamus. Daylight was morphing into dusk, and the French Quarter never looked more beautiful than when pink and purple streaked the sky. All the graceful old buildings had a certain softness to them, like a rubber stamp that had been carefully printed then gently smudged.

A breeze riffled the green awning overhead, and the twinkling white lights in the potted palmettos looked positively welcoming as Carmela hurried through the door into Glisande's Courtyard Restaurant.

The maître d' glanced up from his reservation book with a smile, but Carmela waved him off with a quick "I'm meeting someone." Then she strode into the dining room and looked around. It was old world New Orleans glamour personified. Decorated in a French palette of pale blue, eggshell white, and yellow, it was both posh and plush. White linens graced the tables, diners sat on richly upholstered high-backed chairs. Windows were swagged with linen draperies, and bunches of dried lavender and white roses were arranged in enormous French crocks.

Tonight there were a few early diners, but no Shamus.

But he wouldn't wait for me in here. He's probably . . .

Carmela strolled into the sleek, dark bar with its backlit Greek chorus of bottles filled with rum, brandy, whiskey, and every other spirit you could possibly conjure. And there he was, sprawled at the bar, looking happy and sassy as if he held the deed to the darned place in his hot little hand.

Carmela watched Shamus for a minute, thinking of what might have been. Of promises . . . broken.

Then Shamus turned and caught sight of her. An easy grin lit his face and he waved. Carmela remembered when that grin had set her heart to pounding. Not anymore. Now her heart was just . . . beating normally.

"Carmela!" Shamus called. "Babe!"

Carmela slid onto the bar stool next to

him. "What's going on?"

Shamus frowned. "What kind of greeting is that for your ex-hubby?"

"Sorry." Carmela closed her eyes and took a deep, cleansing breath. When she opened her eyes again, she said, "Hi, Shamus. How are you?"

"Oh yeah," he said. "That's so much better. Practically bordering on sincere."

The waiter set a vodka martini, two olives, straight up, in front of Shamus.

"You want something?" Shamus asked her.

"Just a Diet Coke."

The waiter nodded and disappeared.

"So what have you been up to?" Carmela asked.

"Ack, same old, same old. The only interesting things that've come across my desk lately are a loan app for the new casino in Bogalusa and an interim loan for an oil exploration company." Shamus sipped on his martini, then reached out and dug his hand into a bowl of bar peanuts. He popped them into his mouth, chewed, and went back for a giant helping of popcorn.

Carmela was basically appalled. But then again, she knew Shamus had the digestive system of a goat. When her Diet Coke finally arrived, she took a fortifying sip and said, "What's this little meeting all about?"

Shamus scooped up some maraschino cherries and popped one in his mouth. "So there's this charity event Saturday night . . ."

"Uh-hum." Carmela took another hit of Diet Coke. *Wait for it,* she told herself.

"The Cakewalk Ball," he said, still chewing.

"I'm aware of it," said Carmela. "In fact, I'm going to it."

"Oh, hey," said Shamus. "That makes it even easier."

"What makes what easier?"

"Because of our status in the community, Crescent City Bank is obviously contributing a cake to the auction." He eyed her carefully.

"Ye-e-s-s," Carmela said, drawing out the word.

"And Glory is donating a really gorgeous diamond pendant to top off our cake. So I need someone — hopefully you — to create the decorations. You know, the frosting and all that shit."

"Sweet talk will get you everywhere," said Carmela.

"Anyway, when it comes to decorating and crafts and girly stuff like that, you're the most creative person I know!" The wattage on Shamus's smile almost blinded Carmela.

"Shamus, I know next to nothing about

decorating a cake!"

"C'mon, babe, how hard can it be? You whip up some frosting and spackle it on."

"Plaster with sugar," said Carmela.

Shamus bobbed his head. "Sure."

"And I'm sure Glory would just *love* for me to be involved."

"She's mellowed, Carmela, she really has. She doesn't hate you nearly as much as she used to."

"You call that progress?"

"Sure," said Shamus. He reached over and squeezed Carmela's hand. "Please, babe? As a favor to me?"

"Oh . . . jeez." She was wavering. Why was that? What was the hold Shamus still had on her? "I wouldn't have to actually *bake* the cake, would I?"

"No, no, Duvall's Bakery will take care of that. In fact, I'll have them deliver it right to your place. All you have to do is throw on some frosting and fondant and make it look absolutely stunning." Shamus slipped off his bar stool and dug for something in his pocket.

"Like I know how to do that," said Carmela.

"And incorporate this diamond necklace into the decor," said Shamus. He opened his hand and a necklace suddenly tumbled out, a large diamond pendant on a thin gold chain. It dangled in midair, twirling and glinting and catching the light.

"Wow." Carmela could barely take her eyes off it.

"Nice little bauble, don't you think?"

"It's stunning. How many carats?"

"I think about six, all told. A four-carat emerald-cut diamond set in a frame of pave diamonds. Pretty neat, huh?"

"You trust me with this?" Carmela asked playfully. It was all she could do to restrain herself from hooking the gorgeous little thing around her neck!

"I trust it will be the crowning jewel on your cake."

Carmela held out her hand. "Okay. I'll do it."

Shamus dropped the necklace into her hand, where it made a delightful little puddle of diamonds and gold. "But be careful! Don't lose it! Here, better put it in this." He handed her a small black velvet bag.

Carmela placed the necklace into the bag, then tucked the whole thing into her purse. "Okay." She stood up to leave. "You coming?"

"Naw." Shamus's eyes slid down the bar, where a couple of women were sitting. "I think I'll hang around for a while. See what's shakin'."

"You're incorrigible, Shamus."

"Yeah, whatever." His eyes focused on her. "You know this is my weekend to take the dogs. According to our somewhat laissez-faire custody agreement."

"I know that."

"Okay," said Shamus. "I'm just sayin'." His eyes slid back to the two women.

"Bye, Shamus. Try to be good." Carmela walked back through the dining room, which was filling up rapidly now, and headed for the front door. But before she could push it open, a gentleman inclined his head to her and said, "Please, allow me."

Carmela looked up into the bearded face of Buddy Pelletier.

"Oh," she said, startled. "It's Mr. Pelletier, right?" She remembered him from Margo's party.

"That's right," he said as he pushed the door open for her. "And you're Carmela Bertrand." They walked out into the coolness of the late afternoon. "Margo Leland has told me quite a bit about you."

Buddy Pelletier was tall and strikingly handsome. He was midforties and wore an expensively hand-tailored suit that oozed class. He had the sharp blue eyes of a Samoyed, and they crinkled winningly at the corners.

"My dear," Pelletier continued, "you have my undying thanks. Margo tells me you've been a tremendous comfort to her during her time of need."

"I hope I have been," said Carmela.

"Margo also tells me she's roped you into the investigation?"

"Only because I was the one who found Jerry Earl."

"And a sad state of affairs that was." A sleek navy blue convertible slid to the curb and a valet jumped out.

An Aston Martin, Carmela thought to herself. Hand tooled in England and the very same vehicle that 007 drove.

"Your car is beautiful," she told him. She couldn't help herself. She was a sports car aficionado and knew this one was in a class by itself.

"One of the best things about New Orleans's climate," said Pelletier, "is that you can enjoy tooling around in your convertible practically year-round." Then Pelletier got serious again. "Your kindness to Margo is greatly appreciated. Jerry Earl was a dear friend of mine, and Margo is very special to me, too. If there's anything I can do to help, please don't hesitate to ask." He reached into his jacket pocket and took out his wallet. He extracted a business card and handed it to Carmela. "I mean that. Anything at all."

"Thank you," said Carmela, accepting the card. For some reason, the heartfelt sincerity of this very busy man touched her. And brought tears to her eyes.

The memory box tucked safely inside a cardboard box, Carmela strode up the walkway to Margo's mansion. After her encounter with Pelletier, she'd returned to her shop and picked up her handiwork. Somehow, Pelletier's worry over Margo's well-being had telegraphed to her. Even Baby had remarked how much of a comfort the memory box would be. So here she was, bearing both sympathy and a gift.

Carmela noticed that the grounds looked well kept today. The grass had been freshly cut and the camellias pruned. She inhaled the pleasant fragrance as she rang the bell. Then waited for someone to appear from behind the wrought-iron security door.

A few moments later, Beetsie opened the door. She was wearing a dark dress that hung on her spare frame. Surprise registered on her face. "Carmela. Was Margo expecting you?" Then her manners got the better of her and she said, "Come in."

Carmela followed Beetsie inside. "Is Margo here?"

"Of course, dear, I'll get her. You can wait in the parlor."

Carmela stepped into the parlor, where, only a few days before, guests had danced and drank while a zydeco band cranked out foot-stompin' tunes. Now it all looked subdued and unused. The heavy velvet chairs and sofas looked almost shabby, as if they, too, were in mourning. Carmela glanced at the enormous white marble fireplace and the portrait of Margo that hung above it. It was a very flattering oil painting, one that made Margo look years younger and pounds slimmer. She wondered who the artist had been. Certainly not Sullivan Finch, he of the strange and unusual death portraits.

Soft footsteps caught Carmela's attention. Margo descended a long stairway with Beetsie trailing behind.

"Carmela, darling," said Margo. "I've just been picking out clothes for the funeral tomorrow." She looked hollow and worn out. "You'll come, won't you? It's going to be held at St. Louis Cathedral."

"Yes, you mentioned that," said Carmela.

"Elaborate yet personal," said Beetsie.

Carmela searched her brain for a good

excuse not to attend, but Margo clasped a pudgy hand to her chest and said, "Please, Carmela, you have to come! We're counting on it!"

Carmela gave in. "Then I'll be there. And thank you for the tickets to the Cakewalk Ball. As it turns out, I'm going to be decorating a cake for Crescent City Bank."

"Aren't you the clever one," remarked Beetsie.

"That's just wonderful," Margo chirped. Sad Margo was suddenly gone; happy Margo had just taken her place. Then a wolfish grin spread across her face. "Would you like to see the necklace that *I'm* donating?"

"Certainly," said Carmela.

"Beetsie," said Margo. She did everything but snap her fingers. "The necklace?"

Beetsie hustled out of the room and returned not thirty seconds later bearing a purple velvet box.

"Come take a peek," said Margo.

Carmela and Margo crowed closer to Beetsie as she raised the lid.

An elaborate necklace studded with diamonds, emeralds, and rubies sparkled at them. In the center was a pendant in the shape of a Victorian crown. Carmela thought it looked like something Marie

Antoinette might have worn. Or at least lost her head over.

"Stunning," said Carmela.

Margo raised an appreciative eyebrow. "It is, isn't it? It will no doubt be the highlight of the auction."

Carmela stood there for a couple of seconds, then said, "You know, I didn't mean to interrupt your dinner hour." She thrust her gift box toward Margo. "I just came by to give you this."

"What?" said Margo, accepting the box. "What is it?"

"It's the memory box we talked about," said Carmela.

"Haven't you been the busy little bee," said Beetsie.

Margo carried the box over to a table, then carefully lifted the lid. "Oh," she said as she lifted out Carmela's creation. "Oh my."

"Hmm," said Beetsie.

"Car-*mel*-a," said Margo. She was choked up and finding it difficult to speak. "I can't . . . believe it." Now she pulled out a hanky and wiped away tears. "It's . . . it's . . . I absolutely love it!"

"Thank you," said Carmela. "I was hoping you would."

"You're so very . . . clever," said Beetsie.

But not half as clever as you, Carmela thought. *If you really were carrying on with Jerry Earl.*

"Speaking of clever," said Margo. "How is your investigation coming along?"

"Slow," said Carmela. "There's not a whole lot to go on."

"There isn't, is there?" said Beetsie, staring at her with eyes that were as cold as a silver penny.

"You must keep digging!" Margo pleaded. "I know you can figure this out! I know you can help me!"

Carmela stood there. This wasn't the time or place to bring up the alleged Jerry Earl–Beetsie affair. Besides maybe it was only a rumor. Or maybe . . . Well, she and Ava planned to drive down to Venice tonight. Maybe they'd turn up something there.

"If there's anything you need from me," Margo said.

"Tell me more about Conrad Falcon," said Carmela.

Margo's face turned red and her brows pinched together. "That scoundrel! You know Conrad Falcon and Jerry Earl were archenemies as far back as I can remember."

"Because they both owned construction companies?" said Carmela. "And were fierce rivals?"

Margo nodded. "Exactly. And that's why we weren't surprised when Falcon framed Jerry Earl and had him sent to prison."

Framed? But Jerry Earl really was found guilty. By a court of law. By an impartial jury of his peers.

"When Jerry Earl went to prison," said Carmela, "what happened to all the construction contracts that he had?"

"Are you kidding?" said Margo, her voice rising in near hysteria. "They all went to Falcon. He went around to all of Jerry Earl's clients and bad-mouthed him. Got them to hire him instead. It was awful!"

"What was Jerry Earl planning to do about this?" asked Carmela. "When he got out?"

Margo stared at Carmela. "Why, get even with Falcon, of course."

"And how was he going to do that?"

Margo's smile was almost a snarl. "Jerry Earl was going to ruin him!"

CHAPTER 13

Against Carmela's better judgment, she and Ava were cruising down Highway 23, headed for Venice. She knew she probably shouldn't, since an impromptu little trip like this probably wasn't going to reveal any deep, dark secrets. And Babcock would surely freak out if he found out. But she needed to make this trip anyway, if for no other reason than thoroughness.

Leave no stone unturned.

She glanced at Ava in the passenger seat, who was scrunched up and scrolling her phone for tunes. When she finally found something she liked, she smiled and plugged her phone into the car stereo. When she pressed play, Rihanna's voice filled the car.

Ava warbled happily along, but Carmela gripped the steering wheel a little tighter.

Suddenly sensing her friend's unease, Ava stopped her combination serenade and seat dance and said, "What?"

Carmela kept her eyes on the road ahead. "Something inside me is telling me to turn around right now and head back home."

"You mean like some kind of creepy warning? That something really bad is going to happen? Like an accident or a carjacking?"

"No, more like this is going to be a huge waste of time."

Ava turned the music down a little. "You know what, *cher*? I don't think so. You've got good instincts. Heck, you've got *great* instincts, honed like a doggone jungle predator! And if they tell you to check out these guys in Venice, then that's what you should do."

Carmela wasn't convinced. "I have no idea how we'll even find them."

Ava waved a hand airily. "That's no big deal. When we get there, we'll just pop into the first beer and gumbo joint that we see and start asking questions."

"Sounds a little dangerous to me."

"Then *I'll* do the asking," said Ava. She inhaled deeply and fluffed her hair. "I don't know if you realize this or not, but men often find me highly irresistible. They just looooove to help."

"Like that guy, Mickey, who's always helping you with deliveries and stuff?" Carmela chuckled.

"He's a man with a van," said Ava, practically striking a pose.

"And how about poor Stanley?" said Carmela. Stanley was an aging trust fund baby from the Garden District who trekked after Ava like a lovesick puppy.

"If Stanley likes to take me out for three-hundred-dollar dinners at Galatoire's, who am I to complain?"

"You like to game the system, don't you?" said Carmela.

"Only when it comes to men," said Ava. "And hey, girlfriend, isn't it about time women started taking the upper hand?"

"I suppose turnabout is fair play," Carmela agreed. Ava had perked up her spirits and succeeded in making her laugh. And now as they raced down the thin ribbon of highway, the bayou stretched out low and sparkling on both sides of the road. The sun, which was just about poised to slip over the horizon, cast a warm pink and orange glow that made everything feel peaceful and beautiful and right with the world.

Twenty minutes later, they coasted across an old one-lane bridge as wooden boards buckled and thumped beneath their tires. They had arrived in the heart of Venice, but the place hadn't exactly rolled out the welcome mat.

"Oh my," said Ava, crinkling her brow.

What they could see of the town was more than a little depressing. Many homes looked practically unoccupied; others seemed to have been knocked off-kilter from their foundations. A few homes were just plain flattened.

"This is worse than I expected," said Carmela as they continued on another block.

Here, many houses sported boarded-up windows, chipped paint, and sagging front porches. Others looked slightly more habitable but had often been jury-rigged in places. Obviously, the last two mighty hurricanes hadn't been kind to Venice.

Ava put a hand over her heart. "Honey, you're not going to go knocking on any of these doors, are you?"

"I don't think most of these doors would hold up to a knock," said Carmela. She felt terrible that people were living this way. That many of the people down here were forgotten victims, left to fend for themselves.

"Now what?" asked Ava as they continued to creep down the main street. "Oh man, if New Orleans is supposed to be the city that care forgot, then Venice is the city that *time* forgot!"

"It's looking a little better up ahead," said Carmela. They cruised past what served as the heart of the business section — Boudreau's Rod and Gun Shop, Palermo Pizza, Stritch's Realty, and Sonny Turk's Used Cars (*No Offer Too Ridiculous!*, according to Sonny's hand-painted sign).

"Do you see a bar?" asked Ava.

"Yup. Just up ahead. With lots of cars parked around it, too."

"Finally," said Ava. "Some real vital signs!"

Carmela drove toward the throng of cars and found a parking spot between a beat-up Ford F-16 pickup truck and a rusted Chevy Impala. She heard faint strains of zydeco music as she switched off her engine. "Sounds like something's going on."

But Ava had already scrambled out of the car. "Looks to me like a crawfish boil!" she said excitedly.

And she was right. The vacant lot next to Sparky's Saloon was in full festivity mode. Strings of colored lights had been wound from pole to pole, a zydeco band was thumping out tunes from a makeshift stage, and an outdoor bar in the corner was jammed with happy patrons. But the crown jewels of the party were the steaming pots of crawfish!

"Food!" exclaimed Ava. "Thank goodness they're serving up mudbugs, because I'm starving!"

They bought tickets at the gate from a guy wearing a *Born on the Bayou* T-shirt and pushed their way in. Two long trestle tables were covered with newspapers and piled high with bright red crawfish, red potatoes, and cobs of sweet corn.

Ava looked around at the men. "Not exactly Chippendales material, are they?"

"No," said Carmela. "But the food looks good."

"Then let's do it!"

Grabbing paper plates and a handful of paper napkins, they helped themselves to what was a veritable bayou feast.

"Perhaps a refreshing beverage as well?" said Carmela. You had to drink beer with crawfish. It was tradition, after all.

So they grabbed longneck Abitas from the bar, found two seats at one of the picnic tables, and settled in.

"Mmn," said Ava. She twisted the head off a crawfish and sucked the body meat out greedily. "This is delicious."

A man with more facial hair than a billy goat passed Ava a bottle of Pleasure & Pain hot sauce. The red and yellow label featured a naughty little dominatrix cracking a whip.

"You might want to try this, ma'am. It'll really spice things up!"

"*Merci!*" said Ava.

"This is quite a *fais do do,*" Carmela said to him, using the Cajun word for *dance party.*

"Sparky's has a boil goin' most every Wednesday night," said the billy goat. Then he tucked back into his own pile of crawfish again.

Carmela and Ava ate happily, washing down their food with the cold beer, and watching the dancers whirl madly about. A burly biker in leather swung his partner, a nimble woman in a pink and yellow dress, around the dance floor like they'd taken lessons at Arthur Murray. Other couples did the two-step, and a young, sort of Goth-Cajun couple did a Cajun jitterbug with lots of intricate spins and turns.

As Carmela ate, she watched. Kept an eye on the dancers, noted the people who sat at the surrounding picnic tables, and scanned all the newcomers who seemed to constantly stream into what was becoming a very crowded event.

"I'm going to grab us a couple more beers," Carmela told Ava.

"Sure," said Ava. "Great."

Carmela pushed her way through the

throng, grabbed the beers, and started back toward their table. Halfway there, providence dropped its little gift directly in front of her — a tough-looking man, probably in his midthirties, and wearing tight-fitting blue jeans and a black leather vest. No shirt, just the vest. But what really stood out for Carmela was the blue-inked tattoo on his shoulder.

Is it? Carmela wondered. *Could it be?*

But the man had wandered away. So Carmela had a quick decision to make. Go back and join Ava, or make like a stalker and follow this guy.

It was an easy decision.

Darting through the crowd, Carmela tried to catch sight of him again. She dodged and bobbed, hanging on to her bottles of beer, but wasn't having any luck.

Please don't tell me he just up and left.

She circled around one of the boiling pots, glanced toward the bar, and saw him again. He was stationary now, leaning against a wooden post with his arms folded across his chest. His expression was glum, and he seemed immune to the toe-tapping, upbeat music.

Carmela decided that asking him to dance was pretty much out of the question. So then what?

She knew she had to come up with something quick. She was ten feet away from him, walking straight at him, and closing fast. When she stopped directly in front of the man, she flashed what she hoped was her most dazzling smile and thrust one of the beers toward him. "Would you like a beer?"

The man reached out and swept it from her hand. Like a bear paw coming out of a cage to snatch a hunk of meat.

"Thanks," was all he said.

Carmela smiled again and decided he was actually a decent-looking guy. Aside from the bayou-biker look, he had a tangle of blond hair like a surfer or beach bum, piercing blue eyes, strong cheekbones, and kind of a cute nose. But there was no smile, no hint of encouragement to her at all.

"I bet a smile would light up that handsome face," she said to him.

The man continued to stare at her.

Okay, maybe I should try another angle, Carmela thought. And decided to take a direct route. A very direct route.

"I like your tattoo."

"Who're you?" asked the guy. His tone was suddenly wary.

Carmela's trusty *compadre* in crime suddenly materialized at her side.

"We're just a couple of friendly gals from up New Orleans way," Ava said breezily. "And we're sure enjoying the hospitality around here."

As the man studied Ava, Carmela studied his tattoos. They were faded and his skin was very tan and leathered, but she could definitely see the outline of a sailboat. The other tattoo looked like a complex algebra equation, but Carmela guessed it was really the stars and map.

This could be a guy who served time with Jerry Earl Leland!

Before Carmela could ask him anything, a man with a receding hairline and toothy smile reached in and grabbed Ava's hand.

"Excuse me, Moony," he said, "but if you ain't gonna dance with one of these fine beauties, then I will." And with that, he pulled Ava into the fray of dancers.

Which left Carmela facing her quarry once again.

"Your name is Moony?" she asked.

The man nodded.

"That's your God-given name?" asked Carmela.

"You ask a lot of questions, don't you?" said Moony.

And I'm about to ask a lot more, Carmela thought to herself.

"Look," said Carmela, "I bought you a beer; the least you can do is tell me your name."

"Ah . . ." said Moony, then his shoulders seemed to relax and his face lost some of its earlier tension. "It's Eddy Moon, but everybody around here calls me Moony."

"Is that where you're from? Around here?"

"That's right," said Moony. He took another sip of beer and gazed toward the dancers. "Your friend is having some fun out there."

Carmela followed his gaze and saw Ava shimmying and shaking like she was the second coming of Beyoncé. "Girls just like to have fun," she quipped to him. And then, as the music ended, Ava's partner dropped to one knee. He said something to her that made her throw her head back with laughter. Then she scampered back to join Carmela and Moony.

"What was that all about?" Carmela asked her.

Ava blinked. "What?"

"He was down on one knee," said Carmela.

"Oh that." Ava casually brushed her hair off her shoulder. "He professed his undying love for me and asked for my hand in marriage."

Next to them, Moony snorted loudly.

Carmela raised an eyebrow at him.

"Knowing old Dusty," said Moony, "that's not all he asked for."

Ava dimpled prettily. "No. But I'm a lady and that's all I'm going to divulge in mixed company."

This time Moony laughed out loud, his shoulders shaking.

Carmela took full advantage of his guard being down. "Moony, we were wondering if you were acquainted with a gentleman by the name of Jerry Earl Leland."

Moony's disposition changed in a heartbeat, and his shoulders suddenly hitched up to around his ears. "Why would you ask me that?"

Carmela pointed at his tattoo. "Your tats are showing."

"So what?" said Moony.

"Jerry Earl Leland had the same tattoo," said Carmela.

Moony's eyes flashed an angry green, then turned hard as sea glass. "How would you know that?"

"It was in the *coroner's* report," said Carmela. She and Ava both held their breath as they waited for Moony's reaction.

Finally, Moony said, "Yeah, I heard that old Leland kicked the bucket." Now he had his eyes focused on the ground. "Sounded like a tough way to go."

"That's what his widow thought, too," said Carmela. "That's why we're trying to help her."

Moony's eyes finally rose to meet Carmela's. "You're trying to help his old lady?"

"That's right," said Ava. "She's pretty broken up."

"That's too bad," said Moony.

"If you two had the same tattoos," said Carmela, "you must have been friends."

Moony seemed to pick his words carefully. "Not really friends . . . more like . . . acquaintances."

"But you knew him fairly well," Carmela prodded.

"Yeah, I knew Jerry Earl," he acknowledged. "From when we were in Dixon together."

"You were both in some sort of gang?" asked Ava.

Moony thought for a moment. "I'd call it more of a business arrangement. Me and my guys occasionally helped smuggle out information for Jerry Earl."

"Information? What kind of information?" Carmela asked.

"More like orders," said Moony. "That old fox was running his company from inside a ten-by-twelve-foot jail cell. Pretty funny when you think about it."

Carmela didn't see anything funny about it. "What exactly was it you smuggled out?"

Moony shrugged. "Like I said, information. Notes and shit. You know, the kind of . . ." He twirled his hand around in a circle. "Messages. Stuff a guy like Jerry Earl would need to communicate to the outside world."

"How exactly did you smuggle it out?" asked Ava. "If you were in the joint yourself?"

"Lots of different ways," said Moony. "Sometimes it went out with our lawyers inside their briefcases. Sometimes one of my boys would get his release papers and carry it himself. And sometimes we used visitors or even tennis balls."

"Tennis balls?" said Carmela.

"You had a tennis court?" said Ava. "I've heard of country club prisons but that's ridiculous —"

"No, no," said Moony, interrupting. "From when we were out in the exercise yard. You cut a hole in a tennis ball, stuff in a note, and toss it over the fence to a waiting messenger." He grinned. "That's a good way to get dope *into* the prison, too."

"So the notes were all about business?"

Carmela asked.

Moony shrugged. "Sometimes it was a note to his old lady; sometimes it was this crap about geology. He was loony about geology and dinosaurs. Kept yapping about how he knew where there was a T. rex buried. At least he hoped there was."

"Did he tell you where?" Ava asked.

Moony pursed his lips and made a disparaging sound. "Come on, like you actually believe that stuff? Dinosaur bones buried in Louisiana? If you believe that, then I got some hot property down the street you might be interested in."

"Oh no," said Ava, "I've been down that street. Nothing in my price range."

Moony's mood turned dark again. "Speaking of money, I did a lot of favors for Jerry Earl. And he owed me considerable money. Now that's all gone. Since the jerk went and died on me."

"Do you get up to New Orleans very much?" Carmela asked.

Moony narrowed his eyes at her. "I haven't been up to those parts since I got out of the pen."

Carmela decided she probably would have noticed if Moony had been at Margo's big bash. On the other hand, that didn't mean he hadn't creepy-crawled into the house through Jerry Earl's office and killed him. A man like Moony was used to flying under the radar. He could probably get in and out of Jerry Earl's house before anyone could say "Another champagne, *s'il vous plaît.*"

"Let me ask you something," said Carmela. "How did you know that Jerry Earl was dead?"

"Lady," said Moony, "Venice may be the end of the world. But we still get TV, newspapers, and the Internet!"

CHAPTER 14

Carmela pulled back the gauze curtains in her bedroom and assessed the weather. Raindrops tip-tapped at the window and ran down in rivulets. A sodden gray mist consumed her view into the courtyard. Feeling tired and brought down by the weather, every ounce of her wanted to dive back into bed and burrow beneath the down comforter. Cuddle up with Boo and Poobah and catch a few more *zzz*'s. But this morning was Jerry Earl's funeral, and she'd promised Margo that she'd be there. Front and center. Rain or shine.

She took a shower, standing under the shower head, letting the water wash over her until the pipes started clanking and the hot water dwindled to a tepid trickle. Then she dried off, smoothed on body lotion, and padded barefoot to her closet. Next problem. What to wear?

Well, it was a funeral, so she should probably choose something tasteful and sedate. She searched through her closet and came up with . . . nothing. Why was it, she wondered, that she had been shopping for twenty years and still had nothing to wear?

Okay, time to get serious. Maybe her tailored gray wool blazer and skirt? Sure, why not? Worn with a peach blouse, it had been her honeymoon going-away suit. It hadn't brought her much luck in that regard, so maybe the suit would be put to better use as funeral attire. Couldn't hurt.

Shrugging into the skirt and a black blouse, Carmela returned to the bathroom. She applied the bare minimum amount of makeup — a hint of pink lip gloss and a waft of the mascara wand — so she wouldn't get ticketed by a roving glam squad. Then she turned to her hair, which was caramel-colored and not quite shoulder-length and still dripping water. She considered doing a blowout, but in the end just settled for spritzing it with styling lotion and kind of brushing it into shape. Ava, who was a graduate of Mr. Gary's College of Hairdo Knowledge, would have scolded her. Ava would have advocated using a blow dryer and a curling iron, and pinning in three or four hairpieces, but she wasn't about to spend thirty minutes doing a fancy coif and then end up all bedraggled by the rain.

The doorbell dinged, setting off a cacophony of barks from Boo and Poobah. Canine homeland security at work.

Probably Ava.

Carmela scurried to the door and pulled it open. Ava sauntered in like she was walking the catwalk, wearing a tight black leather skirt and a low-cut hot pink and orange silk blouse. From the bounce in her step and a few other places, it looked as if she also wore a spring-loaded bra.

"Good Lord!" said Carmela. "We're going to a funeral, not trolling for questionable dates at Dr. Boogie's Jazz Club!"

Ava twirled around so Carmela could see and appreciate the full effect. "You like? I know it might be construed as being a trifle edgy by some people with a more conservative bent, but I see my outfit as being rather celebratory."

Carmela stared at her deadpan. "Huh?"

"After all," Ava continued in her confident jabber. "You never know when your time is up. I mean, life is for the living and this is, after all, New Orleans!"

"Okay." Carmela wasn't sure what kind of philosophical prose that was supposed to be, but she wasn't about to argue. The clock was ticking and the dogs were padding back and forth between her and Ava, making nervous little figure eights, as if they were in a figure-skating competition.

"*Cher,* how are you fixed for coffee?"

"Sorry, no time."

"Coca-Cola?" asked Ava. "I always need a hit of caffeine to get my engine purring."

Ava's engine seemed like it was purring just fine. "In the refrigerator," said Carmela. She grabbed a bag from under the cupboard and poured kibbles into two aluminum bowls for the pups. *Petit déjeuner* for dogs. "Help yourself."

Ava found her Coke and wandered over to the dining room table. She plunked herself down, did a sort of double take, and said, "Holy chibata, girlfriend. That's a sweet-lookin' little bauble you got here!"

Oops, Carmela thought. Ava had just spotted the diamond necklace.

"Where did you get this?" Ava had pulled it from the pouch and was practically drooling.

"From Shamus."

Ava's brows instantly puckered. "Oh no! *Problema!* Please don't tell me that lying, scheming skunk is trying to ply you with expensive gifts? Don't you *dare* think about taking him back!"

"Not to worry," Carmela chuckled. *That*

214

was never going to happen. "The necklace is for the top of a cake he asked me to decorate for the Cakewalk Ball."

Ava plucked the little pendant up and dangled it from her fingers. "You're telling me Crescent City Bank is donating this?"

"That's right." Pause. "Would you like to go?"

"To the ball?" Ava nodded. "Sure, why not."

"With me as your date, since I only have two tickets."

"Okay by me." Ava studied Carmela for a couple of seconds, then batted her eyelashes. But in a friendly way. "Carmela dear."

"Yes?" Carmela could pretty much guess what was coming.

"Can I wear this?" Ava asked, giving the little pendant a shake. "Just for the funeral? I mean, it's the closest I've come lately to a gen-u-ine diamond." She fluttered her left hand absently. "Honestly, I thought for sure I'd be married and divorced by now, out of my starter marriage and working on finding a second, more successful husband. And what am I? A single woman with a cat! I'm a cliché!"

"But it's a *prize*winning cat," said Carmela. When her words failed to cheer Ava, she added, "I suppose you can wear it. After

215

all, what Shamus doesn't know won't hurt him."

Ava hastily strung the pendant around her neck, where it glittered and gleamed and caught the light. "Isn't it funny," she said in a breathy voice, "that diamonds are a girl's best friend, but dogs are man's best friend?"

Carmela thought for a moment. "I guess that tells you which sex is smarter."

Carmela and Ava walked across the plaza to St. Louis Cathedral, arguably the heart of New Orleans. With its triple steeple, the cathedral was an architecture gem. It towered above its historic neighbors, the Cabildo and the Presbytere, and looked down benevolently on the green of the Square and the block-long Pontalba Buildings with their lacy ironwork galleries.

Inside, the church smelled distinctly Catholic, a blend of frankincense and sandalwood mingling with the scent of votive candles, oil, and fresh flowers.

"Wow," Ava whispered as she and Carmela stood in the back of the church and looked around. "Margo's turned this funeral into a real shindig."

The great rococo altar was adorned with extravagant floral bouquets of porcelain white camellias and English roses. Enormous candles burned on two six-foot-high brass stands. And front and center, between two rows of wooden pillars, was Jerry Earl's ornate mahogany casket. It rested atop a wooden bier and was draped with a white flag embroidered with a gold Mardi Gras emblem.

"It looks like a state funeral," Carmela whispered. She decided that all that was lacking was some red, white, and blue bunting. The kind politicians seemed to love. Then her eyes searched the crowded church, a veritable sea of darkness with everyone dressed in black like a flock of grackles. Finally, she spotted Gallant, sitting just a few rows ahead of them. "C'mon," she whispered.

Carmela and Ava tiptoed to the pew, where Bobby Gallant was camped out. He looked up expectantly, then scooched over to make room for them.

"Anything new?" Carmela asked him.

But before he was able to answer — or maybe he wasn't going to answer her at all — a hush descended upon the crowd.

There was a clatter at the back of the church, then Carmela and the two hundred or so mourners turned to watch as Margo began her way up the center aisle. Escorted by Duncan Merriweather, Margo was dressed in a flowing black dress and wore a perky hat with a veil. As she stepped smartly along, knowing full well she was being scrutinized by everyone, it became quite apparent that her intent was to show off. Her dress, edged with pale pink lace, was knee-length in front, but fell into dramatic, sweeping, floor-grazing folds in back.

"She's wearing a mullet dress," Ava whispered. "Business in the front, party in the back."

As Margo continued up the aisle, a chill ran down Carmela's spine. She realized that Margo, with her black dress and matching veil, looked more like a bride than a grieving widow. Only she was a bride dressed in black, like a witch bride or a character out of some unholy fairy tale.

Margo finally made it to her seat in the front row. She and Merriweather slid in and settled next to Beetsie, who extended a bony hand to each of them. Beetsie, Carmela noted, appeared more severe than ever. She wore a plain sack-like black dress that hung loosely around her hips, and she sported a fresh-cropped haircut that revealed rather large ears.

Seated directly behind Margo was Eric Zane and two other people that Carmela recognized as household staff.

From the third row on were the hoi polloi of the Garden District. Friends and neighbors, many of whom had been present at Margo's soiree last Sunday night. Carmela even recognized Buddy Pelletier, looking dignified and somber. He was clutching the hand of a petite blond woman seated next to him. Presumably his wife.

Suddenly, organ music burst forth with an impressive rendition of "How Great Thou Art." The priest marched in, accompanied by two altar boys, and the service was under way.

The Requiem Mass was longer and more elaborate than Carmela had remembered. And so, when Buddy Pelletier took the lectern to speak, she found it to be a welcome break. His manner was gentle and caring, and he spoke elegantly and meaningfully about his dear departed friend.

There was more incense as well as prayers and songs. And then, finally, the service came to its inevitable conclusion. The casket click-clacked down the aisle, followed by a weeping Margo, who was barely supported by a teetering Duncan Merriweather.

"Very dramatic," Ava whispered to Carmela.

Carmela nodded. Then turned to speak to Gallant. But like a will-o'-the-wisp, he had suddenly disappeared down the side aisle.

"Doggone," Carmela said under her breath. "I wanted to talk to him."

"Maybe you can catch him at the cemetery?" said Ava.

"That means we have to go to the cemetery," said Carmela. She hadn't planned on that.

"We have to go!" said Ava. "Because . . ." She hesitated.

"What?"

"There's a fancy luncheon afterward. At Commander's Palace. You know I don't get to go there all that often."

So of course, they drove down St. Charles Street from the French Quarter to the Garden District. Or "back to the scene of the crime," as Ava called it.

"Your pink and orange top is a welcome hint of color in all this gloom," Carmela told Ava as they walked through the wrought-iron gates of Lafayette Cemetery No. 1.

"Nothing will ever be dull around me," agreed Ava. "Not even the weather."

In the distance, a bright flash lit up the sky. It was followed by a loud clap of thunder.

Carmela laughed. "Did you do that?"

Ava raised her brows and glanced sideways at her. "That's only a small sample of my bewitching powers."

They followed a group of mourners through the jumble of tombs and markers and mausoleums. Rain pattered down lightly as white gravel crunched underfoot.

"Spooky in here," Ava muttered.

"I thought you liked spooky," said Carmela.

"I like *my* brand."

"Oh," Carmela laughed. "You mean the manufactured kind. The voodoo dolls that come wrapped in plastic from a factory in China."

They assembled with a small group of about thirty people, then waited in the light rain as a cadre of pallbearers carried in Jerry Earl's casket.

"At least this isn't filled with theatrics," Ava whispered.

At which point a flash of lightning blazed across the sky and Margo Leland stepped forward to place the memory box that Carmela had crafted atop the polished casket.

"Ooh, look what's suddenly front and center," whispered Ava.

"Shhh," said Carmela as Margo turned to address the group.

"I'm so glad y'all could come," Margo said in a halting voice. "It means a lot to me, and it would have meant so very much to my dear Jerry Earl." She brushed back tears. "He did so love a good party."

"She's not just the life of the party," Ava whispered. "She's the death of the party."

Margo turned and touched a hand to Jerry Earl's casket. "Now he's gonna join his momma and daddy right here in this magnificent Leland family tomb." Her eyes went a little wonky. "Where I will probably join him sometime in the distant future."

Carmela had seen weird send-offs before — this was New Orleans, after all. But this one took the cake.

"Buddy," said Margo, turning slightly, "would you do the honors?"

Buddy Pelletier nodded at her and stepped smartly up to the mausoleum. As he pushed open the wrought-iron gate, it creaked back loudly on rusty hinges. Then it took another few minutes for the pallbearers to grapple with Jerry Earl's casket once again and muscle it into the tomb.

Carmela knew that family tombs were a grand tradition here in New Orleans. Coffins were often left inside for years at a time to dry out and decay. Then they were discarded and the dear departed's bones shoved down a slide to a repository below. She wondered if Jerry Earl was next in line, or if he was going to have to wait his turn. Then, because she knew her thoughts were dark and grisly, she glanced around to clear her head. And noticed Eric Zane wiping away a tear.

Is he sorry that Jerry Earl is dead? Or relieved that he's gone?

Another thunderclap rumbled, this one closer than ever, and Carmela felt fine droplets starting to hit her head.

Good thing I didn't pop for an eighty-dollar blowout.

They all bowed their heads as the priest stepped up and gave his final blessing, his voice sounding hollow and stark in the old cemetery. Even he seemed to rush through the ritual before the thunderstorm threatened to let loose and soak them all.

When it was finally over, the crowd began to quickly disperse, but Carmela sought out Buddy Pelletier.

"You gave a really lovely eulogy," she told him.

Pelletier tilted his head at her in appreciation. "Thank you, my dear." He placed his hand over his heart and patted it. "It's a very sad day for all of us."

Carmela nodded. "Indeed it is. Though

Margo seemed to hold up fairly well."

"Margo's a trooper," said Pelletier. "She'll carry on no matter what. Of course . . ." He gazed at her pointedly. "She'll need a little help from her friends."

"That goes without saying."

"I wanted to tell you," said Pelletier, "how much I admired the little shadow box you created. Very appropriate."

"Thank you. It was really just stuff that Margo gave me. The coins and photo, a geode plus Jerry Earl's notebook."

"Still, a lovely and meaningful piece of artwork," said Pelletier. "Perhaps I could commission one myself someday. But something a little more feminine in nature, since it would be a gift for my dear wife."

Just then Ava walked over to join them.

"Carmela could do it," said Ava, always the promoter. "She's a real artist."

Pelletier smiled. "I know she is." He paused. "Are you ladies coming to the luncheon?"

"We wouldn't miss it for the world," said Ava. She waggled her fingers. "Bye-bye. See you later." Ava could generally charm the stitches off a baseball.

"Save it," said Carmela when Pelletier was out of earshot. "He's married."

"Why is it that the rich, good-looking ones

always are?" she sighed.

"Come on," said Carmela. "We should say something to Beetsie."

"Why?" said Ava. She pulled a mirror out of her bag and made a big point of checking her hair. "Ooh, I'm getting soaked to the bone. Soaked to the *bone*, get it?"

"Be nice," said Carmela. She forced a smile to her face and called out, "Beetsie."

Beetsie turned toward her, dabbing at her eyes, and Carmela realized that she'd been crying.

"What a lovely funeral," Carmela told her. "It was so kind of you and Duncan Merriweather to help with the planning."

Beetsie nodded tiredly. "Yes, it was quite a fine send-off. But really, aside from ordering flowers and a few minor details, Duncan handled most of the details himself. He's a retired funeral director, you know."

Carmela stiffened. "No. I had no idea."

Beetsie nodded. "I don't think Mr. Merriweather did any actual embalming in the last few years of his career, but he ran a fine, dignified business. Perhaps you know it? Broussard's over on St. Charles?"

"I've heard of it," said Carmela.

"Yes," said Beetsie. "Broussard was his mother's maiden name." She smiled brightly, showing amazingly long incisors.

"Duncan Merriweather comes from a long line of undertakers!"

CHAPTER 15

Carmela and Ava exchanged hasty, astonished looks. This was front-page news for both of them!

"But that's neither here nor there," Beetsie prattled on. "Goodness, I do think it's really going to pour." She hunched her shoulders and tried to shield her head with her clunky black purse. "I guess I'd better dash across the street to the luncheon reception." And without even a polite good-bye, she turned and scuttled over to join Margo, who was still surrounded by a small group of mourners.

"Did you hear that?" said Carmela, her voice rising a couple of octaves. "Undertaker? That means Merriweather probably has a trocar. Just like the murder weapon!"

"It also means he probably knows how to use it," said Ava.

"If Merriweather's an expert, and it sounds like he might be, he could probably kill someone in an instant."

Ava snapped her fingers. "In a heartbeat. Why . . . he could probably stab someone at a party and no one would even know until it was too late!"

Carmela rubbed at the goose bumps on her arms. "Where's Bobby Gallant? Did you see him? I need to talk to him. I think I should tell him about this."

"I know he was here," said Ava. "I just saw him a couple of minutes ago." She glanced at the sky and flinched. "But if he has any common sense at all, he's somewhere out of this weather. C'mon, we should go, too. Let's head over to Commander's Palace and find us a nice cozy table. Ponder this new information where it's nice and dry."

Carmela glanced around. "You go grab a table. I'll be right behind you, I promise. I'm just going to take a quick look around, see if I can find Gallant."

Ava wagged a finger at Carmela. "Okay. But be careful. Stay out of trouble!"

Like that's going to happen, Carmela thought to herself. She was already in too deep and knew it. She probably shouldn't have agreed to help Margo in the first place. Now here she was. Checking out suspects, stumbling on a couple more. Madness, for sure.

Carmela dodged around several tombs and mausoleums, looking for Gallant. She really needed to find him! Making that connection between Merriweather and the trocar had given rise to a very bad feeling!

Could Duncan Merriweather be the murderer?

He was older, she reasoned. But he was big. And maybe still strong enough to wield a weapon like that. If Merriweather got it in his head that he wanted to be Margo's next husband — and inherit the wealth that way — that could be a powerful motivator. A powerful motive.

Voices rose from behind a nearby crypt. Carmela ignored them and was about to call out Bobby's name when she realized the voices had turned harsh and were rising rapidly in pitch.

An argument? Sure sounds like it.

Now she recognized one of the voices!

That's Eric Zane!

Creeping closer to the crypt, Carmela ducked down, hoping to listen in on the conversation.

"It's worth a lot of money!" Zane said angrily.

Carmela pressed herself against cold,

damp marble. *What's worth a lot of money?* she wondered. What was going on? Was Zane blackmailing someone? Trying to strong-arm someone?

But the person's response was a low, angry mumble.

Carmela tried harder to listen in on the conversation.

"I know you have the money," Zane snarled.

Trying to ease her way around the crypt, Carmela wondered if she could sneak a peek without getting caught. She heard another irritated response, this time softer. And realized the conversation was fading out, like a bad radio signal. The two people were drifting away.

Maybe I can still catch a look!

She was about to steal a look when there was a soft crunch of gravel just behind her. Startled, she whirled around in a nervous panic and came face-to-face with a large, imposing figure. She blinked and tried to focus. *Please don't let it be Merriweather. That would be way too spooky.*

It was Bobby Gallant, looking quizzical and a little amused.

"What are you doing over here?" he asked.

Carmela touched a hand to her heart. "You scared me half to death!"

"I didn't mean to," he said. Then, "What are you up to?"

"I . . . I was looking for you," said Carmela.

"Here I am."

She wondered if she should just blurt it out and decided, yes, that was the best course of action.

"I just picked up some information that could be critical to your investigation!"

A look of skepticism crossed Gallant's face. "Oh really?"

Carmela ignored his Doubting Thomas demeanor and continued.

"Beetsie just told me that Duncan Merriweather is a retired funeral director!"

Gallant's expression never wavered. "And you think that's important . . . why?"

"Because of the nature of the murder weapon!" she shrilled. "The trocar. What if he . . ."

"Owned one?" said Gallant. "Knew exactly how to use one?"

"Yes! Exactly!"

"Your information is highly circumstantial," said Gallant.

"Look," said Carmela, "I can't connect all the dots; I'm the first one to admit that. But you've got to look into this!"

"We're looking into everything," said Gallant. "Believe me. Even the mayor is exerting pressure on the department to solve this crime."

"Then we really need to get cracking," said Carmela. "We need to figure this out!"

Gallant gave her a wary look. "We?"

Carmela pursed her lips. "You, I meant you."

"That's right."

Carmela wondered if she should tell him about her visit to Venice last night. But the look on Gallant's face told her no. *Save it. Wait until he's in a more receptive mood. If that ever happens. Don't tick him off any more than you have to, or he'll really slam the lid shut on the investigation!*

"Wait a minute." Carmela stopped dead in her tracks. "Was Merriweather even at the party Sunday night?" Images of canapés of beluga caviar and champagne danced in her brain. And were immediately followed by the grisly memory of Jerry Earl tumbling lifeless and limp out of the clothes dryer. *Tumble dry. How ghastly.*

"He was on the guest list," said Gallant. "But nobody I interviewed remembers seeing him."

"Well," said Carmela. "What does Merriweather say? Was he there or not?"

Gallant stuffed his hands into his pockets.

"That, my dear Carmela, is proprietary information. I can't tell you everything!"

Yes, you can, she thought as he sauntered away. *Or at least you should!*

Commander's palace was a New Orleans fixture. Established in eighteen eighty-three by Emile Commander, this turreted Victorian structure had been a bordello back in the twenties. Now the aqua and white building with the matching awnings served as one of New Orleans's premier restaurants.

Much to Carmela's delight, Ava had snagged a lovely little table near the window. She half stood in her chair and waved as Carmela entered the elegant dining room with its overhead crystal chandelier.

"*Cher!* Over here!"

Carmela hurriedly joined Ava at the table. "I talked to Gallant."

Ava wrinkled her nose. "Do you think we might put the murder on hold for, oh, say about thirty minutes? While we enjoy a cocktail or two as well as the food from this gorgeous buffet that Jerry Earl's widow has popped serious money for?"

"Yes, of course," said Carmela. "Sorry. I guess I am driving you nuts with all this stuff."

"Just a teeny bit," said Ava as they both

233

slipped into the buffet line.

And once Carmela saw the food, and felt her stomach rumble, all thoughts of murder flew out of her head, too.

"Look at that," said Ava. "Wild Louisiana white shrimp, tasso ham, and pickled okra."

"Fantastic," said Carmela. The luncheon was suddenly looking very good indeed.

"Ooh, and beef shish-kabobs. Let's not forget these," said Ava as she piled two skewers on her plate and two on Carmela's.

Carmela eyed a pastry dome and scanned the place card in front. "Do we have room for oyster and absinthe dome?"

"I always have room for oysters," said Ava, pushing aside some shrimp on her plate.

"We'll have to make a return trip for the bread pudding," said Carmela as they sat down at their table.

They ate for a few minutes, relishing their food and chatting amiably. Finally, Carmela said, "So I ran into Gallant and told him about Duncan Merriweather."

Ava nodded. "Of course you did."

"Something else happened, too. I over-heard Eric Zane talking to some guy. Well, actually, it sounded like Zane was trying to extort or blackmail them."

"Did you see who it was?"

"Unfortunately no."

Ava looked over at the buffet line, which was still snaking its way past dozens of steaming chafing dishes. "I just saw Zane a few minutes ago."

"Was he with someone?" Carmela asked, pouncing on her words.

"Not that I noticed. But he did look kind of stressed."

"He's probably working his buns off," said Carmela. "Talking to the chef or harassing the kitchen staff to keep the chafing dishes filled. Trying to make things perfect for Margo."

"So he's working for her," said Ava.

"Sure. I guess. I mean, now that Jerry Earl is dead and buried, he's probably become Margo's personal assistant."

"That's only if Zane decides to stay on."

"He doesn't seem to be making any motion to leave," said Carmela.

Ava pulled out her compact and studied her hair and makeup. "Eeh, I look like I'm wearing a fright wig." She stared at Carmela. "I look awful, don't I? Be honest."

Carmela lifted a hand. "It rained. You were caught without an umbrella."

Ava stood up. "Come on, I need to do a major fix-up." She cocked an eye at Carmela. "And, I'm sorry to say, your hair doesn't look all that lush and springy, either."

"Thanks a lot," said Carmela.

They pushed their way through the dining room and wandered down a narrow hallway hung with all sorts of awards, notations, and autographed photos. Commander's Palace had been honored by the James Beard Foundation, *Wine Spectator, Food & Wine, Southern Living,* and dozens of local groups and media organizations.

"Here we go," said Ava. She put her hand on the aqua-colored door that said *Ladies* and gave a little shove.

Nothing happened.

"Huh?" said Ava. "Is this thing locked?"

"What's wrong?" asked Carmela. She'd been scanning an award given by Zagat to honor what they were calling "modern New Orleans cooking and haute Creole." Very impressive.

"This dang door is stuck," said Ava.

"Here, let me try." Carmela pressed a hand against it, but it still didn't budge.

"See what I mean?" said Ava.

Carmela frowned. "Yeah." She pushed harder on the door. When it still didn't move, she leaned a shoulder against it and put her whole body behind it. It grudgingly opened a few inches. "Well, this is stupid."

"Something's blocking it," said Ava. "See if, like, one of the vanity chairs tipped over or something."

Carmela pushed the door open another couple of inches and eased her head through the narrow opening.

And immediately wished she hadn't.

There, sprawled on the carpet, legs and arms akimbo, was Eric Zane! He wasn't moving, breathing, or even twitching. And the carpet that had once been a plush silver-gray had been turned into a soggy, squishy mess.

"What?" said Ava, seeing the look on Carmela's face. "What's wrong? Let me see!"

Carmela withdrew her head. "You don't want to . . ." Carmela began.

But much like the cat, whom curiosity had killed, Ava had already stuck her head in to look.

Ava's bloodcurdling scream echoed through the whole of Commander's Palace. It bounced off the ceiling, rattled dishes in the dining room, and ricocheted back into the depths of the kitchen.

Carmela grabbed Ava's arms, held them to her side, and hugged her tight. "It's okay, honey. It's okay."

"It's not!" Ava screamed again. "He's in

there and he's dead!"

"I know he is," Carmela soothed. She wondered how she could remain so calm. Had she actually become blasé about finding dead bodies?

But wait. Was Zane dead?

As nervous waiters and a quizzical maître d' immediately rushed to join them, everyone venturing a horrified look and yammering at once, Carmela fought to take another look.

Zane hadn't moved a muscle. Hadn't even twitched. Yup. He was definitely dead.

"We called 911," said the maître d'. He looked pale and stricken and was wringing his hands compulsively.

Another man in a tall chef's hat poked his head in the door to survey the body. "We don't want a problem here," he told Carmela.

"It's too late for that," Carmela responded tiredly. "You've *already* got a problem."

CHAPTER 16

Five minutes later, the front door flew open and Bobby Gallant blew in like an ill wind. His mouth was pulled tight, his brow was deeply furrowed, and his jaw was in locked position.

By that time, all hell had broken loose. A crowd had gathered, and Margo and Beetsie were toddling around like a pair of hysterical zombies. Only Ava seemed to have recovered fairly well from her fright and was sipping a hibiscus martini given to her by a passing waiter.

Gallant thundered down the hallway, two uniformed officers and a full paramedic crew in tow.

"Out of the way, let us through," he barked as waiters and looky-loos scattered like bowling pins.

When Gallant saw Carmela, he said, "You! I should have known."

"I didn't do anything!" Carmela bleated.

"You found him," said Gallant. "That's bad enough."

"I didn't mean to," said Carmela. "We just sort of . . . stumbled upon him."

Gallant stood off to one side while the uniformed officers grappled with screwdrivers and crowbars and pried the entire door off its hinges. Then he pulled on a pair of latex gloves, ducked into the room, and knelt down next to Zane. He studied him for a couple of minutes, then said, "The personal assistant, right?"

"That's right," said Carmela. "Eric Zane."

"Been dead for what?" said Gallant. "Maybe twenty minutes or so?"

One of the blue-suited paramedics nodded. He seemed to concur.

"But how?" Carmela asked. She continued to hover in the hallway just outside the ladies' room. "What happened to him? I don't see a gunshot wound or anything."

Ava had edged down the hallway, the better to be in on the action. "We didn't *hear* a gunshot."

Gallant was grim. "Another stabbing."

"Oh dear Lord," said Ava. "Don't tell me it was one of those trocar things again."

"No, but I'd say this is equally strange," said Gallant. He reached down and gently pointed to a thin trickle of blood on one side of Zane's head. "It appears that some-one jammed a thin piece of metal into his ear. Like a metal skewer or something."

"Oh no!" said Carmela. "You mean a skewer from one of the shish-kabobs?"

"The *what*?" said Gallant. He looked up at them, half-angry, half-surprised.

"They served mini shish-kabobs at the luncheon," Carmela explained. She was suddenly feeling queasy in her stomach.

"Fillet mignon and pearl onions," Ava said helpfully.

"How long were the skewers?" Gallant asked.

"You haven't pulled it out yet?" asked Ava. "Gack."

"It's part of the crime scene," said Gallant. He sounded irritated. "So we have to leave it in place and let the ME deal with it." He looked at Carmela again, waiting for an answer.

Carmela held her hands a few inches apart. "Maybe . . . seven or eight inches long?"

"Enough to do the job," said Gallant.

"You mean enough to kill him?" asked Carmela.

"You pierce the central cortex," said Gallant, "you're talking instant death." He shook his head. "Who would do this? And why?"

"I think I might know something about that," said Carmela. "At the cemetery, just before I ran into you, I . . . I heard Zane arguing with someone."

"Arguing? Arguing with who?"

"I have no idea. If I knew that, I'd tell you."

"Was it a male? A female?"

"Now that you ask, I'm not totally sure."

"Do you think it might have been Duncan Merriweather?" Gallant asked.

Carmela stared at him. Maybe he had taken her seriously.

"I suppose it could have been him," she said. *Then again, it could have been anyone. It could have even been Beetsie.* Carmela tried to shake the feeling of helplessness that had suddenly engulfed her.

"Did Zane sound like he was being intimidated?" Gallant asked.

"Not at all," said Carmela. "In fact, I got the distinct impression that he was the one who had the upper hand. That he might even be trying to blackmail someone."

"Blackmail? Blackmail over what?" Gallant demanded.

"No idea," said Carmela. "Maybe . . . maybe you should try to ask Margo?"

Gallant glanced down the hallway, where Margo was crouched and babbling. "I don't know, she's pretty hysterical right now."

"You have to try," said Carmela.

Gallant shrugged and walked down the hallway. He had a short conversation with Margo, the upshot being she started blubbering and waving her arms around in a spectacular fanning motion.

"I'm guessing Margo's not making a whole lot of sense," said Ava.

"I think you might be right," Carmela agreed.

Gallant rejoined them. "No rational answers to be found there."

"What did you expect?" said Carmela. "Margo's had a bad shock." Heck, *she'd* had a bad shock.

"Why don't —" Gallant caught himself before he said another word.

"What?" Carmela said.

He grimaced and shook his head. He didn't look happy. "I can't believe I'm about to ask you this."

"What?" Carmela said again.

Gallant gazed at her and said, "Why don't you try to talk to Margo? She might respond more positively to a woman. A friend."

"A friendly woman," said Ava.

Carmela was mildly amused. "Me? I

thought you wanted me to stay out of this."

"Well, you're in it up to your armpits now," said Gallant. "So could you at least try? Talking to her, I mean?"

"Sure she will," said Ava. "We'll both try!"

Carmela and Ava led Margo into the manager's office and sat her down on a plush blue love seat.

"Honey," said Carmela. "Can we get you anything?"

"Maybe a drink," said Margo. She was sniffling like crazy and had black rings around her eyes where her makeup had run. She looked like a raccoon with a head cold.

"Water?" said Ava. "Maybe an Evian?"

"Bourbon," said Margo.

Once Margo had sucked down two fingers of good Kentucky bourbon, she seemed to relax a little bit.

"I just want to ask you a couple of quick questions," said Carmela. "Take your time and try to answer them as best you can."

Margo took another long pull on her drink. "Okay."

"Do you know who could have done this?" Carmela asked. "To Eric?"

"I don't know," Margo blubbered. "First Jerry Earl, now poor Eric." Her lower lip began to quiver and she hiccupped abruptly.

"It feels like some kind of *curse* has descended upon me."

"A curse?" said Ava. She sounded interested for the first time.

Margo gripped Carmela's arm tightly. "That's it! There must be a terrible curse on my head!" she hissed. "A curse that latches on to everyone around me. On everything I touch!" Her voice rose and cracked, and she pinched Carmela's arm so hard that Carmela winced.

"Oh no," said Carmela. "There's no such —"

"The psychic," Margo said, her eyes big and fearful. "I've got to talk to her. Please! You have to get me an appointment with that tarot card reader!"

Carmela glanced at Ava.

"We can surely do that, darlin'," said Ava.

"Soon," said Margo. "We have to do it soon! I have to know what's going to happen!"

"How about tomorrow morning?" said Ava. "I'll call Madame Blavatsky and set everything up."

Margo released her death grip on Carmela's arm and gazed at Ava. "Thank you, Eva, thank you so much!"

Ava pursed her lips, but didn't bother to correct her.

Carmela tried to ask a couple more questions, but Margo wasn't having it. Finally she left Margo sitting in the office, having a second drink and commiserating with Beetsie.

"Nothing?" said Gallant.

"She thinks there's a curse on her head," said Carmela.

"Well, *that's* real helpful," said Gallant. "Maybe I should consult a witch doctor?"

"Sorry," said Carmela. "We tried; we gave it a shot." She paused. "Is Duncan Merriweather still around?"

"Yes, he's sitting in the dining room with the rest of the guests who've been stunned into silence." Gallant rolled his eyes. "Now I have to conduct more interviews."

"Too bad," said Ava.

After muttering a few more words to Gallant, apologizing for not getting any useful information out of Margo, Carmela tried to steer Ava toward the door.

"Let's blow this pop stand, Ava. Before something else happens!"

A look of shock crossed Ava's face. "Wait a minute, we're leaving now? But we didn't even get a chance to sample the bread pudding!"

Carmela felt a wave of relief wash over her

the minute she entered Memory Mine. She was finally back in familiar territory, her safety net, her home away from home with its racks of colored paper and rubber stamps and rolls of ribbon. Gabby was, as usual, expertly holding down the fort as she rang up one customer while she demonstrated to another how to make a crepe paper rosette.

When both customers had made substantial purchases and finally exited the shop, Carmela grabbed Gabby's hands in hers and said, "You'll never guess what happened after the funeral!"

Gabby frowned. "Margo freaked out and tried to jump into her husband's grave?"

Carmela shook her head. "Close but no cigar. Rather than putting Jerry Earl's coffin in the ground, they stuck it inside the family mausoleum."

"Then what are you talking about?"

"After the graveside service, right smack in the middle of the funeral luncheon, Eric Zane was murdered in the ladies' room at Commander's Palace!"

Gabby frowned. "Zane? What on earth was he doing in the ladies' room?"

"I don't *know*!" said Carmela. "Dying, I guess."

"Oh my gosh," said Gabby, her eyes going big. "You're not kidding, are you? You're absolutely serious!"

"Hey," said Carmela. "You can't make this stuff up." She paused and thought for a moment. "Well, maybe you could if you were a really bad sitcom writer."

"I think you better start from the beginning and tell me everything!" said Gabby.

Carmela gave Gabby a quick rundown on the entire morning. She gave her the *Reader's Digest* version of the funeral and graveside service, and ended with her account of Eric Zane's bizarre murder.

"Holy frijoles!" said Gabby. "And you say Bobby Gallant did a complete switcheroo and *asked* you to talk to Margo? That's pretty bizarre."

"Isn't it?" said Carmela. "Who would've thought that he'd ask for my help?"

"But maybe you shouldn't be looking into this at all, Carmela. There's a killer out there who doesn't seem to be afraid to take down anyone who gets in his way." Gabby glanced furtively at the shop's front door. "Which means you might not be safe anywhere."

"I hear you," said Carmela. "Which is why I can hardly wait for Babcock to get back."

"Were you able to pry anything at all out of Margo?"

Carmela shook her head. "Nope. Margo

was in the advanced stages of hysterics. She's also convinced herself that there's some sort of evil curse hanging over her head. And that it can be transferred to anything or anyone she touches."

"Wow," said Gabby. "That's kapow crazy!"

"Isn't it? Anyway, to calm her down, Ava and I had to schedule a tarot card reading for her tomorrow."

"A lot of good that's going to do," said Gabby. "I don't think you'll find any real answers in those cards."

"Margo's convinced we will."

"But what about suspects?" said Gabby. "You must have some ideas on possible suspects."

"I'm guessing it had to be someone who was at the funeral luncheon," said Carmela.

"But who?"

"I don't know," said Carmela. "The two people closest to Margo seem to be Beetsie Bischoff and Duncan Merriweather, but . . ." She debated telling Gabby about Merriweather's background as a funeral director, then decided not to. She'd spooked poor Gabby enough for one day. Instead she said, "Beetsie always seems to be around whenever someone gets killed."

"That's nothing," said Gabby. "So are you."

"Thanks a lot," said Carmela. She slipped her jacket off. "You know what? I suddenly have a splitting headache. So I think I'm gonna take refuge in my office for a while. Maybe work on a scrapbook page or start that history scrapbook I promised the French Quarter Association."

"Let everything percolate for a while," said Gabby.

"That's right," said Carmela. "But if we get super busy, give me a holler."

Carmela sank into her chair and kicked off her shoes. There. Much better. It felt comforting to be surrounded by all her familiar things. Even if they were just drawings pinned to the wall, some brocade pillow boxes she'd created, and a handful of decoupaged boxes. She pulled out her sketch pad and turned to a clean sheet.

I should work on a few ideas for Shamus's cake. Not leave it to the last minute like I usually do.

But what could she do for a cake topper? How to incorporate the great little necklace that was still dangling around Ava's slim neck. Carmela thought for a few minutes, then picked up a fat, squishy pencil and started sketching.

What if she did a cake decorated with

twigs and branches that were made out of frosting? What if they swirled their way up the side and around the cake? And what if, at the very top, was a lovely little bird's nest made out of frosting?

The bird's nest would hold the necklace nicely. And for added color and interest she could add a few of the miniature feathered birds she had in the shop.

Yes, I like that a lot. Better yet, I think it's something I can actually pull off. It's kind of cake décor slash memory box.

As she continued to sketch, a light blinked on her phone. She steadfastly ignored it, hoping Gabby would take care of whoever was calling. Then she heard footsteps and Gabby's light knock on the wall outside her office.

Carmela spun around in her chair. "Yes?"

"Bobby Gallant is on the phone."

"Okay, thanks."

Gabby paused. "Carmela. Please be careful."

People keep telling me that, she thought to herself as she picked up the phone. *Maybe I should start listening to them.*

"I shouldn't be telling you this," were Gallant's opening words.

"What?" said Carmela, practically pouncing on him.

"You were one hundred percent correct. It was a metal skewer."

"From one of the shish-kabobs," said Carmela.

"The chef confirmed it, so yes."

"What do you think? Was it the same killer who stabbed Jerry Earl?"

"That possibility certainly exists."

"Then it had to be someone who was at the funeral luncheon," Carmela said.

"Or someone from the kitchen staff," said Gallant. "But that's kind of a stretch."

"Not if they were also on the catering staff from the other night."

"I thought of that," said Gallant. "And we're checking it out."

"Do you have a guest list of who attended the services and luncheon today?" Carmela asked.

"That, of course, was Eric Zane's job," said Gallant.

"Oh."

"And Margo was still pretty weepy, but her friend managed to pull together a list for me."

"You mean Beetsie?"

"That's the one." He paused. "Then I asked Margo if she thought Zane might have been trying to blackmail someone."

"What did Margo say?"

"Basically, nothing. Margo was stunned; she didn't have a single idea in her head."

"She never does," said Carmela. "Which is starting to make me a little suspicious."

"Are you telling me you suspect the grieving widow?"

"I don't know what to think," said Carmela. "For one thing, I'm not even sure about motive anymore. I can understand if someone hated Jerry Earl and wanted him dead. But then to kill his assistant? What's that all about?"

"But if Zane was trying to blackmail somebody . . ."

"Blackmail them over what?" Carmela asked. "Zane was basically a flunky."

"But maybe he knew something," said Gallant.

"Because he spent so much time hanging around the Lelands' home?"

"That's right," said Gallant. "So I need to keep asking questions."

"Did you talk to Duncan Merriweather?"

"Yes, I did. After you told me about Duncan Merriweather's background, I spoke to him and he did admit to having a number of antique mortuary items in his possession. But here's where it gets a little crazy. Merriweather also told me that several of them were stolen from his house when it was burglarized a few months ago."

"What? Do you believe him?"

"I pulled the police report and there was indeed a burglary," said Gallant.

Carmela sighed loudly. "Don't tell me a trocar was stolen."

"A trocar was listed among the stolen contents."

"Dang!" said Carmela. "I still think you've got to look at him hard. Because you know why? He could be Margo's next-in-line!"

"What are you talking about?"

"I didn't think it was strange at the time, but Merriweather escorted Margo to my shop last Monday. And he hangs around her house all the time. And he was comforting her at the funeral this morning . . ."

"That's what friends do," said Gallant.

"Or he could have another motive."

"Which is?"

"What if Merriweather is angling to marry Margo, get her money, then dump her for Beetsie!"

Gallant was shocked "That sounds like a storyline on *Days of Our Lives,* not a motive for a murder!"

"What if it's both?"

"Then God help us," said Gallant. He was quiet for a few moments, then he said, "No, you've got to be overthinking this. It has to be business related."

"What makes you say that?" said Carmela.

"Because Merriweather still strikes me as a nice old guy. Kindly and sweet."

"So was John Wayne Gacy," said Carmela. "He dressed up as Pogo the Clown to entertain kids, yet turned out to be one of the worst serial killers of all time!"

"Point taken," said Gallant.

Carmela worked for another twenty minutes until she was interrupted again. Her Realtor, Miranda Jackson.

"Hey there," said Miranda, "I've got some good news for you."

"You finally sold the house!"

"Noooo, but I've got an offer I'd like to present."

"When?" asked Carmela.

"What are you doing in thirty minutes?"

"Oh," said Carmela. "That soon?"

"You're the one who wanted a quick sale," said Miranda. "And it is a buyer's market out there."

"Good point," said Carmela. "So . . . where do you want to meet?"

"At the property, of course."

"The Garden District house," Carmela said slowly. She wasn't all that keen on going back there. Too many bad memories.

"There are a few contingencies we need to go over," Miranda said breezily.

"Okay," said Carmela. "I'll see you there."

CHAPTER 17

New Orleans's Garden District is considered to be one of the best-preserved collections of historic Southern mansions in the United States. Greek Revival, Italianate, and Moorish-designed homes stand shoulder to shoulder amid lush foliage and abundant flowers. Authors such as Anne Rice and Truman Capote have found inspiration among all these white columns and louvered shutters, and dozens of novels and movies have been set here. The Garden District is, to put it mildly, utterly enchanting.

With tentative movements, Carmela pushed open the front door of her soon-to-be-former home. She stood in the marble-tiled entry, breathed in the scent of sweet jasmine mingled with dust bunnies, and called out, "I'm home, dear."

The voice of Miranda Jackson, her Realtor, floated back to her.

"I'm in the dining room."

Carmela stepped into the living room, or Grand Salon as she'd once jokingly referred to it. She took in the marble fireplace, cove ceilings, arched windows, and magnificent chandelier. Even unlit and unlived in, the home was definitely a beauty. And deep inside her chest she felt a small flutter of . . . what?

Is it regret?

No, she knew she was far better off with her life firmly rooted in the here and now. With her cozy apartment, wacky friends, and chugging-along-fairly-well business. Not to mention her hot cop boyfriend. Carmela tamped down her feelings and ghosted through the house, following the clicking sounds that were coming from the dining room. She found Miranda seated at the expansive pecan table, pecking away on her tablet computer.

Miranda looked up and smiled. She was a pretty woman in her midforties with a mane of curly blond hair and a pair of pink half-glasses perched on her pert nose. Her worn leather briefcase was puddled on the table, and sheets of paper covered every inch of fine polished wood.

"Your new office," said Carmela.

Miranda shoved a pencil into her hair.

"Don't I wish. This is such a grand old place."

"Maybe *you* should buy it."

"Can't," said Miranda. "I just closed on two duplexes over by Tulane. Rental properties, you know."

"You think I should invest in another home? A *smaller* home?"

"Couldn't hurt," said Miranda. "Now's the time to make your move. Before all the homeowner tax loopholes get closed by those greedy Feds."

Carmela wandered absently over to the bay window and gazed out into the back garden. It was lush and beautiful, the low afternoon sun casting a soft glow on the crepe myrtle and azaleas that were in bloom.

"Don't look out at that magnificent view," Miranda warned. "I don't want you getting cold feet."

Carmela chuckled. "I won't." She took a deep breath. "So you brought me an offer?"

Miranda pulled the pencil out of her hair and tapped at a legal-size sheet of paper. Then she indicated the chair next to her.

Carmela came over, sat down, and stared at the paper. It was filled with numbers and line after line of small print. Weasel words, as she liked to call them.

"It's an impressive offer," said Miranda.

"Not full price, but close enough for jazz."

"Hmm." Carmela wasn't sure how to respond, she was so dazzled by all the zeroes that danced before her eyes.

So this is it?

She would sign on the dotted line and be free of the massive home and the nagging memory of Shamus? She suddenly felt a strange hollowness deep in the pit of her stomach.

Probably just need something to eat!

Miranda's phone buzzed.

"Where do I sign?" Carmela asked.

Miranda fumbled with her phone and sent the call into voice mail. "Not so fast." She held up a hand. "Your buyers are asking for a few sweeteners."

"Sweeteners?"

Miranda sighed. "They walked in and absolutely went gaga over your furniture. So they're asking you to throw in a few pieces."

"How few?" Carmela asked.

"This dining room table and chairs, as well as the mahogany secretary and side table from the living room."

Carmela drummed her fingers on the table, thinking.

"We can always counter," said Miranda. "Remember, this is all about negotiation."

"No," said Carmela. "I want to get this done. So . . . they can have the furniture." She didn't really want to deal with it and had already talked to Jekyl about selling whatever pieces seemed worthwhile. He'd promised to place them on consignment in various antique shops up and down Royal Street.

"All right," said Miranda, surprised by Carmela's decisiveness. "We'll include those few pieces." She made a few notations on the document. "Oh, and one more thing."

"What's that?"

"The buyers also want you to share in the closing costs."

Carmela frowned. "How much would that be?"

"They usually run a couple thousand dollars. Maybe three at the most."

"So I'd pay half?"

"Yes."

Carmela pulled a pen from her purse. She was almost ready to agree, but then caught herself. "Anything else?"

Miranda smiled. "No. They love the house and they're good solid buyers. We should have a quick escrow."

"I'm willing to concede on those two points just to make this sale happen," Carmela told her.

"Excellent." Miranda's phone buzzed again and she sent another caller into voice mail. She tapped a manicured finger against the paper. "Then all you have to do is sign right here."

Carmela signed.

"Good," said Miranda. "Perfect."

"Now you have to relocate your office," Carmela said, hiding a smile.

Miranda gathered up all her papers and shuffled them into a tidy little stack. "Not a problem. I'd do just about anything to make this sale happen."

Carmela nodded. "Me, too."

After signing the paperwork, Carmela floated out of the mansion, feeling surprisingly free and light. As if a very heavy weight, namely a hulking mansion, had been lifted from her slender shoulders. Now she had a nice tidy bit of cash to invest or use to buy another house. Whatever. She didn't have to decide today or even tomorrow.

It was early evening as she climbed into her car, the sky a darkening blue behind a parade of just-lit streetlamps that stretched, block after block, like a glowing rosary.

Carmela started her engine and slowly cruised around her old neighborhood, gazing at the enormous homes and enjoying her mingled feelings of awe and relief. Selling the home meant marking a decisive end to one very strange chapter of her life!

One door closes, another door opens, she reminded herself. *That's the way it usually works.*

She drove slowly past her friend Baby's huge Italianate home. Everything looked quiet there tonight. Baby was probably enjoying a leisurely dinner with her husband, Del. Or maybe she was off on a play date with the grandkids.

Turning the corner onto Prytania, Carmela came up on Margo Leland's home. With both outside and inside lights ablaze, Margo's home was lit up like party central.

I wonder what Margo's up to right now?

Was she still in hysterics? Or lying in bed all conked out on bourbon and Xanax? Or was she crazy like a fox and had really wanted Jerry Earl dead and buried? And Eric Zane, too? Was a second murder just way too much of a stretch? Or was it icing on the cake?

Carmela decided that Margo could probably manage one murder. But two seemed to be pushing it. Somehow she just didn't see Margo luring Zane into the ladies' room for a whispered conference, then jamming a shish-kebob skewer into his ear.

That kind of cold-blooded murder required . . . what? A cold-blooded killer, she supposed. But also a certain steely nerve and decisiveness. It was one thing to grab a gun and pop somebody from a distance. But to get up close, look them in the eye, and watch them die . . . that was indicative of a dangerous psychopath.

So who?

Who indeed.

Carmela drove down the block and hooked a right turn. A large, black Range Rover had just pulled into a driveway, and Carmela was amazed when she saw Conrad Falcon scramble out of the vehicle.

Falcon! He lives across the back alley from Margo?

Why hadn't Margo ever told her about this?

Carmela thought for a moment, then realized that Margo *had* mentioned to her that Falcon lived in the neighborhood. She just hadn't said how close he was!

Carmela pulled to a stop across the street and killed her headlights. She watched as Falcon stalked up to a side door and disappeared inside his house. Two minutes later, the light in his front room snapped on.

So he was probably home by himself . . .

Carmela waited a few minutes, then slipped out of her car. She glanced up and down the street, feeling guilty and pulsing with nervousness. No cars were coming; no pedestrians or dog walkers were in sight. *Okay, good,* she thought as she crossed hurriedly.

Carmela chided herself about feeling guilty. After all, she was only trying to get a closer look at his property, right?

Gosh, I love a good rationalization, she told herself as she dashed past Falcon's car and slid around the side of his house.

The backyard was a veritable jungle of magnolias, oleander, and gardenias with a few pecan and sweet olive trees tossed in for good measure. She had just waded through a spongy flowerbed and was tiptoeing across the lawn when a yard light flashed on. She heard the back door snick open. Then her breath caught in the back of her throat as she heard a disgruntled mumble followed by the loud bark of a dog!

Nerves fizzing, Carmela flattened herself against a tree.

What would she tell Falcon if he stormed out and caught her? If he accused her of trespassing and called the police?

She heard grunts and sniffles and knew the dog was heading right for her.

Oh no!

Carmela peeked around the tree, ready to confront a hulking Doberman or German shepherd and saw . . . a fluffy little bichon! Who trotted right up to her and happily wagged its tail.

Carmela bent down and let the little cutie sniff her hand.

"Are you going to give me away?" she whispered.

The dog rubbed his head against her hand as she stroked him between the ears. He chuffed and sniffed and his hind end shook happily.

Carmela stood up and whispered to him, "Now you be good and stay here." She stepped quietly down the garden walk toward a wooden gate that had an arch overhead. She pressed her hand to the gate, grimacing as it creaked loudly, then pushed it open.

The gate led out to a narrow cobblestone alley bordered by a tall hedge of prickly junipers. Carmela stepped forward, rose up on her tiptoes, and peeked through the hedge.

And found herself looking directly into Jerry Earl's office!

Wow. So close. And so easy to access, especially if you know the neighborhood.

Carmela wondered if Conrad Falcon had stolen across the alley on the evening of Jerry Earl's big party. Had he stood in the shadows waiting and watching with murder in his heart? Then snuck into Jerry Earl's office and stabbed him? And stuffed his body into the clothes dryer?

Maybe. It could have happened that way.

Carmela ducked back across the alley into Falcon's backyard. She looked around for the little bichon, but it had disappeared and the yard light had gone off.

Good. Lucky.

But as she rounded the corner of the house, poised for a clean getaway, a light inside snapped on!

As light from the window suddenly spilled out to illuminate part of the garden, Carmela flattened herself against the outside wall. She felt cool bricks press against her and heard a muffled voice.

It was Falcon's voice. Talking low but with great intensity.

Taking a chance, Carmela leaned in and peered through the window. She could see the back of Falcon's head as he sat at his desk in a wood-paneled office. A Siamese cat was curled languidly in his lap. Probably the prize-winning cat from two nights ago.

Suddenly, he spoke loud enough for Carmela to hear.

"That's right," Falcon said, his voice booming. "We can move our equipment in there first thing Monday." There were a few moments of silence, then he added, "Yes, I'll have all the paperwork signed and sent over."

Where were they moving equipment to? Carmela wondered. Another construction job that he'd stolen from Jerry Earl? Or something else entirely?

Falcon hung up the phone and dumped the cat onto his desk. Then he stood up and stretched, arms above his head, neck lolling from side to side.

Carmela ducked down hurriedly, deciding she couldn't make a move until his office light went off.

Several minutes passed, and she was starting to get a nasty cramp in her calves from crouching in the oleander.

What on earth is he doing in there?

As she waited, her paranoia began to get the best of her. Had Falcon seen her? Did he know she was hiding and was planning to . . .

The light winked out, leaving Carmela in the relative safety of darkness. She stood up, unkinked herself, and thanking her lucky stars that she hadn't been caught, quickly scurried away.

Once she got home, still thankful she hadn't been caught, Carmela scrounged around the kitchen for dinner. She wasn't terribly hungry, but finally decided on some baked shrimp. It was a simple, one-pan dish with shrimp, butter, lemon juice, seasonings, and parsley. She usually served it over pasta or rice, but tonight she'd have to make do with toast.

While her shrimp concoction bubbled and baked, Carmela poured a cup of kibbles into each of Boo's and Poobah's dishes. Five seconds later, their dinners inhaled, they were looking at her once again with pleading brown eyes.

Carmela could just imagine what they were thinking: *Please, give me another helping of food and I'll never ask for anything ever again.* And then, when she gave them another serving: *Please, give me another helping of food and I'll never ask for anything ever again.*

She tapped her foot while she waited for her shrimp. And wondered — who had been hanging around Commander's Palace today, waiting to pounce? There was Duncan Merriweather, of course. In her mind, he still wasn't off the hook. And good old

Beetsie. Had *she* been the one that Eric Zane was trying to blackmail? Because of her supposed relationship with Jerry Earl?

And then there was Eddy Moon down there in Venice, probably drinking Abita beer and poaching alligators.

Or was he?

Moon had been powerfully angry about Jerry Earl owing him money. So could he have snuck into the funeral luncheon? There was always that possibility.

But why would he do that?

To kill Eric Zane? That seemed a little far-fetched. Unless there'd been bad blood between Zane and the Venice gang? She let that thought percolate for a few minutes.

Could Zane have functioned as their go-between? Was his killing some sort of retaliation?

The oven timer dinged so loudly, it made Carmela jump. Still thinking about the Venice-Zane connection, she quickly served herself a portion of baked shrimp. She ate half of it as her mind continued to wander, thinking about all the strange goings-on of the past five days. Feeling anxious and more than a little on edge, Carmela set down her fork, walked into the kitchen, and poured herself a half glass of Chablis.

This should help calm me down. Unless . . .

She hesitated for a moment, then poured the wine into the sink without taking a sip. And decided her restlessness wouldn't be completely quelled until she took another trip down to Venice and had a serious, all-cards-on-the-table talk with Moony.

"Boo? Poobah?" she called out. "You two want to feel the wind in your fur?"

CHAPTER 18

Driving down to Venice, Carmela had plenty of time to think. About Margo and Beetsie. Jerry Earl's murder. Conrad Falcon. Eric Zane's murder. And about Duncan Merriweather. Lots of egos and lives had intersected. Still, nothing seemed clear; it was like some tricky Chinese puzzle.

As she zoomed along a stretch of bayou, the sky a spectacular pinky-purple backdrop, she considered the foolishness of going back to Venice yet again. After all, what did she really know about Eddy Moon? And what if she couldn't locate him? What if he didn't hang out at Sparky's every night?

What if I start asking too many questions and . . .

Before she could ponder that thought to the fullest, she was bumping across the old one-lane bridge into town. She slowed down and drove through the business section again, passing Boudreau's Rod and Gun

272

Shop, Palermo Pizza, and the used car place, finally pulling into Sparky's parking lot.

Just like the other night, the parking lot was jammed. Carmela figured that Sparky's, such as it was, must be the social center of town.

She parked, pulled out her phone, and tried to call Ava. Nothing. Her call just went to voice mail. Okay, then she'd send her a quick text. The thought that she could disappear into the bayou with no one knowing where to search for her sent a chill up her spine.

After sending the text, Carmela steeled herself and fought to dismiss any and all irrational fears. She was here to get a few answers and that was all. There would be no spooky disappearance in a bottomless swamp. No murky figure who . . .

A vision of a shish-kebob suddenly wafted through her brain!

Carmela grimaced and shook her head to dispel the image. No. There would be no blood, no trocar, no lethal skewers, or anything else that was threatening or grisly.

"You guys stay here and hold down the fort," she told Boo and Poobah. They were both wagging their tails like mad, ready to jump out and enjoy a romp down main

273

street with the local mutts. "Be good. Try not to bark your furry little heads off."

Carmela slithered out of the front seat as paws and muzzles strove to wedge their way into her exit. She closed the car door carefully, crossed a dusty expanse, and pulled open the front door of Sparky's.

The place smelled like stale beer, burned cheeseburgers, and last month's cooking oil. Music blared from a jukebox in the corner, and lights were dim except for a galaxy of neon beer signs. A crowd was ponied up to the bar, and most of the tables were occupied.

Oh dear.

Carmela headed directly for the bar. Maybe if she talked to a friendly bartender?

The bartender saw her coming and gave a perfunctory swipe of his dirty rag at the expanse of bar in front of her. He was late fifties with a long, thin ponytail, a gold earring, and one wonky eye. He looked like one of Jean Lafitte's pirates who had somehow managed to hang on through the last two centuries.

"Help you, miss?" the bartender asked.

Carmela pushed closer to the bar. "I'm looking for a guy by the name of Eddy Moon. Can you help me? Can you tell me if he's here tonight?"

The bartender looked suddenly bored. "*Who* are you?"

She touched a finger to her chest. "Carmela. I was here last night? For the crawfish boil?"

"You were?" said the bartender.

Carmela nodded. "Sure. With my friend Ava."

A man on the bar stool next to her turned and smiled a gap-toothed grin. "Ava! I remember her. Seems to me we danced together."

"You probably did," said Carmela. "She's quite the dancer."

"Quite the looker, too," said the man.

The bartender interrupted. "If you want to talk to Moony, he's in the back room. Got himself a card game going."

"High stakes?" said the guy at the bar, looking interested.

"Penny-ante," said the bartender.

"In the back?" said Carmela. She gazed toward the rear of the smoke-filled bar. Two guys in leather vests were playing pool. Her nervousness suddenly returned.

"That's right." The bartender hooked a thumb and gestured toward the back of the bar, where two curtains hung limply in a narrow doorway.

Feeling self-conscious, Carmela walked

the length of the room and paused when she got to the curtains. Then she stuck out a hand and parted them.

Moony was there all right. He was seated at a dilapidated round table with three other men. They all held cards and had small stacks of poker chips in front of them. Nobody looked particularly happy . . . or flush.

Carmela cleared her throat. "Um . . . Moony?"

Moony tilted back in his chair and took his own sweet time in looking over at her. When he finally did, he said, "You again?"

"That's right," said Carmela. "I wonder if we could have a word."

Moony made a rude sound that caused the other men to snigger. Then he said, "Go ahead and have your word."

"Look, do you mind if we step outside?"

The player seated next to Moony, a man in a camo-printed trucker cap, said, "Some guys have all the luck."

Moony tossed his cards facedown onto the table. "Not me. I'm out." He shuffled his feet and rose from his chair. "This better be good," he told Carmela.

They walked back through the bar together and out the front door. In the fading darkness, they faced each other under a yellow streetlamp. The minute Boo and Poobah spotted Carmela, they started barking and yipping with joy. They stuck their noses out of the top of the window that Carmela had cracked open and snorted happily.

Moony saw their antics and managed a sardonic laugh. "Are those your dogs?"

"How on earth did you ever guess?"

"Can they hunt?"

"They can dig through the pillows on my sofa for treats, yes."

"No," said Moony. "I mean really hunt. Flush out game. You know, like partridge and wild boar."

Carmela chuckled. "Not hardly. Boo is basically a lapdog, and Poobah is . . . well, he's a little lazy and prefers not to get his paws wet. But he's very sweet."

"Now that we've established you've got dogs," said Moony, "what exactly did you get me out here for?"

"I've got a few more questions for you," said Carmela.

Moony's lips formed a straight line and he grumbled, "Now what's bugging you?"

"Unfortunately, there's been another death connected to Jerry Earl Leland."

Moony frowned. "What are you talking about?"

"Eric Zane, Jerry Earl's assistant, was

murdered today."

Moony looked surprised. "The prissy guy?"

"You knew him?" Carmela asked. Now it was her turn to be surprised.

Moony shrugged. "Met him a couple of times."

"Where?" Carmela asked.

"At Leland's house."

"Really," said Carmela. *So Moony's been there. He knows exactly where Jerry Earl called home. Isn't that interesting!*

Moony stared at her. "So what was your question?"

"Hmm?" Carmela was still processing this new information.

"You said you had a couple of questions for me. So . . . shoot. Time's a-wastin'."

"Did you, um, deliver some of Jerry Earl's messages to Eric Zane?" Carmela asked.

Suddenly Moony seemed fascinated by his shoes. He scuffed up some dirt and studied the sole of his boot. After a moment, he said, "Maybe a couple, yeah."

"So where else were messages delivered?" Carmela asked.

Moony stiffened. "I'm not sure. I don't keep no notebooks or records or anything like that. And I already told you, I had some of my guys working on that stuff, too."

"Which guys?" Carmela asked. "Could I talk to them?"

"Lady, you are way too cuckoo for words. What do you want, huh? You want me to take you to meet 'em?"

"Well," said Carmela. "I guess I do." Her heart caught in her throat. What was she getting into?

Moony took a step back and considered her words. "You really are crazy. But heck, if you want to take a ride . . ."

Carmela looked at him expectantly.

"What can I say?" said Moony. "I've always had a soft spot for the ladies. Come on, I'll drive. You can leave your car here; it'll be safe enough." He sauntered toward a dusty red Jeep Wrangler that was parked haphazardly on the street. In fact, half of the Jeep rested on the curb.

Carmela reconsidered the idea of Moony taking her anywhere. Even if he didn't have malicious plans for her, she could wind up dead or maimed just because he was a terrible driver.

Moony glared at Carmela. "Come on. The longer you make me wait, the easier it is to change my mind."

That was enough for Carmela. She hopped into the passenger side of Moony's

Jeep while Boo and Poobah whined from her car.

"Oh man," she worried. "I really hate leaving them behind."

"Get 'em," Moony said. "That's okay with me."

Carmela jumped from the Jeep and ran to her car. When she pulled open the door, Boo and Poobah spilled out happily. "Come on, guys. We're going for a little ride."

Carmela hefted the dogs into the back of the Jeep, then climbed in herself.

"Buckle up," said Moony as they lurched forward. "We're about to navigate some real Louisiana back roads!" As they tore down the main street, two bearded men in camo gear were just coming out of Boudreau's. They lifted their hands in a knowing wave as Moony's Jeep shot down the street.

At least, if I disappear, there'll be a couple of witnesses, Carmela thought grimly to herself. *And I do have the dogs for protection.* She glanced back at the dogs, who were slobbering on the upholstery and couldn't have cared less.

They crossed the rickety bridge, a tide of dark water swirling below as Boo and Poobah danced with excitement. Soon they hung a left turn onto a dirt road that was rugged with grooves and treacherous dips.

Branches swept against the sides of the Jeep and scratched overhead as they hurtled down a dark tunnel of foliage, swaying from side to side as if they were on a roller coaster.

At one point the bayou closed in so tightly that the road was just a puddle of muck in Moony's headlights. Carmela figured they'd get stuck for sure, but Moony navigated the muck and ruts like an expert, like someone who knew this road like the back of his hand.

As if reading Carmela's mind, Moony said, "I go hog hunting out here all the time."

The narrow road rose a bit as they approached a fork. Without hesitating, Moony downshifted and turned down the right fork. They wove their way past stands of bald cypress and tupelo, eventually ending up at a ramshackle camp house.

"This here is Jake Ebson's house," Moony said as they rocked to a stop in a patch of hardpan dirt. "But most everybody around here just calls him Squirrel."

Carmela gazed around. Under a dim yard light, the camp house was a weathered silver-gray with a corrugated metal roof and an array of animal hides and antique traps nailed to the outside walls. A yellow bug light glowed on the porch and a man in cut-off jeans and a T-shirt with three days' worth of growth on his face lounged in a hand-made rocking chair. Next to him was an old blue cooler with a rip down one of its seams.

Moony climbed out of his Jeep. "Come on. You can let those dogs stretch their legs, too."

"You think?" said Carmela. What if they wandered off, never to be seen again?

"They'll be fine," Moony assured her.

Carmela let the dogs scramble out, just as a brown and white hound came bounding over to inspect the newcomers. In about two seconds flat, the dogs were playing and jumping around together. Fast friends already.

When the man on the porch caught sight of Moony, he dipped a hand into his cooler and fished out a can of Dixie Beer. "Hey, Moony," he called out. "How's about a cold one?"

"Don't mind if I do, Squirrel," said Moony as he stomped over and accepted the beer.

"Whatcha doin' out this way?" Squirrel asked. Then he turned his curious gaze on Carmela, who had followed closely behind Moony. "And who's the lady you brought along?"

Moony pulled back on the tab and said,

"Aw, I got this lady nagging on my butt."

Squirrel tipped his bushy head back and laughed. Then he scratched at his belly. "Well, she's a very pretty lady. I'd sure enough let her nag at me if she wanted."

Moony held up a cautionary hand. "Don't say that. She'll start right in."

Carmela laughed good-naturedly, then stuck out her hand. "Hi, I'm Carmela Bertrand."

Squirrel shook hands with her politely. "How do. Nice to meet you."

"And I hope you don't mind," said Carmela, "but I have a few questions to ask you."

Moony snorted. "Here she goes."

"As you can see," Carmela continued, "Mr. Moony was kind enough to drive me out here."

Squirrel, ever the gentleman, reached in and grabbed another can of beer and held it out to Carmela. When she declined, he shrugged and opened the beer for himself. "Questions about what?" he finally asked.

"Jerry Earl Leland was murdered last Sunday," Carmela began.

Squirrel watched her intently. "So I heard."

"And now," Carmela continued, "his assistant, Eric Zane, was killed right after his funeral this morning."

Squirrel sat up straighter. "You don't say."

"So I'm trying to figure a few things out," said Carmela. "Kind of . . . well, I guess you'd call it investigating."

Squirrel narrowed his eyes. "Are you some kind of cop?"

"No," Carmela said. "No way. I'm just looking into things for Jerry Earl's widow. She's pretty broken up about things." She hesitated. "So Moony told me you did some deliveries for Jerry Earl when he was in prison?"

"I might have," said Squirrel.

"I was wondering," said Carmela, "who else you might have delivered messages to besides Eric Zane?" She glanced off into the dark woods, where she could hear the dogs yipping and yapping at something.

Squirrel thought for a few minutes. He took a swig of beer, then brushed at the back of his hand. Finally he said, "I do remember some guy by the name of Beck."

"Is Beck his first name or his last?" Carmela asked.

Squirrel cocked his head to one side. "I really can't recall."

"But this Beck person lived in New Orleans?" Carmela asked.

"Oh no," said Squirrel. "He lived somewhere up in West Feliciana Parish. Near . . . ah . . . Laurel Hill." He nodded, sure of himself now. "Yeah, I think that was it."

Carmela continued her line of questioning. "Can you think of anything else regarding this guy Beck?"

Squirrel shrugged, then finished his beer in one long gulp. He crushed the aluminum can in one hand and tossed it in the corner, where it clanked noisily and joined a half dozen of its equals. "Not really," he said. "Sorry."

"Too bad," Carmela murmured as the three dogs came strolling back and settled in the dust at her feet.

Moony stepped forward and said rather aggressively, "Look, Carmel . . ."

"Carmela," she said tiredly.

"Carmela," said Moony. "We just gave you a whole bunch of information for free!"

Carmela gazed at him. "This seems to be an ongoing concern of yours. That you're not getting paid."

Moony's face flushed bright pink. "That's right!" he said, his voice a cranky scratch. "*I* never got paid and I was supposed to! Jerry Earl even told me he was gonna sell this fancy, antique necklace his old lady had. Something . . . victorious."

Carmela stared at him. "Wait a minute . . .

you mean Victorian? Was it a Victorian necklace?"

"That might have been it, yeah," said Moony. "Anyway, Jerry Earl even described it to me. It was some kind of elaborate crown with a whole bunch of rubies and emeralds stuck in it."

"He was going to *sell* it?" Carmela said, her voice rising in a squawk. *Why would Jerry Earl do that? Because he needed money? Or . . .*

"I think it was on account of his wife didn't wear it anymore," said Moony. "She was tired of it, I guess. Rich lady like that, he figured she'd never miss it. Or she didn't care anymore."

"That's so weird," said Carmela. "I mean about the necklace."

"How so?" said Squirrel. He was glancing back and forth between the two of them like a spectator at a tennis match.

"I think it's the same necklace Margo Leland is using to decorate her cake," said Carmela.

Now Moony looked disbelieving. "A cake? Who puts a necklace on a cake?"

"For the Cakewalk Ball," Carmela explained. "It's a charity event this Saturday night at the New Orleans Art Institute."

"A *cake* ball?" said Moony. He lifted a

hand and scratched his head. "That sounds like the kind of stupid thing rich people would do!"

CHAPTER 19

"You're looking a little tuckered out, *cher,*" observed Ava.

"I need to squeeze in a nap to get rid of these bags," Carmela grumbled. She pressed her fingertips lightly against the skin under her eyes as she examined herself in the glass countertop at Juju Voodoo. Two dead bodies and several late nights in a row had wrecked havoc on her beauty sleep. The Cakewalk Ball was tomorrow night, and Babcock would be back in town. Needless to say, she had to look fabulous.

"I can't believe you took off for Venice last night without me," Ava said.

Carmela lifted her head. "Where were you anyway? I tried calling a couple of times."

Ava offered a pussycat grin.

"Was it that guy Charlie?" Carmela asked. "The crime-scene tech?"

Ava nodded. "He is kind of a cutie. I'm thinking I wouldn't mind if he Lewis-and-

Clarked my body."

It was ten o'clock Friday morning and they were waiting for Margo and Beetsie to show up for the tarot card reading. Madame Blavatsky had already arrived and was fussing around in the back of the shop, preparing the reading room and, even more important, brewing up a pot of much-needed chicory coffee.

Ava fingered a purple and gold saint candle that sat on her counter. Saint Christopher, patron saint against floods. She'd sold a lot of those in the past couple of years. Now she always kept them on order.

"So," Ava said, "were you able to pick up any hot new information?" She pulled her tight glitter skull T-shirt a little lower, the better to show off her assets.

Carmela thought for a minute. Had she? No, not really. "No, not really," she told Ava. "Well, maybe one thing. Moony took me to meet this guy, Squirrel. And it turns out Squirrel delivered some of Jerry Earl's messages to a guy named Beck somewhere up in West Feliciana Parish."

"I used to date somebody who was from there," said Ava. "Nice fella, except he wore his pants a little too short." She shook her head. "I just don't enjoy seeing a man's ankles."

"Do you know how picky you sound?" Carmela asked.

"I prefer to think of it as exacting," said Ava. "Really, sweetie, do you want me to *lower* my standards? And who are you to talk? You spent last evening with two guys named Moony and Squirrel. Give me a break! It sounds like a reality show on the Discovery Channel."

Footsteps sounded behind them as Madame Blavatsky suddenly whisked out from behind the green velvet draperies that separated the reading room from the shop. She was dressed in a flowing midnight blue skirt, matching peasant blouse, and leather boots. Several long necklaces clanked around her neck, and a red-beaded shawl was wrapped around her slim waist. Best of all, she held a tray with two steaming mugs of high-octane coffee.

Carmela made a one-handed grab, snatching a cup off her tray. "Thank you," she gasped.

Madame Blavatsky held the tray out to Ava.

"Thanks," said Ava as she accepted a mug. "But aren't you having any?"

Madame Blavatsky waved a hand. "I'm going to abstain. I find that any sort of caffeine clouds my instincts."

"Wow," said Ava. "Even Diet Coke? I couldn't live without a hit of Diet Coke in the morning. Those bubbles really wake you up."

Carmela took a sip of coffee. "Thank you, that really hits the spot."

"You had a rough night," said Madame Blavatsky.

"I did," said Carmela. "I went on kind of a wild-goose chase."

"Be careful," warned Madame Blavatsky.

Carmela was instantly on alert. "What do you mean?"

"It's just a feeling I'm getting from you," said Madame Blavatsky. She reached over and gently touched Carmela's arm. "A feeling that perhaps you shouldn't stray too far from home."

Ava pointed a manicured index finger at her fortune-teller. "You. You are *good.*"

At which point the front door squeaked open, and Margo and Beetsie came clattering in.

Margo, true to form, was turned out in a gold brocade jacket, gold chains, and gold bangles. Even her gilded fingertips matched her accessories. She was in full hyperactive mode with hands and arms flapping about and greetings shouted in sharp, shrill tones.

Beetsie, on the other hand, looked like an

extra from *Death of a Salesman.* She wore a dowdy gray dress and carried a sensible, black leather frame bag. Similar to what the Queen of England carried, only nowhere near as stylish.

Once the introductions were over, Margo pounced on Carmela. "Carmela, darling," she said. "Have you made *any* progress at all in your investigation?"

"It depends," said Carmela. "Do you know anyone by the name of Beck?"

Margo's lips pursed together and she made a big show of feigning thoughtfulness, her eyes rolling to the back of her head as if searching out an answer.

"Doesn't ring a bell," Beetsie said.

"No," Margo agreed. "I don't know anyone by the name of Beck." She hesitated. "Why? Have you learned something new?"

"It doesn't really look that way," said Carmela. "Sorry."

Margo patted her hand. "But you're trying. That's what really counts."

"That's right," Beetsie agreed.

"Why don't we get started," said Ava. She raised both arms as if to herd everyone in the direction of the reading room.

"This is very thrilling," said Margo as they wound their way through Ava's shop.

"Scintillating," said Beetsie. She stared

thoughtfully at a wooden Day of the Dead ferris wheel that featured tiny pink and purple skeletons snuggled in each dangling car.

Ava's octagonal-shaped reading room was kept cool and dark by voluminous swags of velvet draperies. The only bit of natural light came from a pair of stained glass windows that depicted an angel carrying a small lamb. The windows had been scrounged from a church, and then Ava had scrounged them from the scratch-and-dent room of a local antique shop.

In the center of the room was a low round table covered with a purple paisley shawl. A deck of tarot cards was centered on the table.

Everyone filed in, eyes darting, shoulders hunched, expectations running high.

Madame Blavatsky wasn't about to disappoint them.

"Please, everyone sit down," she intoned. "Margo, you sit right next to me."

Margo took her seat, with Carmela sitting on the other side of Madame Blavatsky. Beetsie sat across from Margo. Ava stood by the door and slowly dimmed the lights, creating a moody ambience.

"And now, a few moments of silence," said Madame Blavatsky.

They all sat in silence and stared expectantly at Madame Blavatsky, who had closed her eyes and was engaged in some kind of rhythmic yogic breathing.

Carmela smiled to herself. She knew that Madame Blavatsky — aka Ellie Black — was centering her energy. But she always imagined this moment as a good opportunity to grab a quick catnap, too. On the other hand, maybe it was just wishful thinking on her part, since she was feeling so dang pooped.

Suddenly, Madame Blavatsky's eyes flew open and her right hand hovered above the deck of tarot cards.

"Margo, I want you to pick up the deck and select five cards," Madame Blavatsky said in a low voice.

Margo reached out tentatively, her fingers not quite touching the deck. "Any five cards?"

Madame Blavatsky nodded. "That's right."

Margo picked up the deck, handling it like it was a hot potato just out of the microwave. "Should I shuffle it?"

"If you wish," said Madame Blavatsky.

Margo did a slow shuffle and plucked out five cards. "Okay, now what?"

"I want you to place the cards in a cross formation," said Madame Blavatsky. "The first tarot card in the center. Then the second card at the top and the rest going around in a clockwise pattern."

Margo's necklace and bracelets clanked as she studiously placed the cards facedown in the cross pattern. "Now what do I do?"

"Turn over the center card," Madame Blavatsky instructed. "This will reveal your present situation."

Margo flipped the card over and gasped. It was *The Hanged Man* card! Her hands flew instantly to her neck and she shrieked, "What does it mean? What does it mean?"

Carmela and Ava both grimaced at the high-decibel level.

"The card indicates a crossroads," Madame Blavatsky said quietly. "You find yourself wanting to do *something,* but having no idea what it is or how to do it. Your hands are tied. You feel powerless."

Margo's eyes grew wide. "Yes, yes, you're so right! That's *exactly* how I feel!" She gazed toward Beetsie for confirmation. "Wasn't I just saying that this morning?"

Beetsie nodded. "That's right, you were in a terrible quandary."

Madame Blavatsky nodded sagely. "Good, good. Now turn over the top card. This represents potential."

Margo's hand shook as she flipped over

the top card. "The five of wands," she said. "What does that mean?"

"Competition," said Madame Blavatsky.

Margo frowned. "Competition? With who?"

Madame Blavatsky shrugged. "It could be in the areas of work or career, or even a romantic rival."

Margo went a little cross-eyed. "A rival?" she sputtered.

"Now the next card," Madame Blavatsky said. "That represents the cause."

"Cause of what?" asked Margo.

Madame Blavatsky's eyes drifted closed. "The cause or reason for the situation in which you find yourself."

Margo's lips pressed together as she flipped over the card and revealed a reversed four of pentacles.

Madame Blavatsky studied the card. "This one implies that you are holding on to things, people, money, or . . ."

"Greed!" Beetsie suddenly squawked. "That's what it means. Greed!"

Ava raised an eyebrow. "Wow, honey, you really know your stuff."

Margo looked supremely insulted. "Greed?" she said. "I sincerely doubt *that*!" She hastily flipped over the last two cards. "Please tell me what these are supposed to represent?" Now she sounded petulant and abrupt.

"A recent death as well as anxiety," said Madame Blavatsky.

Margo stood up suddenly, practically knocking over the table. "You're telling me my life is filled with death and anxiety?" she quavered.

"Don't be upset," said Madame Blavatsky. "Death is natural, and anxiety is something to guard against."

Margo reached down and clasped Carmela's hands. "Oh, Carmela," she cried. "Please help me figure out what happened to Jerry Earl and Eric. As you can see, I won't be able to rest . . . to find peace . . . until I have an answer!"

"How did your tarot reading go?" asked Gabby. She was restocking paper bins when Carmela came cruising into the shop.

"Don't ask." Carmela tucked her handbag behind the front counter and let loose a heavy sigh.

"Ooh, that bad?"

"You know Margo," said Carmela. "Frankly, squeezing into my skinny jeans this morning was far more productive than her tarot card reading."

"The thing is," said Gabby, "I really *don't*

know Margo. But from the little I've seen of her, I have a feeling she's awfully demanding."

"You have no idea." Carmela picked up the morning mail and idly sorted through it.

"So you're still working on this . . . thing?" said Gabby.

Carmela looked up. "Go ahead and say it. It's an investigation. I know I shouldn't have gotten involved, but I did. And now everything's in a muddle and I don't seem to be getting anywhere at all."

"Then you should just quit," said Gabby, ever the practical one. "Hang it up and let Detective Gallant grapple with it."

"I would," said Carmela. "Except . . ."

"Except now it's become a personal challenge," said Gabby. A smile stole across her face. "I know you, Carmela. "You love a challenge. You're like a cantankerous mule when it comes to a challenge. You won't give in, you won't give up."

Carmela fingered a packet of floral stickers. "Why do you make tenacity sound like such a bad thing?"

"Because when you obsess over something, like these two murders, it becomes, well, obsessive," said Gabby. She studied Carmela carefully. "I don't know. You usually come up with *some*thing."

"But not in this case. I feel absolutely stumped. I feel like . . ." Carmela rubbed a hand through her hair.

"Like you've hit a dead end?" said Gabby.

"Ha-ha, very funny," said Carmela.

"Maybe you should lock yourself in your office and doodle for a while. Try to clear your head."

Carmela was nodding in agreement. "Blow out the cobwebs. Yeah, well, I suppose I could give it the old college try."

"Oh," said Gabby as Carmela headed for her office. "I put a couple of those little feathered birds on your desk. The ones you wanted for cake toppers." And under her breath she added, "Maybe they'll put you in a better frame of mind."

Carmela grasped a squishy red marker and sketched a quick layout for a scrapbook page she was working on for Chart House Antiques. If she put a large photo at the bottom of the page and a smaller photo intersecting the top half of the large one . . . then her copy could go . . .

The marker hit her desk with a clatter. No. Doodling and working weren't putting her in a better frame of mind at all. They were only delaying the inevitable.

Which is . . . what? More investigating?

Carmela spun in her chair and tried to think in a more practical manner. What would be the next step? Talk to Margo again? Try to pry more information out of Bobby Gallant? Or . . .

She straightened up, and her hands suddenly flew across her keyboard. Maybe she should try to follow up on the lead that Squirrel had given her. The guy named Beck who lived up in West Feliciana Parish near Laurel Hill.

Wait a minute. West Feliciana Parish? Where else had she heard that mentioned in the last few days? She racked her brain. Somewhere . . .

First had been the party and the murder. Then she'd gone to Margo's home to commiserate. And she'd been introduced to Eric Zane.

Poor Eric Zane.

But . . . wait! It was Zane who had mentioned West Feliciana Parish! They'd been talking about dinosaurs and fossils, and Zane had said the jawbone of a mastodon had been dug up in West Feliciana Parish!

Could Jerry Earl's crazy fossil hunting be behind his messages to Beck? Would someone murder Jerry Earl over a fossil? She supposed it depended on how much a fossil could be worth!

Carmela tip-tapped away, searching white pages, people finders, and LinkedIn. But the only Beck she was coming up with, the only one near Laurel Hill, was Beck's Tire Store.

A shot in the dark maybe, but a shot worth taking.

Carmela dialed the phone number. Two seconds later, a chirpy voice came on the line.

"Beck's Tire Store, this is Cindy."

"Hi, Cindy," Carmela began, then faltered. What exactly should she say?

"Hello?" said Cindy.

Carmela cleared her throat and gave it another shot. "I'm looking for Beck. Is he there?"

"You mean Bill? Sorry, he's with a customer right now. May I have him return your call?"

Bill Beck. Looks like she'd happenstanced upon a possible lead!

"It's pretty important," Carmela said. "I really need to talk to him."

Cindy made a noise and Carmela wondered if she was chewing gum. "Uh-huh. Do we have your car here in the shop?"

"No," said Carmela. "I'm calling about a personal matter."

Now there was a distinct popping sound. "Maybe you should call back," came the slightly disinterested voice.

"How long will Bill be there?" Carmela asked, looking at her watch. It was a bit of a drive up to Laurel Hill, but she didn't want to just sit there and twiddle her thumbs. She needed answers!

"He'll be here until closing," Cindy said.

"And that's what time?"

"Six o'clock," Cindy said as she hung up.

CHAPTER 20

Laurel Hill was above Baton Rouge, practically on the Louisiana-Mississippi border. It was an easy drive through beautiful pine-studded countryside, and Laurel Hill itself was a small, picturesque town that was simple enough to navigate.

Five minutes after Carmela hit town, she was cruising the street in front of Beck's Tire Store. The store was a small stucco building that had seen better days. Definitely a mom-and-pop-type setup. She pulled into a small parking lot at the side of the store and hopped out. An old-fashioned Coke machine buzzed noisily nearby while clanking sounds came from the back of the shop. Probably, she decided, that's where the service entrance was. That's where she'd find Bill Beck.

A burly man in khaki coveralls wiped his greasy hand on a towel when he saw Carmela approach. "Our showroom and main office is around front," he called out.

Carmela nodded. "I'm looking for Bill Beck."

The man squinted at her, then stuffed the rag into his back pocket. He had a friendly hangdog face and a ring of gray hair with a little bald spot on top of his head. Like a monk. "You're in luck, you just found him."

"I'm here on a kind of fact-finding mission," Carmela told him. "And I'm hoping you can help out."

Beck squinted at her. "That so." His tone was flat, barely interested.

"I'm looking into a few business dealings that concerned Jerry Earl Leland. I understand you were fairly well acquainted with the man?" Beck didn't look like any sort of killer to her. Then again, you never know.

"Why are you asking?" said Beck. "Who are you anyway?"

Carmela put a friendly smile on her face. "My name is Carmela Bertrand and I'm looking into a couple of things for Leland's widow."

Beck cocked an eye at her. "Widow?" He looked confused.

"That's right," said Carmela. "Jerry Earl was murdered last Sunday." She let her words wash over him. "And buried yesterday."

A shocked expression crossed Beck's face. "Murdered? You don't say. By who?"

"We don't have any answers on that yet. The police are working on a number of leads, but the whole case is rather complicated." Carmela hesitated, then decided to be very, very direct. "I know you had some kind of business deal with Jerry Earl." She lifted a hand casually to indicate she was just trying to tie up some loose ends.

Beck pulled the rag out of his back pocket again and wiped his hands unnecessarily. "I did have something going with the man. But that was a while ago."

"Can you tell me what kind of arrangement the two of you had?"

Beck stuffed the rag back into his pocket. "Well, I suppose I could. Nothing really came of it, so . . ." His voice trailed off. "And you're helping out his widow . . ."

"If you could just outline the basics," said Carmela, hoping he'd continue.

"Mr. Leland wanted to lease some land from me," said Beck. "Thirty acres off of County Road 714."

"Land?" Carmela thought back to Jerry Earl's little notebook with all the intricate maps and jottings. Could all this be about a fossil hunt? "Does he still hold a lease on it?"

"Oh no, heck no," said Beck. "After we'd hammered out the terms, Mr. Leland had that turn of bad luck and was sent to prison before the lease was ever signed." He shook his head. "It sounds like he had a lot more bad luck after that."

"So you still own that parcel of land?"

"Nope," said Beck. "I sold it six months ago."

"Was it farmland?" Carmela pressed.

"Hardly. It's more like swampland next to a big gravel pit. The company I sold it to said they were gonna build a shopping center there. Some kind of discount mall."

Carmela immediately thought of Conrad Falcon, Jerry Earl's neighbor and nemesis. Had he beat Jerry Earl out of another contract? When she'd overheard Falcon late yesterday afternoon, he'd mentioned something about moving his equipment in . . .

"Who was the buyer for your land?" Carmela asked.

"Let me jog my memory," said Beck. He crossed over to a wide wooden shelf that ran along the entire back wall of his shop. An aging computer sat there amid a tangle of tools. Beck wiggled the mouse and brought the computer to life. He tapped a few keys and muttered, "Just a sec." Then, after a minute, he said, "Spangler Enterprises was the buyer."

"Spangler?" said Carmela. She'd never heard of the company. "Are you sure the buyer wasn't a man by the name of Conrad Falcon?"

Beck shook his head. "I don't think so, ma'am."

"But you've heard that name before?" Carmela asked hopefully. "Falcon?"

Beck should his head. "Nope. Sorry. Doesn't ring a bell."

Carmela followed Highway 714 out of town, determined to take a bit of a detour and look at the land that Jerry Earl had been so anxious to lease. She followed the directions Beck had given her and came upon the parcel of land with a minimum of fuss.

Beck had been right. The land was part swamp, part gravel pit. Not much to look at. Her curiosity at a fever pitch, Carmela wondered just what Jerry Earl's interest had been. Were there fossils buried here? Dinosaur bones? Somehow that didn't seem very likely. So . . . had something else drawn him?

Determined to get a closer look, Carmela parked the car on the side of the road and jumped out. Because she was still wearing pumps, she exchanged them for a pair of sneakers that were in her backseat. As she laced up the sneakers, she noticed a spot of dried dog drool staining them.

Oh well. What else is new?

Then she stepped off the blacktop and crossed into what appeared to be a miniature Badlands. The land was challenging terrain at best, lots of mounded earth and deep trenches where it had been roughly gouged up. And tall, prickly grasses that made her wish she'd strapped a couple of Poobah's flea and tick collars around her ankles. She pressed on, came to a stream that burbled down through a rocky streambed, and skipped across it.

Why, she wondered, would Jerry Earl want to lease this land? Could he really find fossils here? Or was he looking for something else? Or had he been the one who planned to build a big shopping center? Although this place seemed like it was in the middle of nowhere.

Up ahead, an enormous mound of gravel rose up. Carmela headed that way, thinking that the ground might be a little drier that way, and that if she climbed to the top of the mound, she could get a bird's-eye view of the entire property.

Halfway up the mound, her tennis shoes displacing little avalanches of gravel, a loud noise suddenly started up. A *kerpuckety-*

puckety kind of noise.

What on earth?

Startled, she glanced up and was stunned to see a giant yellow bulldozer shudder to life on top of the mound. Suddenly, the noise turned into a loud roar, and the front bucket of the bulldozer rose up like the trunk and tusks of an enraged bull elephant!

Rivulets of gravel began to stream past her like crazy! The dozer was pushing gravel down the hill! Directly at her!

"Stop!" Carmela yelled. "Stop it, please!"

As more gravel continued to pour down, the loose gravel beneath her feet gave way. Stumbling, scrambling to gain a better foothold, Carmela fought to keep from falling as gravel rained down from above.

"Stop!" she cried again, waving her arms, trying to catch the attention of the machine's operator.

But it was useless. More gravel tumbled her way, streams and streams of it, this time burying her up to her ankles. Thrown off balance, she fell forward and sank to her knees as more gravel piled up around her.

Frantic now, Carmela began pawing at the stones around her.

Dear Lord, if I don't get myself out of here, I'm going to be buried alive!

She struggled to get upright again as dust

blew into her eyes and filled her nose. The roar of the engine above was deafening.

Small stones pelted painfully against her as she pulled one foot free and spun to turn her back on the bulldozer. A massive push of gravel came hurtling downhill and shoved her forward. Helpless now and at its mercy, she rode the avalanche down as if surfing a wave, somehow managing to keep her balance. At the bottom of the hill she was rudely upended and bounced painfully onto her backside.

Pulling herself up, dazed and shaking with fear, Carmela backed away from what was now a major rockslide. Then she spun on her heels and sprinted for the safety of her car.

Still shaking and trembling, spitting out grit, she gunned the engine and raced away from there as fast as she could!

Instead of heading home to relative safety, Carmela drove back over to Laurel Hill. She was dazed and dusty and hopping mad — determined to find out who owned the land and figure out what exactly was going on there! After a few wrong turns and more than a couple of inquiries, she found her way to the county clerk's office.

The office was housed in a sleepy-looking

red brick building with white trim, and Carmela prayed that someone was still working there. It was late Friday afternoon, so there was no knowing if the office would be open or closed.

Hoping for the best, she pushed her way through the front door, saw two service windows with closed signs on them and one window still open. Luck was with her.

She glanced around the deserted office and called out, "Hello?" Her voice echoed in the empty building. Walking up to the open window, she grimaced when she noticed that her shoes were leaving scuff marks on the tile floor. She kicked at the spots, hoping to erase them, but only made it worse.

After a moment, a woman with short wavy hair and thick glasses that gave her a bug-eyed look appeared behind the counter. She let out a startled gasp when she saw Carmela and put a hand to her heart.

"I'm sorry," said Carmela. "I didn't mean to frighten you."

"I didn't hear you come in," said the clerk. Her eyes remained large and startled. "I was just about to lock up." She glanced at a wall clock in a black metal cage. "We close at four thirty," she said primly. It was four twenty-eight now, clearly an imposition.

"This will only take a minute," Carmela said. "I was hoping you could look something up for me." She held her breath, hoping the woman would comply.

The clerk seemed to hesitate, glancing at the clock again, probably willing it to spin ahead faster.

Then Carmela said, "I just need you to check the ownership of a parcel of land out on Highway 714. It's approximately thirty acres and was sold by Bill Beck maybe five or six months ago."

The clerk let out a sigh and crossed over to a computer station. "Let me bring up the plot map."

Carmela breathed a sigh of relief. "Thank you."

The clerk fiddled on the computer as Carmela squinted through the service window, trying to read the screen.

"That's . . . yes, that's it right there." Carmela pointed out the grid that corresponded to the land where she'd nearly been buried alive.

The clerk copied down the parcel number. "I have to look this record up in back. It'll take a few minutes." Her look was stern, indicating that Carmela was causing her to stay late. And on a Friday yet.

"I sure do appreciate this," Carmela said

smoothly. "It's very important."

"Is this information for personal or business use?" asked the clerk.

"Business," said Carmela. "For the Crescent City Bank Corporation." She crossed her fingers at her little white lie. What Shamus and his cohorts didn't know wouldn't hurt them.

"Oh sure," said the clerk, recognizing the name. "I think we've done searches for them before." She scurried to the back room and returned two minutes later with a smile on her face. She glanced at the pad of paper she carried and said, "That parcel was purchased by Spangler Enterprises."

"That's it? That's the only name?"

"That's the corporation it's registered to."

"Do you know if they have plans to build some kind of shopping center?" Carmela asked.

The woman shook her head. "No idea. The information we have so far indicates the land is pending development. So it's currently taxed as undeveloped land."

"Thank you," said Carmela. "You've been a big help."

Now if I could just figure out the link between Conrad Falcon and Spangler Enterprises, I might actually get somewhere!

Carmela skirted Lake Pontchartrain on I-10, heading for home. She felt tired, dusty, and achy, and couldn't wait to jump into a nice hot shower. But when she hit the French Quarter and spotted a familiar beat-up van parked outside the Click! Gallery, she cranked her wheel sharply and pulled over to the curb.

That van belonged to Sullivan Finch, Ava's death portrait friend, and Carmela had just developed a sudden hankering to talk to him. She found a lucky parking spot, jumped out of her car, and let her eyes rove up and down the street. She figured Finch was either hanging out at Click! or he was up to no good at Shooters Oyster Bar, which was right next door.

She tried the Click! Gallery first and — bingo — there he was.

Finch was standing at the far end of the blazingly white gallery, looking blasé and shooting the breeze with the young female receptionist, who sat behind a stark white desk. Carmela walked slowly through the gallery, noting the new photographs that were hanging on the wall. They were black-and-white, moody and gritty. Lots of shots of barges on the Mississippi, dilapidated warehouses, and tough-looking dock workers. Interesting and well composed, but not exactly her taste.

Finch had his back to her and was waxing prosaically to the young receptionist about his favorite subject, postapocalyptic and dystopian art.

Then, in a purely calculated move, he leaned forward and reached a hand out, gently smoothing a strand of the young woman's long blond hair.

Honestly, if Ava thinks she has a lock on this guy, she is so mistaken.

When she was about ten feet away from him, Carmela called out, "Finch!" Her voice was loud and authoritative, but not so menacing that she'd unnerve him.

Sullivan Finch whirled around, caught unaware. And even though his watery blue eyes looked startled, he managed to project the scruffy, I-don't-care look of a serious artist. Shoulder-length hair, drooping mustache, and tweedy but slightly frayed jacket worn casually over blue jeans.

"Carmela," Finch said when he finally recognized her. He didn't sound happy.

"I need to talk to you," said Carmela. She crooked her finger and motioned for him to come join her. She wasn't about to air

Margo's dirty laundry in front of the receptionist.

Finch walked slowly toward Carmela, his tennis shoes making little squeaking sounds on the polished wood floor. "What's up?" he asked.

"You gave Margo Leland a quote on a painting?" said Carmela. She saw no need to mince words.

Finch's head lolled to one side. His nose wrinkled and his lips puckered. "Oh jeez," he said. "First the cops and now you."

Carmela gazed at him. So Babcock had followed up on Margo's death portrait commission. Good. "That's right," said Carmela. "Now me. I'd like some answers if you don't mind."

Finch looked suddenly surly. "You got a problem with an artist trying to make a decent living? I got rent to pay, you know, just like everybody else. And business expenses."

"I'm not concerned with the rates you charge," said Carmela. "I'm concerned about your basic arrangement with Margo."

"Oh."

"Tell me," said Carmela, "was Beetsie Bischoff the one who pressured Margo Leland into giving you the commission?"

"You mean the skinny older woman?"

"I guess you could call her that."

"Yeah," said Finch. "I'd say so. She was the one who really flashed on my paintings. She was the one who kept urging on her friend."

"It didn't concern you that the death portrait was for a living person?"

Finch shrugged. "Why should it?"

"Let me guess," said Carmela, lowering her voice. "You saw dollar signs when you laid eyes on Margo Leland. And don't tell me you don't know who she is — I'll bet the society pages are your Bible."

Much to his credit, Finch didn't try to bluff his way out of it. "Like I said, an artist's gotta make a living. We're in a reccssion, in case you hadn't noticed. It's not like five years ago when anybody with money was practically salivating to *invest* in art."

"Poor you," said Carmela. She turned to leave, assuming that Finch, with his line of art *patois,* was probably surviving just fine.

"Hey," said Finch, just as Carmela was almost to the door. "Tell your friend Ava I've been thinking about her."

"Tell her yourself," Carmela shot back.

CHAPTER 21

Carmela was just out of the shower and bundled in a fluffy robe when the doorbell rang.

Boo and Poobah came unglued.

"Shh," Carmela warned them as they spun and barked. "If you don't show a little more reserve, you're going to get us all evicted!" She opened the door for Ava and said, "I swear you must stuff dog biscuits in your purse!"

Ava laughed. She was dressed in a purple leather halter top and tight blue jeans and waving a bottle of Chardonnay. "*Cher,* I'm a natural woman. I don't stuff anything anywhere!"

"Come on in and let's uncork that sucker," said Carmela, indicating the wine. "After the day I've had, I could use a drink."

Ava handed the bottle over to Carmela. "First I have to spread the love." She leaned down and stroked Boo's ears, then rubbed

Poobah's tummy.

Standing in her kitchen, Carmela jammed her corkscrew into the top of the bottle. She twisted it hard and the cork slipped out, making a soft popping sound.

Ava, posed next to the dining room table, tipped her head back and sniffed the air. "Wait," she said with all the dramatic flourish of a Shakespearian actor. "What's that I smell?"

Carmela frowned. "What?"

"Nothing!" said Ava. "I don't smell a darned thing!" And then, "Why aren't you cooking dinner for us, *cher*? Stuffing the heck out of a pullet or braising some short ribs with a splash of Jack Daniels?"

Carmela raised an eyebrow and stared at her. "Was I supposed to? I don't remember that we . . . why, are you hungry?"

"Please," said Ava. "Does a chicken have lips?"

"I don't know," said Carmela. She grabbed two Reidel wineglasses, which she'd filched from Shamus. "Tell you what, let's have a drink first. Then I'll scrounge around and see what we can have for dinner."

Ava waved a hand. "Ah, don't worry about whipping something up. We can just order takeout. Pizza or chicken drummies. It'll be a nice change. Give me a chance to break out the Pepcid AC."

"Someday," said Carmela, "you're really going to have to learn how to cook."

"No way. In fact, I'm thinking of having the landlord rip out my stove and refrigerator and install a couple of vending machines."

They settled on the sofa, music playing softly, wineglasses in hand. The dogs lay attentively at their feet, like court dogs in a Velázquez painting.

"Okay," said Carmela. "After our riotous tarot card reading with Margo this morning, I went back to my shop and did a little research."

"On what?" said Ava.

"For one thing," said Carmela, "I located that guy Beck. The one Squirrel mentioned to me. He's the guy that Moony and Squirrel delivered a couple of messages to."

Ava looked askance. "From the deep recess of a bright yellow tennis ball?"

Carmela sipped her wine. "Something like that, yes. Anyway, this guy Beck was going to lease a parcel of land to Jerry Earl. But the deal fell through when Jerry Earl got sent to jail."

"Okay," said Ava. She stared at Carmela, then waggled her fingers. "What else? I know there's something else."

This time Carmela took a generous gulp of wine. "I went out to look at the land, just to sort of satisfy my curiosity . . ." She stopped and gave a nervous hiccup.

"What happened?"

"Um . . . some guy was running a bulldozer and he pushed a bunch of gravel down on top of me and I almost got buried alive." Carmela tried her best to downplay the drama. "But see! I'm okay now."

Ava wasn't having it. "What! You're telling me that the operator didn't *see* you?"

"I suppose that's what happened, yes. I mean, he was probably plugged into his iPod or something and just way too distracted."

Ava was staring at her with great concern. "You *think* that's what happened."

Carmela felt goose bumps practically exploding on her arms. "I'm pretty sure that's what happened."

"What if it wasn't?" Ava snapped back.

"What do you mean?" Ava had just voiced the one terrible thought that Carmela had been trying desperately to hold at bay. The thought that had been swirling around in the nether regions of her mind.

"What if somebody followed you up there and tried to get rid of you?" said Ava.

Carmela worried her bottom lip with her teeth. "Who would do that?"

"Duh," said Ava. "The killer?"

That pretty much put the kibosh on the evening's fun. They were suddenly back to talking about the investigation big-time.

"You shouldn't have gone out there alone," Ava scolded.

"I never thought I'd be in danger," said Carmela. "It never crossed my mind."

"Two people are dead and it never crossed your mind that you could be the third?"

Carmela shook her head. "Not exactly."

"Holy hominy!" said Ava. She reached a hand down and stroked Boo's ears. "Did your momma park her brains in her sock drawer this morning?" She turned back to Carmela. "Okay, what else? You were obviously out on some secret-agent-CIA-NSA-fact-finding mission."

"Well," said Carmela. "I found out that Beck has since sold the land to a company by the name of Spangler Enterprises."

"Who are they?"

"No idea," said Carmela. "But I think they're in the construction business. I think the plan is to build some kind of discount mall there."

"Construction," said Ava. "The same as Jerry Earl's business."

"That's right."

"Interesting," said Ava. "We should try to find out who they are."

"I agree."

"Do you think Shamus would know anything about Spangler Enterprises?"

"No idea," said Carmela.

"Call him," said Ava. "He's a business guy. He gets around."

Carmela made a face.

"I know," said Ava. "The last thing you want to do is talk to your sad sack husband. Especially on a Friday night when neither of us have hooked up with a hot date. But I want you to give him a call anyway. And put it on speaker phone so I can hear."

So Carmela picked up her cell phone and called Shamus. It rang three times then went to his voice mail: "Hi, this is Shamus. If you're calling about business, get back with me first thing Monday. If you're a good-lookin' gal, get over here right now!"

"Gack!" said Carmela, tossing the phone down.

"No luck there," said Ava. She frowned and poked a finger into her mass of dark, curly hair and scratched thoughtfully. "Hmm."

"What hmm?" said Carmela.

"We're missing something," said Ava.

"Wait a minute, do you think Margo might know something about Spangler Enterprises?"

"I don't know. I suppose I could call her."

"She was pretty upset this morning," said Ava. "So, hint hint, maybe we should go over there and check on her?"

Carmela laughed. "You just want to stop and have dinner on the way."

Ava dimpled prettily. "Nothin' wrong with that. My stomach is growling so loud I sound like a circus act."

"What do you feel like eating?" Carmela asked.

Ava rubbed her hands together in anticipation. "Chang's Golden Dragon is right on the way."

Carmela finished the last of her wine. "You won't catch me saying no to General Tsao's chicken."

"Or moo goo gai pan," said Ava. "Hurry up and throw some clothes on, will you please?"

Chang's Golden Dragon on Magazine Street was redolent with spicy peppers, sizzling duck, and steaming noodles. Carmela and Ava ordered three different entrées and ate family style, enjoying the hot Szechuan-style food and washing it down with bottles of Tsingtao Beer. Ava even managed to negotiate her dinner using chopsticks.

When the waitress finally delivered their tab along with a couple of fortune cookies, Ava made a grab for hers and immediately cracked it open.

"You think fortune cookies are more accurate than tarot cards?" Ava asked.

"No, I do not," said Carmela. She wasn't a big believer in cards, fortune-telling, or even the *I Ching*.

"Don't be so hasty to judge," said Ava.

"Fortune cookies are made in a *factory*," said Carmela. "Where the same fortunes are probably inserted into every twenty-fifth cookie. Then they're randomly packaged."

Ava stared at her. "You like to suck the magic out of things, don't you?"

"I had no idea I was ruining it for you. Sorry, go ahead and read your fortune."

Ava peered into her teacup. "Maybe I'll just read my tea leaves instead."

"What do you see in there?"

"Hmm," said Ava. "I think it's something about Margo." She tilted her teacup and gave a wicked smile. "It says, 'Oolong time no see'!"

The garden district was a flurry of activity. Lights blazed inside many of the larger homes, cars were double-parked in drive-ways and lined every curb, while couples strolled up front walks to attend fancy soirees and dinner parties.

Only Margo Leland's home looked quiet. A small light burned over the front door, and flickering blue light shone through one of the front windows. A television set, no doubt.

"It looks awfully dark," said Ava as they walked toward her door. "You think she's home?"

Carmela shrugged. "Probably. The Cakewalk Ball is tomorrow night. I imagine she's fretting over what to wear."

Ava suddenly gave a knowing smirk. "I wonder what *we're* going to wear."

Carmela, who'd been planning to wear a long black dress, stopped in her tracks and said, "I hadn't really thought too much about it." Then, "Why? Do you have something up your sleeve?"

Ava shrugged. "I might have."

Carmela knew Ava must have hatched some sort of dress-up plan. She was acting so mysterious. Had she borrowed dresses from The Latest Wrinkle? Or was she going to raid her own closet, which rivaled that of a Las Vegas showgirl?

"Never mind," said Carmela as they

stepped up to the door. "I don't want to know. My only rule of thumb is that I won't wear anything crazy from Oddities."

"Oddities?" Ava drawled. "Why would your ball gown come from there?"

"Because Joubert is now carrying a line of steam punk fashion."

Ava looked suddenly interested. "Steam punk? You don't say. A touch of Goth meets Victorian? Lace meets studs? I *like* it."

"I'd really prefer something soft and frilly," said Carmela.

"Ah, yes," Ava said knowingly. "Babcock will be back home tomorrow night."

Carmela pushed the doorbell. They heard a deep *bong* resound inside the house. They waited a few seconds but no one appeared at the door. No Beetsie, no housekeeper, no live-in maid. Could it be that Margo was all by her lonesome?

"Maybe she's . . ." Carmela began. Then the door suddenly creaked open and Margo peered out. She was clad in a red silk kimono robe embroidered with gold dragons. Her face was scrubbed clean and devoid of makeup. She looked as if she was ready for bed.

"Carmela!" Margo said with a surprised gasp. "And Eva."

"Sorry to call on you so late," said Carmela, though it really wasn't all that late. "But I got involved in a little more research today and wanted to ask you a couple of questions."

Margo opened the door wider. "Of course. Come in."

Carmela and Ava followed Margo through the dark parlor, down a long hallway, and into a small TV room. There was a sofa, two chairs, and a table. A glass half-filled with amber-colored liquid sat on the table. Probably bourbon.

Carmela felt a wave of sadness for Margo. Tonight, Margo looked like a woman who'd just lived through a horrible week. A botched party. The murder of her husband and his assistant. And countless rumors. Not to mention two failed marriages. In New Orleans social circles, any one of those things could signal the end of a career as a glamorous hostess.

"Can I get you ladies something to drink?" Margo asked. "Carmela? Eva?"

Ava's lips pulled back in a semi-snarl.

"Maybe a glass of Chardonnay?" Carmela asked quickly.

Margo nodded and promptly disappeared.

"That lady better start getting my name right," Ava snarled.

"Just don't start with her now," Carmela

warned. "Let me ask my questions first, okay?"

"Yeah, whatever."

Margo returned with two glasses of wine in elegant crystal goblets that were so heavy Carmela knew they had to be Baccarat.

Once Margo was settled in a chair, her bourbon in hand, she said, "What did you want to ask me?"

Carmela gave Margo a quick, sanitized version about locating Bill Beck today as well as what she'd found out about the land deal.

Margo sipped on her bourbon and said, "I really don't know a lot about Jerry Earl's business dealings."

"The thing is," said Carmela, "are you familiar with a company by the name of Spangler Enterprises?"

Margo closed her eyes, thought for a minute, and shook her head no.

"You're sure?" said Carmela.

Margo blinked at her. "You said the company might have something to do with construction?"

"That's right," said Carmela.

Margo was suddenly incensed. "How much do you want to bet that rat, Conrad Falcon, is involved! He was always sniffing after Jerry Earl's deals, trying to get a step up on him. Trying to crowd him out!" The ice cubes in her glass rattled with outrage. "It has to be owned by Falcon!"

CHAPTER 22

"I was also wondering," said Carmela, "if we could look around your husband's office."

Margo's eyebrows were double apostrophes above her sunken eyes. "What on earth for?"

"Perhaps he had some information about that land deal or his proposed project in his files or on his computer," said Carmela. It was a shot in the dark, but certainly one worth taking.

"That's not such a terrible idea," said Margo. She got to her feet and padded down the hallway, listing like a sinking ocean liner. "You know where his office is, so help yourself. I'm just going to, um, run into the kitchen and grab myself a refresher."

So Carmela and Ava trooped into Jerry Earl's office once again. It hadn't changed one iota as far as Carmela could tell. Same black-and-persimmon-colored carpet, same bookshelves dotted with fossils and gold trinkets, same French doors that led out to the secluded backyard.

Carmela peeked out the French doors. Across the alley, on Conrad Falcon's second floor, a light shone. Was he up there right now, watching their comings and goings? Or was she just being paranoid? And when was paranoia really just your brain warning you to be careful?

"This house feels so empty," said Ava.

"Without Eric Zane around? Yes," said Carmela.

"Do you think Margo feels responsible for his death?"

"No idea," said Carmela.

"You think she's going to plan his funeral?"

"Are you serious?" said Carmela. "She didn't even plan her own husband's funeral." She slipped into Jerry Earl's chair and ran her fingertips across the keyboard of his computer. "Time to get to work."

"Is his computer password protected?" Ava asked.

As if in answer, his desktop files suddenly appeared.

"Nope," said Carmela.

"So what do you see?" asked Ava. She

leaned forward and studied the screen along with Carmela. They hunted and searched for a few minutes but came up with nothing. Just files of blueprints that had been digitized and boring notes on several past projects.

The clatter of Margo's fresh ice cubes heralded her return. "Did you find anything?" she asked as she flopped down into a chair.

"Not yet," said Ava. "But we're still working on it."

Carmela pulled open the file drawer on the right side of Jerry Earl's desk. There were maybe a dozen folders there, all neatly arranged in Pendaflex hanging files. She scooped them all out and stacked them on top of the desk. "Maybe we should each take a couple of these files and go through them?" she suggested.

Margo pursed her lips. "Honestly, I can never make head nor tails out of any of that stuff. Not unless I get my reading glasses and . . ." She took a sip of her drink and crossed her legs. "You know, I haven't the foggiest idea where they could be."

"Don't worry," Ava told her. "Carmela and I can whip through these pretty fast. She grabbed a stack and settled into the leather armchair next to Margo.

Margo sipped more bourbon. "Jerry Earl was always so interested in geology. I imagine you'll come across quite a few plot maps and topography maps. Different charts, too."

Ava held up a sheet. "You mean like this one?" It was a map illustrating rainfall averages in Louisiana.

Margo nodded. "That's my Jerry Earl. He liked to keep on top of things."

"Do you know anything about this?" Carmela asked. She held up a handful of papers that she'd been reading. "They look like some kind of laboratory report."

"A lab report?" Ava asked. "Was Jerry Earl on some sort of medication?"

"Not that I know of," said Margo. "Although he did have bunions and a nasty hammer toe. What report do you exactly have there, dear? You're starting to worry me. Was it blood work?"

"No, nothing like that," said Carmela, studying the pages. "These look more like results from a land sample."

"Ah," said Margo. "It's probably an analysis on the age of some soil." She nodded, half to herself. "Jerry Earl was always taking soil samples. And he was crazed about finding fossils."

Carmela shook her head as she pored over

them. "I don't really know what they are. I'm no whiz kid when it comes to science, and these reports look like they're written in a foreign language."

Ava stood up and leaned across the desk. "Let me see whatcha got there."

Carmela spun the pages around for Ava to see.

Ava scanned them. "This looks like some kind of mineral content analysis," she said. "Wait a minute, hold everything . . ."

"What?" said Carmela.

She tapped a finger against one of the sheets. "This one's a geological survey. And it's for . . ." She looked up, her eyes suddenly wide and questioning.

"What?" Carmela repeated.

"It's for West Feliciana Parish," said Ava.

Their eyes locked together. Now it was Carmela's turn to jump up. "What else is here?"

"Looks like receipts," said Ava, fingering a few more pages.

"Jerry Earl was always buying me jewelry," sang Margo. "He was generous to a fault."

"I don't think you'd want to wear this," said Ava. She squinted, trying to make out the fine print. "This receipt is for some pieces of heavy equipment. A trammel and a power sluicer."

"A juicer?" said Margo.

"Sluicer," said Carmela. "What on earth would that be used for? It doesn't sound like something you'd use for digging up ancient dinosaur bones."

"It sounds more like it would rip them apart," said Ava.

"Let me go online and look that up," said Carmela. She sat down at the computer again, brought up a search engine, and typed in "power sluicer." Watched a few hits spin out.

"Here we go," said Ava.

" 'A power sluicer, sometimes called a highbanker," Carmela read out loud, "is a piece of gold-prospecting equipment that uses a pump to force water through a sluice box to mimic the natural flow of a stream.' " Carmela looked up and stared at Ava. "Apparently a power sluicer is used for separating gold particles from sand and gravel."

"Gold?" said Ava.

"Gold!" said Margo.

Three sets of eyes suddenly focused on the floor-to-ceiling bookshelves that were crammed with boxed sets of shimmering gold coins, glass tubes filled with gold nuggets, and gold-encrusted statuary.

"Holy Coupe de Ville!" said Carmela. "Jerry Earl was going to hunt for gold on that property!"

"Wait a minute," said Ava. "There are gold deposits there? Really?" She sounded skeptical. "I thought you only got gold from . . . um . . . maybe the Sierra Nevada Mountains. Or is it the Superstition Mountains in Arizona?"

Carmela turned back to the computer. "Let's just see about that." She executed another search. And then another. After a few minutes she had some of the information clear in her head. "It turns out," she said, "there were small deposits of gold found in West Feliciana Parish some hundred and twenty-five years ago."

Margo squinted at Carmela. "You can tell all that from the computer?"

Carmela smiled. "It's just a search engine."

"But aren't you a whiz," Margo marveled. "Almost better than a tarot card reading!"

Ava frowned. "The computer can spit out facts and information about the past, but it can't see into the future."

Fearing that insurrection was about to break out, Carmela interrupted with, "It says here, ladies, that the price of gold is well over sixteen hundred dollars an ounce!"

Margo gasped. "Holy Hannah!"

"But is there any gold still to be found in

northern Louisiana?" asked Ava. "That's the real question, right?"

"Who knows?" said Carmela. "But the information I'm getting here is that lots of old mines and gold deposits are being given a careful second look. Especially now that there are new ways of extracting gold."

The three women stared at each other again.

"So who is Spangler Enterprises?" asked Ava. "And why did they buy that exact parcel of land?"

"The land that Jerry Earl first spotted!" put in Margo.

"I don't know," said Carmela. "Maybe they're also . . . prospecting for gold?"

"Ask that thing again," Margo instructed. "See if that rat Conrad Falcon is involved."

Carmela did a quick search on Spangler Enterprises cross-referenced with Conrad Falcon. And came up empty-handed. "Nothing," she said.

"Agh," said Margo. "That thing's not so smart after all."

On their way out the door, Ava muttered, "She could be a real Lady Macbeth."

"You mean Margo?" said Carmela. "Yeah, she's still on my suspect list."

"What about the guy she got all frothed

up about? He lives next door, right?"

"Conrad Falcon?" said Carmela. "His house is kind of around the block. But backed up to this place."

Ava lifted one shoulder delicately. "Maybe we should . . ."

"Pay him a visit?" said Carmela. *What if he's the killer?* she thought. *What if he's . . .*

"Come on," said Ava. "What are you waiting for? Let's take a chance."

Conrad Falcon answered the door wearing an elegant navy cashmere sweater with a dark paisley ascot tucked in the neck and dove gray slacks. He looked, Carmela thought, like Sean Connery if he starred in an updated version of *Gone with the Wind.*

"Yes?" said Falcon. His face registered nothing. They could have been there to sell Girl Scout cookies. But, of course, they weren't.

"I'm sorry to interrupt," said Carmela.

"Me, too," said Ava.

"Do I know you ladies?" Falcon asked. He seemed ready to close the door on them.

"We met the other night," said Carmela. "At the Star of the South Cat Show?"

Falcon's eyes were cold and flat. Then he said, "Yes, now I remember you. You were the impertinent one."

"And I'm the sweet one," said Ava, offering her most dazzling smile.

"What is it you ladies want?" asked Falcon, clearly ruffled by their presence.

"The answer to a question," said Carmela.

"And what might that be?" said Falcon.

Carmela gave him a tight smile. "Why did you buy the parcel of land up by Laurel Hill?"

Now Falcon looked even more confused. "What? Laurel Hill?" If he was acting, it was masterful. Worthy of the Actor's Studio.

"In West Feliciana Parish," said Carmela. "Thirty acres."

Falcon frowned. "I didn't buy any land in West Feliciana Parish."

"Sure you did," said Carmela. "Under the guise of building a discount shopping mall. But instead of stores that sell tube socks and tennis shoes, you're really going to mine for gold!"

"That's right," said Ava. "You somehow got wind that Jerry Earl was looking there and you stepped right in and bought the land out from under him."

"Right after you blew the whistle on him," Carmela added.

"Are you crazy?" said Falcon. "Get out of here. Stop bothering me before I call the police." He started to shut the door.

"That's a great idea!" said Carmela. "In

340

fact, I'm going to call the police myself!"

At that, the door slammed with a resounding bang.

"Good girl," said Ava. "You've got him running scared now."

Carmela gave her a sideways glance. "You think? He didn't look all that scared to me. He mostly looked ticked off."

"He's compensating," said Ava. "With all that bravo and machismo."

"Maybe so," said Carmela. "But if he's really the killer, we just tipped our hand."

Ava thought for a second. "Maybe you should call Bobby Gallant," she suggested. "Kind of fill him in on what's happened. What you figured out so far."

"Maybe tomorrow morning," said Carmela as they walked to her car in darkness.

"Okay," said Ava. "But make sure your lock your door tonight."

"Will do. You, too."

CHAPTER 23

Even kisses from Boo and Poobah couldn't rouse Carmela from her dreams this Saturday morning. In fact, it wasn't until the insistent ringing of the phone finally insinuated itself into the far recesses of her brain that Carmela finally pried one eye open.

She sighed, sat halfway up in bed, and fumbled for her phone. "Hello?"

"Turn on your TV right now!" Ava shrieked.

This uncalled-for, noisy intrusion prompted Carmela to open both eyes. "Why?" she said. "What's going on?" Was there a fire in the building? Had another hurricane swept through town?

"There's a news alert," said Ava.

"So?" Carmela yawned.

"Duncan Merriweather has been apprehended and taken in for questioning in the murder of Jerry Earl Leland!"

Carmela sat straight up in bed. She was

wide awake now. "What?" she blurted. "Why?"

"Because a trocar was found in the garbage can just down the block from Merriweather's house!" cried Ava.

"Dear Lord!" Carmela exclaimed. "You're telling me that Duncan Merriweather is the killer?"

"Looks like. Isn't that something? He was right under our noses all along. And, of course, you knew about his background as an undertaker."

"Beetsie told us," said Carmela. "She was the one who really pointed the finger at him."

"But you were smart enough to put it all together and tell the police," said Ava. "And now . . . the case is solved!"

Carmela was still brushing sleep crusties from her eyes. "I guess."

"Gotta go, kid. Lots going on. But I'll be over this afternoon with some gowns for us to try!"

Carmela crawled out of bed and padded into the living room. Boo and Poobah followed her, relentlessly wagging their tails and grumbling to be let out.

"Just a minute, sweeties, your momma has to figure out what's happening."

Plunking herself down onto the chaise

lounge, Carmela flipped on the TV and found the typical mindless Saturday morning programming. Cartoons, infomercials for tummy toners, infomercials for pimple products. Needing none of it, she flipped to KBEZ-TV, their local station, and caught the tail end of the big news story. There was a grainy photograph of Duncan Merriweather looking dapper in a tuxedo. Choppy red letters across the photo screamed *APPREHENDED!* The morning news anchor, a chirpy twenty-five-year-old, was saying, ". . . and now it looks as though we may finally have some answers in the gruesome slaying of Garden District resident Jerry Earl Leland."

As the anchor happily switched to sports highlights, Carmela grabbed her phone and punched in Gallant's office number from memory. She fidgeted nervously as it rang.

Gallant could be talking to Duncan Merriweather at this very moment, she thought.

But he wasn't. After bluffing her way through two different gatekeepers, Carmela finally got him on the line.

"What?" Gallant said. His tone was hurried and quiet.

"I just heard that Duncan Merriweather was picked up," said Carmela.

"That's right. He's being questioned right

now, even as we speak."

Carmela was still confused. "But how did you know . . . how did you locate the murder weapon? The trocar?"

"We got a tip," said Gallant.

"Anonymously?"

"Is there any other kind?"

"I don't know," said Carmela. "That seems awfully convenient to me. Maybe you were getting too close to the truth and —"

"Hey," said Gallant. "It's what we got."

"But what if it's classic misdirection? What if somebody planted the trocar and then called in the tip?"

"It's possible, anything's possible," said Gallant.

"Was there blood residue on the weapon?"

"We're working on DNA right now."

"But you're still going to hold Merriweather."

"Absolutely. For as long as it takes."

"Listen," said Carmela. "I have some information that may or may not impact this case."

"Now what?" said Gallant. He didn't sound happy.

Carmela hastily told him about the land deal and Spangler Enterprises and her theory that Conrad Falcon stole the land right out from under Jerry Earl.

"Are you sure about all this?" Gallant said in a tone dripping with skepticism. "That Falcon is behind Spangler Enterprises?"

"I'm . . . well, it's all a *theory*," said Carmela. "Which is why I need your help. I need you to please muster your resources and dig into this! See if it's true."

"Why are you so bent out of shape about this investigation?" Gallant asked. "When we probably already have our man?"

"I'm worried you might have the *wrong* man! And that Conrad Falcon will get off scot-free!"

"I can *try* to find a connection, but I can't promise anything. It's crazy around here. Really . . . I have to go."

"If you find out anything at all, call me!"

But Gallant had already hung up.

Carmela changed into jeans, a sweater, and tennis shoes, and headed off on a morning walk with Boo and Poobah. They skipped down Dauphine Street and cut down Conti Street, going past the Pharmacy Museum and the Historic New Orleans Collection, skirting close to the Voodoo Museum.

A lot of museums here, Carmela thought. A lot of history. But what was the history behind prospecting for gold? Or digging up old dinosaur bones? Somehow, those things had to tie in with Jerry Earl's murder, right? And with the murder of Eric Zane?

She kicked it into high gear then as she jogged along with the dogs. Of course, they were doing an easy lope while she was rattling her fillings loose, sweating profusely, and chugging along like the little engine that could. Or at least was trying very hard.

As they came flying through the porte cochere and into the inner courtyard, Carmela found a delivery boy standing at her door. He was shifting about uncomfortably, looking uncertain, while he tried to balance an enormous white cake box.

"My cake!" Carmela called out. She'd almost forgotten about it!

The delivery boy turned. "Are you Carmela Bertrand?" He looked supremely hopeful.

"That's right. Are you from Duvall's Bakery?"

He nodded.

"Let me put the dogs inside then I'll give you a hand with that cake."

So, of course, Boo and Poobah got tangled up in their leashes and almost tripped the delivery boy. But Carmela finally got everything straightened out. The large white cake box was deposited safely on her dining room table, the delivery boy was tipped, and the dogs were . . . well, they were definitely eyeing the large box, their pink tongues hanging out.

"No," Carmela told them. "This cake is totally off-limits. There will be no begging, sniffing, or nibbling at frosting. There will be no *accidentally* knocking this cake over. This cake is for an important charity event tonight. Now, do you understand? Please nod if you understand."

That said, Carmela gingerly opened the box and peered inside. The intoxicating smell of sugar, butter, chocolate cream, and fondant wafted up at her. She closed her eyes and inhaled.

Boo and Poobah edged dangerously close to the cake.

Carmela held up an index finger and glared at them.

They hunched their shoulders and slunk back.

Carmela smiled to herself as she feasted her eyes upon the cake. It was a four-tiered beauty, iced in vanilla frosting and each layer edged with small bouquets of pink and yellow flowers. Bands of fondant pearls coursed down the sides of the cake. Gorgeous. On the bottom layer, Crescent City Bank had been grandly spelled out in poufy fondant. Not so gorgeous, but it was what she had to work with. That was the trouble with a commercial project like this. It was . . . well, commercial.

Carmela headed for her kitchen. "First coffee and kibbles, then we'll whip up our frosting." Boo and Poobah followed her, watching as she measured out a nice strong ration of coffee, set it to brew, and then portioned out food for them.

While the coffee brewed and the dogs snarfed their breakfasts, Carmela whipped together batches of chocolate frosting and buttercream frosting. When both frostings were thick and ready to work with, she poured them into plastic pastry bags.

Now came the tricky part.

Squeezing gently, Carmela formed a crooked twig-like line of frosting on top of a sheet of waxed paper. She went over it a couple of times until it took on the appearance of nubby bark. Then she squeezed out another six crooked twigs.

She surveyed her handiwork. Pretty good. Using a silver knife, she carefully lifted one of the twigs, carried it over to the cake, and placed it across the top tier. It looked good. Very realistic, in fact. The other five twigs followed.

Changing to a smaller tip on her pastry bag, Carmela began the painstaking process of creating the bird's nest. She basically squirted out five skinny lines of chocolate frosting, then crosshatched over them with lines of buttercream frosting. Then she repeated that process three more times. Since the frosting was still sticky and pliable, it was fairly easy to join the four sides together, round them out a little bit, and fashion them into a nest.

"It's working," she told the dogs. "It's really working."

She carried the nest to her cake and, holding her breath, carefully placed it on top. Again, it looked pretty good.

Now she took her miniature feathered birds and placed two on either side of the nest and three more birds on the tier below. Because of her careful placement, the birds looked as if they were perched on her twigs.

Carmela didn't want the necklace to get lost in the nest, so she fashioned a piece of pink silk around a puff ball of cotton and stitched it closed on the bottom. The pink silk pillow went into the nest, and the beautiful diamond pendant puddled right on top of it.

Easy to admire, easy to bid on.

"Ta-da!" she sang out, with Boo barking her approval. "We did it."

She glanced at the clock, stunned that it

was already past one o'clock.

"Holy mackerel." She looked at the dogs. "Did you guys forget? You're supposed to be packed!"

The words were barely out of her mouth when there was a sharp knock at the door.

"Daddy!" said Carmela. She pulled open the door and let the dogs launch their assault on Shamus.

"Jeez!" he cried out. "Take it easy. We've got all weekend to party, kids." He glanced at Carmela, then dug his hand into the bag of Fritos he was carrying. "Did the cake get here? Did you decorate it?"

"Nice to see you, too, Shamus. Yes, I decorated the cake. Just finished it, as a matter of fact."

Shamus sauntered over to the table and took a peek at it. "Hey, it looks good! You do nice work, kid. I knew I could count on you." He stuck a finger out to grab a bit of frosting.

Carmela slapped his hand and said, "Frosting and Fritos? Give me a break."

"Hey, the Fritos are organic, right?" He rolled up the bag, tossed it toward the trash can, and missed. He made an "Aaaaah" sound.

"You want to take the cake with you?" Carmela asked.

Shamus rolled his eyes. "It's hard enough to stuff two dogs with all their beds and toys into a Porsche."

"You could always get a more sensible car," Carmela pointed out.

"Please. That would be so bad for my image."

Carmela smiled. "I can see that. You wouldn't want to look *too* sensible."

"Huh?" Shamus said. Then he made a kind of gangling motion toward her, which Carmela deftly sidestepped. "So I understand you sold the old homestead?"

"That's right. It's over and done with."

"What a pity."

"You didn't really want it, Shamus. In fact, you didn't particularly want to live there with me."

"Still, that house had been in my family for years."

"Yet nobody stepped up to buy it."

Shamus glared at her. "Tell me, do you have the buyer's check in your hot little hand?"

"No, not yet."

"Then the sale's not complete," said Shamus. "It's not technically final until you sign the papers and *deposit* the check!"

"Whatever," said Carmela.

"I suppose I'll see you at the Cakewalk

Ball tonight," said Shamus.

"Wait," said Carmela. "You're going?"

Shamus nodded. "Of course. Crescent City Bank needs to be properly represented."

"But what about the dogs? I thought you were going to spend time with them tonight."

"They'll be just fine," said Shamus. He bent down, grabbed a dog bed, and tucked it under one arm. He struggled to grab the second one. Hunched over like Quasimodo, he headed for the door and said, "Okay, kids, let's haul anchor."

"Wait!" said Carmela. "You can't forget their toys."

"They've got plenty of toys at my place," Shamus growled.

"You can't forget Boo's little red gingerbread doll. She can't go to sleep without it."

"Aw crap," said Shamus. He sighed and dropped the beds. "Where is it?"

Carmela looked around. "I'm not sure." She gazed at Boo. "Boo Boo, where's your dolly?"

Boo lay down and proceeded to lick her front paws, seemingly unconcerned.

"Come on, Boo, I don't have all day," said Shamus. He glanced sharply at Carmela.

"Do we *really* need the darn thing?"
"What do you think?"
They finally found it under the bed.

CHAPTER 24

When the door closed behind Shamus and the dogs, Carmela sank into the couch. At one time, she would have felt sad to bid good-bye to the little family that she'd made. But today she just felt relieved. Still, Shamus had liked the cake, so there was that one little bit of positivity to hang on to. And hopefully, his curmudgeon sister Glory would be impressed as well. If she wasn't . . . well, tough.

But things were bound to improve. Because tonight, Edgar Babcock would presumably join her at the Cakewalk Ball. A little shiver of anticipation tingled deep within her. It had been a long week with her sweetie being out of town, and she couldn't wait to catch up. Not only bending his ear about the two murders, but doing some remedial snuggling, too.

When the phone rang, she was almost too tired to pick it up. Then she remembered

Bobby Gallant. Was he calling her back?

He was indeed.

"You were dead wrong," was Gallant's opening salvo.

"What are you talking about?" said Carmela.

"Conrad Falcon doesn't own that land you told me about. In fact, he has nothing to do with it."

"Sure he does," said Carmela. "It's not X marks the spot, but he probably owns it in some tricky kind of way. It's owned under a different entity than Falcon's aboveboard corporation. Probably that other company I told you about — Spangler Enterprises."

"I checked," said Gallant. "There's absolutely no connection between Conrad Falcon and Spangler Enterprises."

Carmela was shocked. "You're sure about that?"

"Positive."

"Then what can you tell me about Spangler?"

"Nothing at the moment," said Gallant. "I just wanted to give you a heads-up."

And rub my nose in it. "Oh. But can you —"

"Sorry. Gotta go."

Click.

"Doggone!" Carmela almost tossed the

phone across the room, except there was another knock at the front door.

She stormed over to the door and yanked it open. "What?" she cried.

A young man in a delivery uniform shrank back. "I was supposed to pick up a cake? For delivery to the Art Institute?"

"Oh. Right. Come on in." Some of her anger began to dissipate. This kid hadn't done anything to her. Why take it out on him? "It's right here on the table."

The delivery boy hefted the box an inch off the table. "Could you maybe get the door for me, ma'am?"

"Sure enough," said Carmela. She held the door open as he eased his way out. "Thanks. Don't drop it," she told him.

"I'll try not to," he called back.

Stiletto heels rang out like gunshots from across the courtyard. Carmela looked and did a double take. An enormous black plastic bag was moving slowly toward her.

"Is that you?" Carmela asked.

Ava's head cranked out from one side. "*Cher,* help me!" came her plaintive voice.

Carmela ran over to help, grabbing the bottom half of the garment bag that was dragging on the ground. "This weighs a ton!" she exclaimed. "What have you got in here besides dresses? Gold bars?"

"See!" said Ava. "You have gold on your mind. Aren't you excited about the arrest? Aren't you glad they finally caught him?"

"Maybe they caught him," said Carmela as they squished and punched the garment bag through the doorway, then threw it down on the chaise lounge. "It's just that after finding out about the land lease and all . . ."

Ava waved a hand as if solving the murder were a done deal. "Merriweather was on your radar all along, you smarty. In fact, that's what I told Jekyl when I talked to him earlier today. He says kudos, by the way." She looked around. "Where are the dogs?"

"Daddy's weekend. He was just here to pick them up."

Ava grimaced. "Ugh. Did he give you grief?"

"No more than usual." As Ava dug through the garment bag, Carmela was still thinking about the land and the gold exploration and Spangler Enterprises. "I just don't think these murders are one hundred percent solved. I don't know where Merriweather fits in . . ."

Ava pulled out a short canary yellow party dress. "He doesn't fit into this, but you will." She held it up and said, "You like?"

"Yes, I do," said Carmela. "It's absolutely

gorgeous and it matches a pair of too-tight shoes that I impulsively splurged on. But will it fit me?"

"We can always suck you in with Spanx and a few strips of duct tape if need be." Ava pulled out a long, slinky red jersey dress. It had a plunging halter neckline and a breathtakingly open back.

Carmela gasped. "Ava! That one would look fabulous on you."

"I totally agree. The gown is fab. Kind of a harlot's delight."

"It's not *that* racy," said Carmela. Actually, it did look a little hoochie momma.

"Then how about this?" said Ava. She held up a black, strapless number that was completely slit up the side. "Kind of Angelina Jolie, wouldn't you say?"

"Red carpet worthy, for sure. You might even get a mention from Perez Hilton."

"Mmn, what else?" said Ava. "Okay. No, I'm not loving it." She held up a navy satin dress with a sweetheart neckline, a bow at the waist, and a floor-sweeping hem. "This definitely goes in the 'don't even consider it' pile."

"I kind of like it," Carmela said in a small voice.

"You do?"

"I think it's pretty. Very feminine and

demure with that floor-sweeping length."

"Let's leave the floor-sweeping to someone else, girlfriend," said Ava. She pulled out a strapless, orchid-colored dress with a high-low hemline. "This one's got the best of both worlds," said Ava. "Party girl in front, a lady in the back."

Carmela wrinkled her nose. "I don't think orchid's exactly my color."

"And here I thought you were a little hothouse flower," chuckled Ava. "Okay, I've got one more in here."

"Let's see it."

Ava dangled a one-shouldered, champagne-colored gown in front of her. The tulle overlay was brushstroke jacquard, and the underlay was a metallic fabric. The dress was gathered at the right hip and had a flared skirt with a dramatic train.

"Now there's a dress!" Carmela exclaimed.

"But it's *my* dress," said Ava. "And I think this is the one I'm gonna wear tonight."

Carmela made a playful grab for the dress. "No, Ava! Champagne isn't your color. You've told me a million times, it's something you drink, not wear."

"Nice try, cookie. But you know perfectly well there's an exception to every rule. You see how that metallic underlayer warms the whole thing up? Why, it's practically gold in color."

"You win," said Carmela. "Especially since it's your dress."

Ava shook her head, and oversized gold earrings in the shape of dollar signs shone and twinkled in the light. "And I'm gonna wear these earrings tonight, since you made me give up that diamond pendant."

"*Those* earrings?" said Carmela.

"Yeah," said Ava. "I think they lend just the right touch of gangster."

"Okaaaaaay," said Carmela. She fingered the short yellow dress. "So what do you want to do now?"

"Let's have us a little fashion show and finalize our choices. And while we're at it, maybe enjoy a cocktail or two to loosen things up."

"Now you're talking," said Carmela.

By four o'clock, their dresses selected, a pitcher of frozen strawberry daiquiris consumed, Ava drifted back to her own apartment to shower and fix her hair.

Carmela was also feeling no pain. She climbed into her shower, cranked up the hot water, and under the needlelike spray, felt her entire self begin to decompress.

This is good, she told herself. *I'll take a*

couple of hours to relax and get ready. Then I'll get all prettied up for tonight. And be ready to dance the night away when Babcock finally shows up.

She washed her hair, threw in a little cream rinse for good measure, then stayed under the shower until the hot water dwindled and the pipes began their familiar clank.

This is the life. Well, it was anyway.

She stepped out of the shower, wrapped a towel around her head, and cozied up in her terry cloth robe. With the bathroom door still closed tight, the room was steamy and warm, the mirror completely fogged.

I suppose I have to think about makeup, she told herself. Maybe she'd do the Full Monty. Not just tinted moisturizer and mascara, but eyeliner, blusher, lip liner, the works. Really glam it up.

Carmela gazed into the mirror, but it was so fogged up that all she could see was an ethereal, wavering image. She reached out a hand and began to wipe away the steamy residue and beads of moisture. There, that was a little better.

She leaned forward, wondering if she should line her lower eyelids, too. Go for the cool catwalk look she'd just seen illustrated in *Vogue.* She tilted her head to one side, trying to decide.

Only her image didn't tilt with her!

What?

Her heart banging out a timpani solo inside her chest, Carmela suddenly realized that there was *another* image in the mirror. An image that didn't belong to her!

Carmela whirled around and stared in horror at the tiny bathroom window that was positioned directly across from her mirror.

A shadow wavered for an instant and was gone!

Was someone just looking in at me? Dear Lord, I think so!

She fought to quell the rising tide of fear.

But who could it have been?

Without thinking, Carmela kicked into overdrive. She tore through her apartment, dashed out the front door, and scampered around the side of her building. She knew she looked like a crazy woman, but she didn't much care. Someone — and she was pretty sure there *had* been a someone — had been watching her!

Her bare feet felt the hump and bump of every cobblestone as she tore down the narrow alley. There were garages here, old corrugated tin things, where people parked their cars. Some of the garages were leased by the people in the surrounding apartments; others were used by people who lived blocks away. Parking was always at a premium in the French Quarter.

But who had been watching her?

She slowed to a walk. And where had they disappeared to? Was someone lurking right now behind one of the hulking, rusted Dumpsters at the end of the block? Or waiting quietly in one of the open garages? Some of the garages had been broken into so many times, their doors no longer closed.

Maybe it was a bad idea to be out here.

And I left my door standing wide open. My apartment completely unlocked!

That thought got Carmela moving again.

She tiptoed back down the alley and slid around her building. A woman with a small, curly-haired dog, a Schnauzer she thought it was, was walking toward her. Carmela racked her brain, trying to remember the woman's name.

Mrs. Peabody. That was it. And her dog's name was Antoine.

"Mrs. Peabody," Carmela said breathlessly. "Did you see someone run by here?"

Mrs. Peabody stared at Carmela as if her face had just been spray-painted green.

"Why, no," she replied. Then she seemed to register that Carmela had basically just stepped directly out of the shower. "Is something wrong? Is there a problem?"

"I was . . ." Carmela faltered, not sure what she was trying to say. "I just thought I saw . . . um, someone."

With that, Carmela turned and walked back inside her apartment. But she didn't pull her door closed tight until she'd checked inside all of the closets and knelt down to look under the bed.

After all, a girl couldn't be too careful.

CHAPTER 25

The evening was warm and languorous as Carmela and Ava strutted down the street, headed for the Cakewalk Ball. Correction, Ava strutted while Carmela tiptoed. Her three-inch-high Louboutin pumps matched her canary yellow dress perfectly, but they were a bear to walk in. Narrow and strappy, dazzling and pinchy, they were a distinct contrast to the one-inch-high comfy shoes she usually drubbed around town in. But fashion was a petulant mistress, and Carmela had decided she should make a few sacrifices in order to impress Edgar Babcock.

Babcock. Where is my little cupcake anyway?

He hadn't called or checked in with her yet, and Carmela wondered if maybe his plane had been delayed.

Please, no. It's been such a long week.

"This is gonna be one terrific night," Ava

sang out as they stepped into the lobby of the New Orleans Art Institute. "We look great. We're gonna *crush* it!" Dozens of couples dressed to the nines in black tie and evening gowns swanned around them, exchanging excited greetings and elaborate air kisses.

"I hope so," said Carmela. Her self-confidence wasn't as blatant as Ava's.

"Can't you just smell the money?" whispered Ava.

Carmela dug in her jeweled clutch and presented their tickets to the tuxedoed doorman. Then they were sailing down the main hallway, where Greek statues, Renaissance paintings, and Chinese vases mingled in artistic harmony.

"Don't you love being a patron of the arts?" asked Ava as they whooshed past four grand pillars and entered the museum's grand Sky Ballroom.

"I do when I don't have to pay for the tickets," said Carmela. She looked around at the breathtaking décor. Swags of pink and white tulle — like decorations on a cake — were draped everywhere. A jazz quartet, looking dapper in purple tuxedos, played soft, sexy tunes from their perch on a raised bandstand. A large bar was arranged on one side of the vast room along with conversation groups of shiny black tables and comfy club chairs for relaxing. The dance floor, already crowded with couples dancing cheek to cheek, featured a towering ten-layer cake as a centerpiece. Flickering candles and colored lights also added an ethereal, dreamlike feel to the room.

"I love the Moby Cake that's sittin' right square in the middle of the dance floor," said Ava. "But where are all the decorated cakes? The ones with all the tasty jewels and gems?"

"They're on display in the room next door," said Carmela. "Patiently awaiting their turn until the auction begins."

"And when do you think that will be?"

"Probably not until all the guests are sufficiently liquored up. Then everyone will be in a hale and hearty good mood, ready to show off and try to outbid each other."

"That's not a bad fund-raising tactic," mused Ava.

"Trust me," said Carmela, who'd seen her fair share of these benefits. "It works every time."

"Hmm," said Ava, making a Mae West–type cooing sound as she scanned the crowd for eligible men. "Maybe I'll meet Mr. Right tonight."

"Or at least Mr. Okay for Right Now,"

said Carmela.

"Like that cute little stud muffin over there," said Ava. She cast an interested glance at a tall man in a tuxedo with wavy, over-the-collar blond hair. He had that well-scrubbed preppy look, complete with Roman nose and dimpled chin.

"Kind of East Coast meets Louisiana businessman," observed Carmela.

"Who's about to meet me," said Ava. "Lucky thing I've got a black belt in sassy!" And just like that she pranced over to Mr. Roman Nose and struck up a conversation.

Then Gabby and her husband, Stuart, spotted Carmela and came speedballing through the crowd to greet her.

"Carmela!" said Gabby. "I just saw your cake. It's fabulous!" She was dressed in a gorgeous hunter green gown that had tiny pearls sewn into the sweetheart neckline. "And I love your dress — you look beautiful tonight!"

"So do you!" Carmela said, kissing Gabby's cheek. She turned and greeted Stuart, who graced her with his standard, somewhat bored expression. "Stuart, lovely to see you."

Stuart delivered a chaste peck on Carmela's cheek. "Always good to see you, too, darlin'."

"How's business?" Carmela asked him. Stuart liked nothing better than to talk about business.

A smile spread across Stuart's broad face. "Pretty dang good," he enthused. "Most of our primary lease terms are three years now, so our vehicle remarketing program has added significantly to our bottom line."

"That's wonderful," said Carmela. She had no idea what Stuart had just said.

"You know, Carmela," Stuart continued, "I could put you in a brand-new Celica for three ninety-nine down."

Before she could respond, Jekyl suddenly appeared at her right elbow. In his black sequined jacket and bright red bow tie, he looked like a stylish game show host.

"Little bird!" Jekyl cried. "You look so delightfully perky in yellow!"

Carmela laughed. "I better look good, because these shoes are killing me."

Jekyl grabbed her by the hand and pulled her away. "Speaking of killing, m'dear, I'd say *beaucoup* congrats are in order!"

Carmela stared at him. "What do you mean?"

Jekyl led her closer to the bar, where a waiter tipped his tray toward them and offered a choice of shrimp pâté on crackers or blobs of shiny black caviar on toast points.

Carmela helped herself to one of each. She figured it was going to be a long night and she needed to fortify herself.

"Darlin'," said Jekyl, his dark eyes lighting up. "You solved the murder!" He popped a cracker into his mouth and chewed thoughtfully. "Of course, I always knew you would. You have the raw and natural instincts of a real-life investigator. And here I suspected meek little Beetsie all along. I guess it just goes to show how off base *moi* can be."

"Jekyl." Carmela tapped a finger against his shiny lapel. "I don't think I did solve the murder. Yes, the police picked up Duncan Merriweather for questioning, but . . ."

Carmela's cell phone buzzed from inside her beaded bag.

"One second," she told Jekyl. "I have to get this." She grabbed the phone, checked her Caller ID. Yes, it was Babcock! "You're here!" she said.

"I'm back in town, yes." His voice sounded mellow but tired. "My plane just landed."

"Just in the nick of time," said Carmela. "Why don't you jump into your tux and get over here, okay?"

"A tux," he said. There was a giant sigh attached to that.

"That's right," said Carmela. "That same one you wore to the Rex Ball would be absolutely perfect."

"Carmela, I'm pretty beat . . ."

"Please," she said. "Just get your sweet self over here, okay?" She lowered her voice. "I'm really . . . dying to see you."

Now Babcock gave a low chuckle. "With a heartfelt invitation like that, how can I resist?"

"Ooh, wait a minute," said Carmela. "You don't have an invitation. I mean, like, tickets."

"I've got a gold shield," said Babcock. "That should be invitation enough."

As Carmela hung up, Jekyl rolled his eyes. "I take it your sweetie is back in town."

"Finally," said Carmela. She linked her arm through Jekyl's and they strolled around the ballroom.

"Carmela!" called Baby, giving an eager wave.

Carmela and Jekyl quickly joined Baby and her husband, Del. Baby was dressed in a burgundy gown with a yellow sash that perfectly matched her sleek blond hair.

"You're the talk of the walk!" Baby exclaimed.

"Why is that?" said Carmela, somewhat guardedly. *Oh no. Not more talk about the murder and Duncan Merriweather!*

But Baby was all jacked up over Carmela's

cake. "Your delightful little bird cake is getting tons of attention. I've heard from a couple of people that it's their number one favorite, so I'll bet you get the highest bid!"

"I think the attention is probably being paid to the diamond pendant and not my cake," said Carmela. She knew the pendant was a real stunner. Who wouldn't want it? Heck, *she'd* love to have it!

"We'll see!" chirped Baby.

Baby's husband kissed Carmela fondly on the cheek. "It's a good thing the auction isn't silent," he said. "Then we'd have nothing to gossip about."

"Nothing ever remains silent in New Orleans!" Carmela replied.

Carmela and Jekyl moved on. Then, when Jekyl spotted a bunch of friends from the Pluvius krewe, he suddenly dashed off to greet them. Leaving Carmela standing alone.

But not for long.

Buddy Pelletier, Jerry Earl's old business pal, suddenly had her in his clutches. "Carmela," said Pelletier. "I'd like to introduce you to my wife, Melba."

Carmela greeted Melba warmly and they made small talk for a few minutes. Then Pelletier pulled her aside.

"Thank you so much for helping Margo,"

Pelletier told her.

"I'm not sure I did all that much," said Carmela.

"Dear lady, you did far more than you think. You were a friend during her time of need and, from what I've been hearing, pointed a firm finger at Duncan Merriweather."

"Yes, but I . . ."

"Don't downplay your good work, Carmela," said Pelletier. "You made a significant contribution to this investigation." He hooked a thumb and pointed at Margo Leland across the dance floor. "Look at Margo over there. Merriweather's arrest this morning came as a terrible shock to her, but it's also lifted an enormous weight off her shoulders."

"You think?" Carmela didn't think Margo looked all that happy or relieved.

"Absolutely," said Pelletier. "Now she knows. Now she's got closure and can start rebuilding her life." He smiled his handsome smile.

"I suppose you're right," said Carmela. Somehow, deep in her heart, she didn't feel like there'd been any sort of closure. Then again, maybe she was still coming to terms with the two murders.

"I'm going to make sure all Margo's

friends continue to rally around her," said Pelletier. "I'm going to ensure there's a good, solid support group."

"That's very sweet of you," said Carmela.

Pelletier was gazing at her intently.

"I think I'm going to go over and say hello to Margo," said Carmela. "Thank her for the tickets."

Pelletier nodded forcefully. "Do that. I know she'd love it."

When Margo saw Carmela coming toward her, she stretched out a hand and said in a quavering voice, "Carmela. You dear, dear girl."

Carmela put her arms around Margo and gave her a big hug. "How are you holding up?" she asked. "I can't believe you're even *here* tonight."

"I know, I know," said Margo. "But at least this whole terrible ordeal is practically over with now." She stepped back and turned plaintive eyes on Carmela. "Can you believe it? Duncan Merriweather? *Our* Duncan? It surely came as a complete shock!"

Now Beetsie chimed in. "He was always right there, always so close to us!"

"I get chills every time I think about it," said Margo, making google eyes. "Duncan was always with us — our little troika, he liked to call us. He was at every party, every social engagement, pretending to be helpful, pretending to be solicitous."

"But we had a viper in our midst!" said Beetsie. She wore a long black dress and low, squashy heels. Margo, on the other hand, was dolled up in a flamboyant fuchsia-colored dress with her trademark gold accessories and super-high stilettos. Her forehead looked smooth and a little puffy, and Carmela wondered if she'd just had a hit of Botox.

"Being part of our inner circle gave Duncan access to everything and everyone!" cried Margo.

"At least he'll be behind bars now," Beetsie added sharply.

"I should hope so!" said Margo. "It's utterly chilling that we were associating with such a vicious killer!"

Carmela said nothing. It was obvious the two of them were still in shock over the discovery of the trocar and Merriweather's subsequent arrest. Still, she couldn't help wondering if any actual evidence had come to the surface. After all, the phone tip had been anonymous, there were no eyewitnesses to the murders of Jerry Earl and Eric Zane, and the arrest seemed to have been prompted by pure emotion. So was the jury still out on this?

Goodness, Carmela thought, *the jury hasn't even been selected yet!*

CHAPTER 26

"Shamus!" said Carmela, suddenly startled. She'd been elbowing her way through the elegant crowd, trying to hunt down Ava. And instead, she'd run into the two people she really had no interest in talking to — Shamus and Glory Meechum.

"Glory wants to see her cake," said Shamus. He was dressed to kill in a black Armani tuxedo with a tartan plaid cummerbund. Glory, his older sister, had mean, wary eyes sunken into her doughy face, a lacquered helmet of gray hair, and wore her version of a sensible evening gown. In other words, it was brown, long, and shapeless.

Carmela peeked down at Glory's shoes. Her feet looked like two gunboats encased in brown leather. Good heavens, even Beetsie could give this woman pointers!

"Well?" said Glory. She was mean as a puff adder and rich as Croesus. She'd never liked Carmela and liked her even less now that she'd been forced to relinquish the Garden District home in the divorce settlement. "I'd like to see my cake if it's not too much trouble, Carmela."

"All the cakes are on display in the adjoining room," Carmela told them in a neutral tone. *Keep calm and carry on,* she vowed to herself.

"Then lead the way, darlin'," said Shamus. "Let's take a gander."

"How are the dogs?" Carmela asked.

"Just fine," said Shamus. "The little darlings settled in just fine."

"The cake?" demanded Glory.

Carmela trooped out into the hallway and into the next room with Shamus and Glory following in her wake like a couple of disapproving ducklings. Her gaze wandered across six long tables that each held an opulent arrangement of cakes and jewels — and then she finally spotted hers.

"Over there," she pointed. "With the bird's nest."

Shamus saw it and beamed. "It looks pretty good, huh, Glory? It turned out okay."

Carmela rolled her eyes. Poor Shamus was always trying to please his older sister. Always kowtowing to her every whim. Then again, Glory controlled the purse strings that allowed him to live his indolent and often frivolous life.

Glory took a look, nodded, then lifted her glass and drained it.

Carmela, meanwhile, tried to share the thinking behind her creative endeavor. "I thought the bird's nest would really highlight the necklace," she told them. "Give the impression of a rare jewel." She looked around. "I know some of the other cakes incorporated jewelry into the actual frosting, but I felt that might be downplaying your pendant's beauty and importance."

"It looks nice," Glory said in a grudging tone. "It works."

"Carmela's right," said Shamus, trying to muster a little more enthusiasm for Carmela's work. "A lot of the cakes that were donated by individuals and corporations are all fancy and elaborate, but they don't show off the *real* reason for the auction — which is, of course, the jewelry."

Glory looked around for a waiter. "Where are the servers when you need a drink?"

"Anyway," said Carmela, picking up where Shamus had left off. "A lot of the other cakes are just bling-bling-a-go-go while your cake really features the diamond pendant."

"Yup," said Glory, barely stifling a belch. "Okeydoke."

"I bet it'll be high bid at the auction tonight," chortled Shamus.

Glory waggled her empty glass back and forth. "Shamus?"

Shamus clapped a hand on Carmela's shoulder. "Gotta go, babe. Have to freshen Glory's drink."

Carmela watched them wind their way back through the tables of cakes, thanking her lucky stars that she was no longer part of the crazy, dysfunctional Meechum clan. That she was her own free person and had escaped unscathed. Well, reasonably unscathed.

Wandering amid the cakes, Carmela took a careful look at her competition. There were some lovely cakes here as well as some very spectacular jewelry!

Here was a cake with a Grecian-inspired theme that had a pair of gold Bulgari earrings on it. Really fantastic.

Another cake featured five teetering tiers and had a pearl necklace dangling from a fondant Eiffel Tower.

One cake had been done all in Tiffany blue and had a lovely diamond and gold tennis bracelet on it. Was the bracelet from Tiffany's? Had to be.

Oh, and here was Margo's cake, a buttercream confection with her Victorian crown jewel necklace proudly displayed among mounds of whipped frosting.

The cakes were all really quite amazing, Carmela decided. The auction should raise a pretty penny tonight, especially if . . .

A chocolate cake suddenly caught Carmela's eye.

What!

It was covered with whipped chocolate frosting mounded in little swirls with small fondant barrels of oil scattered across it. A gold mesh bracelet was wound around the center barrel of oil.

But the décor and jewelry weren't what drew Carmela's rapt attention. It was the lettering on the side of the cake — the lettering that spelled out Spangler Energy!

Spangler Energy? What on earth?

Could Spangler Energy be somehow related to Spangler Enterprises, the company that bought the land Jerry Earl had tried to lease?

It has to be!

Heart pounding, mouth suddenly gone dry, Carmela studied the cake more carefully. There were lots of little fondant barrels of oil, which seemed to point to a company that did oil drilling. Also, the words *Tuscaloosa-Marine Shale* were written across the bottom layer.

Carmela's brows puckered together. What on earth was Tuscaloosa-Marine Shale? And more important, who had donated this cake? She needed to find out! Immediately!

Dashing back into the ballroom, her heart skipping beats, her skirt flying, she glanced around frantically. She saw passing waiters, two security guards, a knot of good-looking men passing around unlit cigars, and . . . Conrad Falcon.

For once and for all, I'm going to get a straight answer out of that man!

Breathlessly, Carmela approached Falcon.

"Mr. Falcon, a word please." Carmela's wished her nerves were as steely and controlled as her voice.

Conrad Falcon practically sneered when he saw her. "You," he said.

"That's right," said Carmela. "I was just looking at your cake in the other room and found it extremely interesting."

He cocked an eye at her. "Oh really?"

"The Spangler Energy cake?" she spat out.

Falcon stared at her. "Excuse me?"

"What I want to know," said Carmela, "is how Spangler Energy, or Spangler Enterprises, or whatever you want to call it, relates to your company?"

"It doesn't," he said.

Carmela fought to keep from slapping him

across the face. She knew he had to be lying, pure and simple. Of course he was. There was no way he was going to admit to any criminal activity now that Duncan Merriweather was under arrest!

She leveled her gaze at Falcon, though her anger was doing a slow burn. "I'm going to get the proof I need," she told him. "And when I do, rest assured you're going to jail for a very long time. Probably for the rest of your life."

Falcon's reply was a low hiss. "I think you should take whatever prescription you've run out of and get it renewed!" Then he turned and stalked off.

Carmela spun around and pushed her way through the growing throng of people. What to do? How to really resolve this? The noise level was rising in pitch as the jazz band pumped out music like crazy. She could barely make herself heard, let alone think clearly!

Maybe if she could find Ava. Ava could sometimes be the voice of reason. Or at least a catalyst for action!

Carmela looked around frantically. There were lots of women in gold floor-length gowns, but none of them was Ava. So where was she?

Carmela hastily inspected the crowd again

and suddenly spotted Angela Boynton. Angela was one of the curators who'd helped honcho this event. She was also a good friend.

Carmela quickly hatched a plan as she ran up to greet her.

"Angela, I need your help!"

Angela turned toward her with a broad smile. But her smile faded when she saw the worry and distress etched on Carmela's face.

"Carmela, what?" Angela was a serious-looking woman in her midthirties, with shoulder-length light brown hair, green eyes, and a slight bump on her nose that made her look interesting and highly approachable. Tonight she wore a pale peach gown with a dramatic pair of Etruscan-looking earrings.

"I have to know who donated the Spangler Energy cake!" Carmela blurted out. "I have to know who's behind it!"

Angela stared at her. "I don't know offhand. I'd have to go back to my office and check the donor list."

"Can you do that? Can we do that?"

"Carmela, what's wrong?" Angela was busy and a little harried, too. "Is it real important?"

"Yes, it is," Carmela insisted. "Please."

"I'm right in the middle of . . ." Angela hesitated, then removed a chain from around her wrist and quickly handed it to Carmela.

It took Carmela a split second to realize that the keys to Angela's office were attached to that chain. "Thank you!" Carmela breathed.

Angela clutched her arm. "Promise you'll tell me what this is all about when you get a chance?"

Carmela's head bobbed frantically. "I will. I promise!" Then she scurried off.

All the lights were turned off, but Carmela still managed to find the back hallway that led to the curators' offices. Though her shoes were biting into her feet something awful, she ran lightly down the dark corridor and stopped in front of a wooden door marked *Curatorial B.* Key ring jingling, she tried the first one in the lock. No go.

Okay, the second one.

No.

The third one?

There was a sharp click and then Carmela was inside the small office that Angela shared with one of the textile curators. She tiptoed over to Angela's desk and turned on the small tensor lamp. Posters, brochures,

Japanese obis, and small Buddhist sculptures were suddenly lit up in the spill from the lamp. There was a wall of books and another wall where an elaborate brocade wedding kimono hung from a bamboo rod.

Carmela sank into Angela's desk chair and pawed through the stacks of paperwork that were spread across her desk. She found acquisition lists, minutes from a recent budget meeting, exhibition notes, and . . . yes! The donor list!

A sudden noise sounded from down the hallway.

Footsteps. Somebody coming?

Carmela froze as she strained to hear. It sounded as if someone was walking very cautiously and deliberately down the hallway. Then, much to her horror, they stopped right outside the office door!

Who is it? Who's out there?

All thoughts of the donor list were suddenly forgotten. Carmela stood up and looked around with wild eyes. How to escape? As panic rose in her chest, she spotted the door to a small adjacent storeroom. She switched off the lamp and then, with an ungainly lurch, dove into the storeroom and pulled the door shut behind her!

Standing in the dark, trying to control her breathing, Carmela wondered who had followed her!

Is it Conrad Falcon?

If it was, then Conrad Falcon must be guilty as sin! Her teeth began to chatter and she bit down hard to control it. Was he the killer? Was the man who killed Jerry Earl and Eric Zane after her, too? Dear Lord, he was a man who had pulled off murder right in the middle of two crowded events! And now she'd fallen prey to him, too!

What if he opens the door and finds me in here? I'm a sitting duck!

Even with her panic and racing thoughts, Carmela's eyes adjusted to the darkness in the storeroom. And now she could just make out a narrow crack of light at the opposite end of the small room.

There's another door? A way out? Looks like it!

Carmela slipped out of her shoes. Quietly, carefully, she climbed and fumbled her way over an enormous stack of boxes and then a pile of books, hoping to get to the other door. Just as she eased past something tall and metal — a file cabinet? — her toe brushed against something soft. A mouse? No, probably just some rolled-up fabric. She continued on stealthily, stepping over more boxes as she carried her shoes in one hand and beat the air in front of her with her other hand, trying to feel for the door. For her escape hatch! Another foot, another few more inches . . . and there it was!

Just as the door behind her flew open, she scrambled out the second door and shut it quietly behind her. And found herself standing . . . in a large dark sculpture gallery.

She could hear faint sounds of someone fumbling about and cursing inside the storage room that she'd just fled. There was a loud crash and she knew they'd stumbled and fallen down!

Good! Maybe they even broke their arm!

Slowly, stealthily, Carmela tiptoed across the floor, taking refuge behind a large winged metal sculpture, then dodging out and ducking behind a large marble statue.

She heard more sounds! Whoever it was behind her must have righted himself and was still trying to follow her!

Her breath caught in her throat and her nerves fizzed with fear. She willed herself to try to remain calm. She wouldn't go down without a fight.

How close was her pursuer? Were they out the door yet? Into this room?

Carmela took a daring risk and tried to sneak a peak from behind a metal statue of a rearing horse. But she didn't see anything. Her heart still thumping wildly, she backed up some more. This gallery emptied out into a wide hallway, which led directly to safety.

I'm so close. If I can just ease my way out of here . . .

She backed up a few more feet. Then, like a shadow in the moonlight, she slid behind a tall, zigzagging Japanese screen. She held her breath, hesitated, and listened. Heard nothing.

Time to make my move?

She backed slowly toward the hallway. Three more steps, maybe four more, and then she could turn and run. Make a mad dash for safety.

Ever so carefully, Carmela backed up two steps, then three. She hesitated. Nobody coming after her yet, thank goodness. Hoping this was her one big chance, she took a final step backward.

And that's when a pair of arms came out of nowhere and wrapped themselves tightly around her!

CHAPTER 27

Carmela let out a startled scream and spun around, wriggling like mad, fighting frantically to pull herself free.

It was only when she suddenly recognized the man who held her captive that she stopped her frenzied struggle.

What?

Another familiar face bobbed nearby like a small weather balloon.

"Moony?" Carmela said, her voice rising like a falsetto singer. "Squirrel?"

Moony put a finger to his mouth, partially releasing her. "Shhh! Keep quiet!"

"What are you *doing* here?" Carmela hissed. Clearly, they had snuck into the Art Institute. But why? What could they possibly want here?

Moony released his grip on her and gave a cagey smile. "We came here to get our payment."

Carmela stared at him. "What?" She

understood the words okay, but she wasn't tracking their meaning.

"The *necklace*," Moony explained patiently, as if he were trying to teach remedial reading to a fifth grader.

"The one on the *cake*!" said Squirrel. "The Victorian necklace. Heck, you were the one who told us about it."

Carmela's mind was spinning, trying to make sense of this. Her mouth felt dry as sandpaper. "You can't take that necklace," she choked out. "It's not yours."

Moony shook his head. "Oh no, little lady. It's rightfully ours. We earned it."

"It was promised to us," said Squirrel. "It's our payment."

"Are you two totally crazy?" Carmela squawked. Then she remembered her pursuer. She reached out and pulled Moony close to her, said, "There was somebody after me." She pointed toward the sculpture room. "In there!"

"Heck you say," said Squirrel. He took a couple of steps into the dark sculpture room and glanced around. "Nobody in here now." His voice echoed hollowly in the empty room.

"Thank goodness," said Carmela. Maybe her pursuer had slipped back through the storeroom? Maybe it had been nothing at all? No, she told herself, someone had been after her for sure.

"You showed up just in the nick of time to help us," Moony said to Carmela. He scratched his chin with the back of his hand. "And it seems to me you got the lay of the land pretty well figured out here."

"I can't help you steal that necklace!" said Carmela.

"It's not stealing," Moony insisted. "It's payment."

"Fair and square," said Squirrel.

"Oh jeez." Carmela set her shoes down and stepped into them. "What a mess."

"Not if you give us a helping hand," said Squirrel. "Then it'll all be copasetic."

"First I've got to talk to somebody," said Carmela. She cast an appraising eye at the two men. "But . . . you're not exactly dressed for this," she told them. They both wore saggy blue jeans and wrinkled T-shirts. Squirrel wore a plaid shirt open over his T-shirt and Moony had a trucker cap that said *Fat Boy.*

"Take off that stupid cap," she told Moony. "And follow me."

Carmela had luck on her side. The cake and jewelry auction had just kicked off and most of the guests had crowded up toward the bandstand, their backs turned toward them. Excited murmurs ran through the crowd as they clutched their bidding paddles. Three gorgeous cakes were on display up on a dais.

"Nice place you got here," said Moony as they sauntered into the ballroom.

Carmela poked an index finger in his face. "You," she said. "You let me do the talking!"

From the front of the room, the auctioneer's voice boomed out: "First cake up for auction was donated by Holden Industries. I understand this is a lemon chiffon cake topped by an eighteen-karat-gold charm bracelet. Do I hear one thousand?"

"Dollars?" squeaked Squirrel.

"One thousand dollars," intoned the auctioneer. "From the lady in hot pink."

"Holy shebang," said Squirrel, ducking his head.

A waiter carrying a tray of champagne flutes cautiously approached the three of them. "Champagne, ma'am?" he asked. He raised an eyebrow. "Gentlemen?"

"Don't mind if I do," said Squirrel. He grabbed a champagne flute, stuck his pinky finger out, and took a sip.

"How is it?" asked Moony.

"Bracing," said Squirrel.

"Come on," said Carmela. She proceeded

to haul them to the bar, where Shamus was lounging, as if to the manor born. He was drinking bourbon and shooting the breeze with one of the bartenders.

"Shamus!" said Carmela.

Shamus turned, a smile on his handsome face. Then it slipped off completely and was replaced by stunned surprise when she saw Moony and Squirrel. "Ah . . . what?" he said, suddenly at a loss for words. Unusual for Shamus.

"I need to ask you something," said Carmela. "I need you to pay attention!"

But Shamus couldn't pull his eyes from Moony and Squirrel. "Who are these ring dings anyway?"

"This is Moony and Squirrel," said Carmela.

"Don't tell me," Shamus said in a droll tone. "You and Ava brought dates."

"No, Shamus, they're on the *decorating* committee."

Shamus gave a slow, reptilian blink. "Really?"

Carmela grabbed Shamus by the arm and gave him a rough shake. "Snap out of it, Shamus, I need to ask you something!"

His gaze finally focused on her. "What, babe?"

"What do you know about Spangler Enterprises?" Carmela asked.

Shamus stared at her. "You mean . . . uh . . . Spangler Energy?"

Carmela jumped on his words. "Yes! What is that? Are they the same company?"

Shamus, pleased to be the center of attention, playing the learned banker now, chose his words carefully. "Well, the energy group is a *division* of Spangler Enterprises." A slow, sloppy smile spread across his face. "Fact is, we're working with them on an interim loan."

"For oil drilling?" Carmela demanded.

Shamus nodded.

"Oil drilling where, Shamus?"

He took another sip of bourbon. "Parcel up in West Feliciana Parish as I recall."

"There's oil there?" said Carmela.

"That's right," said Shamus. "Supposed to be part of the Tuscaloosa-Marine shale play. If it all pans out, the upside is a potential for seven billion gallons."

"But who's the head of Spangler?" Carmela asked. "Is it Conrad Falcon?" She knew it had to be him.

Shamus's face suddenly went blank. "Falcon?" He shook his head. "No, no way."

"Then who, Shamus? Who is it?"

Shamus took another swig of his drink and gave a low chuckle. "Well, you know him,

Carmela. Heck, you were just talking to him a few minutes ago." Shamus glanced around.

"Who, Shamus? Who is it?" Carmela couldn't stand the suspense!

"There. Over there," he said.

Carmela peered through the crowd just as Shamus lifted a hand and pointed directly at . . .

Buddy Pelletier!

At that very same instant, Pelletier saw Shamus pointing at him. His face registered sudden surprise, then darkened when he saw Carmela. A look of alarm turned his handsome features into dark saturnine anger.

He knows he's been made, Carmela thought. *He knows that we know he's the killer!*

Pelletier spun around quickly and lurched off, weaving past tables and elbowing his way through the throng of bidders, ignoring their startled glances.

"C'mon, we have to grab him!" Carmela cried.

"Who? Why?" said Ava, who had just come up to join them.

"Buddy Pelletier!" said Carmela. "He's the killer!"

"What?" said Shamus.

"Killer?" said Squirrel.

"Holy guacamole!" said a stunned Ava.

Carmela launched herself like a grenade, waving for Moony and Squirrel to follow. "You guys gotta help me grab this guy!"

"Now you're talkin'!" cried Moony.

They dodged through the crowd as the auctioneer called out for another round of bids. Long skirts rustled and feathers were ruffled as they formed a flying wedge through the crowd.

"There he is!" cried Carmela. She could just see the top of Pelletier's silver head as he dashed into the hallway.

"He's heading for the cake room!" cried Ava.

En masse, Carmela, Ava, Squirrel, Moony, and Shamus wheeled wildly in the hallway as they followed Pelletier's mad dash into the cake room.

Pelletier glanced back at them as he dipped and dodged his way past tables laden with elaborate cakes. When he realized with a start that there was an entire posse after him, his mouth pulled into a snarl and he grabbed the end of one table. Giving a hard grunt, he heaved the table upward until it flipped over completely!

A landslide of gorgeously wrought cakes slid and toppled in a monumental rush of buttercream, devil's food, vanilla cake, elaborate fondant, and glittering jewelry.

Carmela, who was at the head of the pack, didn't break stride, even when she skidded dangerously through an oil slick of frosting. Now everyone was yelling, the commotion growing by leaps and bounds!

Grimacing in anger, eyes like a trapped animal, Pelletier spotted an emergency exit and hurtled his way toward it. As his hands slammed the lever that stretched across the door, a buzzer blasted loudly and the door flew open. Then Pelletier disappeared into the darkness of the night!

"Come on!" Carmela pleaded. "We have to stop him!"

"Don't let him get away!" came Ava's cry.

They all flew out the door after Pelletier and clattered down a short flight of metal steps.

Carmela's heel caught in the lower rung. And just as she was about to stumble badly, Moony's arm shot out and grabbed her. She glanced sideways at him, a quick, appreciative look, and saw that he'd somehow managed to grab the cake with the crown pendant on it. The crazy coot was hanging on to his prize and balancing it precariously as he ran!

"Are you crazy?" said Carmela.

"It's mine!" Moony huffed, fighting to keep stride alongside her.

Pelletier hurtled down the sidewalk, his shoes sounding like firecrackers as they slapped against the pavement. Halfway down the block, Carmela spotted an Aston Martin convertible parked at the curb.

"That's his car!" she screamed. "Don't let him get away!"

"Nice ride!" Shamus huffed as he followed after them.

"Focus, please!" Carmela begged as they all tore down the dark street.

But Pelletier had already jumped into his car and was revving the engine. The headlights flashed on, the car let loose a throaty roar, and it started to lurch forward!

"He's getting away!" Ava shrieked.

Red-lining his engine now, Pelletier popped it into second gear, and cranked the steering wheel hard. Just as he was about to explode out of his parking spot like a Formula One car, a burgundy Crown Victoria sluiced in front of him and blocked him!

"What the devil!" Shamus yelped as the front fender of Babcock's car was smacked so hard it crumpled.

"It's Babcock!" Carmela cried. Relief flooded her entire being. Her fear and anxiety were suddenly evaporating.

Babcock leapt from his car, looking handsome and stunning in his tuxedo. His ginger-colored hair was slicked back, his eyes were pinpricks of intensity, and his shoes shone in the glow from the streetlamps like a modern-day Fred Astaire action figure. The only thing that seemed out of place was the startled expression on his face.

Babcock took in Pelletier, who was still gunning his engine, trying to rock his sports car back and forth so he could push the car behind him out of the way and still make a break for it! And then he threw a questioning glance at the throng of people that was rushing toward him.

"What's going on?" Babcock yelled. He threw his hands up and shook his head in disbelief.

"Buddy Pelletier!" Carmela cried. "He killed Jerry Earl Leland!"

"And probably Eric Zane!" Ava added.

But Pelletier was making progress, rocking to and fro, basically smashing the grill of the car behind him. Another two inches and he'd be able to squeak out and make his getaway!

"Stop him!" Carmela cried. "Somebody do something!"

Moony dashed past Carmela, grim determination on his face and the cake held high above his head. Then, in a moment of pure brilliance, he reared back and hurled the cake directly at Pelletier!

The cake soared through the air like a sugar-coated missile, flipping end over end, bits of frosting flying everywhere. Then, like a scene out of a Bugs Bunny cartoon, the cake smashed directly into Pelletier's head and exploded!

Chunks of cake flew everywhere and there was an ungodly screech of glass and grinding metal as Pelletier blindly lurched forward and locked bumpers with the car ahead of him. Bellowing like an enraged bull, Pelletier alternately howled, stomped on the gas pedal, and fought to wipe cake goo from his eyes and nose!

That was enough for Babcock. His gun was out of his shoulder harness in an instant and trained directly on Pelletier.

As Pelletier was rudely dragged from his car, Moony swept in and grabbed the crown jewel pendant, which had somehow magically draped itself on the Aston Martin's rearview mirror!

Carmela felt a rush of adrenaline as she watched her handsome boyfriend put handcuffs on Buddy Pelletier and stuff him into the backseat of his banged-up Crown Victoria. "You got him!" she cried.

Ava was doing her victory dance in the middle of the sidewalk. "We did it! We did it. We got him! We got him!" Squirrel threw her a goofy smile and joined in, dancing and bumping hips with her.

Babcock looked around. "Anybody else need arresting?"

Carmela watched as Moony grabbed the necklace and stuffed it into the back pocket of his jeans. He turned and gave her a slightly guilty look, but she just shrugged. A small payment, she decided, for helping apprehend a dangerous killer.

"I think we're good," said Carmela. She beamed at Babcock. "Thank goodness you showed up when you did!"

"I think you've got some serious explaining to do," Babcock told her. His gaze was stern but his voice was gentle.

Shamus ambled up. "Wow." He pointed to the dent in the Crown Vic. "It's a dang shame about your car."

"Taxpayers won't like paying for that," Babcock agreed.

Ava let out a gasp and pointed at Carmela's shoes. "And look at your poor shoes! They're completely ruined!"

Carmela glanced down. Her yellow silk

shoes were streaked with white frosting and dappled with pink and white cake jimmies. Chances were, she'd never dance in them again.

"Don't worry, babe," said Shamus, puffing out his chest, trying his best to act important. "I'll buy you another pair."

In an instant, Babcock was at Carmela's side. He draped a possessive arm around her waist, pulled her close to him, and gave her a big kiss.

"No," he said, "*I'll* buy her another pair."

SCRAPBOOK, STAMPING, AND CRAFT TIPS FROM LAURA CHILDS

Dimensional Paper Images with Rubber Stamps

Take about 6 Kleenex tissues and get them nice and damp. Now lay the tissues over one of your favorite rubber stamps. (A simple image works the best — I used a teapot image.) Press carefully so the image begins to show through. Now carefully remove the tissue and let your piece dry overnight. When the embossed image is completely dry, you can cut it into any shape you want, then paint it, gild it, or leave it plain. These embossed images are a great addition to handmade cards or add interest to scrapbook pages.

Greeting Card Pockets

When you're scrapbooking a special event — such as Christmas, Mother's Day, etc. — why not include the greeting cards that you received? Just create a pocket on your page and stick the cards in there. Your photos from that day, along with the cards, will make for a more memorable page.

There's Life in That Old T-Shirt!
Fun graphic emblems from the front of a T-shirt can make a great cover design for an album. Just cut them out and adhere with hot glue.

A Hot Look!
To achieve a sort of "burned" look on your photos or papers, tear the edges so they have a nice rough look, then use a brown ink pad to color the edges.

Leftover Bits of Paper
Don't toss out all those smaller, leftover pieces of colorful scrapbook paper. Use them to make napkin rings and place cards.

Adding Instant Age
Want to make a black-and-white photo look like an heirloom? Take a wet tea bag and smear it across your photo. Depending on how much tea you smooth on, you can adjust your sepia tone from very light to a medium tone. And, of course, you have the pleasure of drinking a nice cup of tea!

Wineglass Charms

Have you seen those expensive wineglass charms that are sold in gourmet shops? You can easily create your own using a few colored beads and memory wire! You can even laminate tiny photos and use them in conjunction with your beads. Cheers!

Just Your Type

If you are creating a scrapbook page featuring a certain sport or sporting event, hunt through the sports section of your newspaper and snip out some of the various sports words. (Think WIN, VICTORY, and BIG FINISH!) Arranged as a background collage, they'll look great with your sports photos.

Repetition's the Thing

An image is always much more powerful when it's repeated. For example, a stamped image of a bunny is great on your scrapbook page. But several bunnies hippity-hopping across the page is even more fun. Ditto for images such as pumpkins, hearts, or flowers.

Wraps for Gift Soaps

Small bars of handmade soap become wonderful hostess gifts when you create your own "wrap" to go around them. Just use fun paper and stamp it with images such as flowers, bubbles, or hearts. A short, hand-lettered poem would be delightful, too. For example: *Soap smells so sweet when splashing bubbles with your feet.*

FAVORITE NEW ORLEANS RECIPES

BAKED SHRIMP WITH PARSLEY
1 lb. raw shrimp
1/2 stick butter
1/4 cup oil
1/2 tsp. garlic powder
1 Tbsp. lemon juice
1/2 tsp. salt
2 Tbsps. chopped parsley
2 Tbsps. grated Parmesan cheese

Preheat oven to 400 degrees. Clean, wash, and dry shrimp. Melt butter in a 9-by-13-inch pan. Add oil, garlic powder, lemon juice, salt, parsley, and Parmesan, then mix. Add shrimp and mix some more until shrimp are well coated. Bake for 9 to 12 minutes. Serve over pasta or rice. Serves 2.

BANANA NUT BARS
1 1/2 cups flour
1 cup sugar

1/2 tsp. baking soda
1/2 tsp. salt
1/2 cup butter, soft
2 eggs
1 banana, very ripe, sliced
1/3 cup milk
1/2 cup chopped walnuts

Preheat oven to 350 degrees. Beat all ingredients except walnuts at medium speed for 2 minutes. Stir in walnuts, then pour into a greased 9-by-13-inch baking pan. Bake for 25 to 30 minutes or until toothpick comes out clean. Cool and slice into bars. Excellent when topped with whipped cream!

EASY OVEN-FRIED CAJUN CHICKEN
1 frying chicken, cut up
1 cup flour
1 tsp. black pepper
1 tsp. Creole seasoning
1/2 tsp. paprika
1/4 tsp. cayenne pepper
1/2 cup butter, melted

Preheat oven to 425 degrees. Wash and pat chicken dry. In a large ziplock bag, combine flour, black pepper, Creole seasoning, paprika, and cayenne pepper. Add chicken and shake well until coated. Line a 9-by-13-inch baking dish with foil and pour in butter. Place chicken in baking dish, skin side down. Bake at 425 degrees for 30 minutes. Then reduce heat to 325 degrees and bake for an additional 45 minutes. Chicken should be golden brown and very tender!

GRILLED PEANUT BUTTER SHRIMP

1/4 cup creamy peanut butter
1/4 cup soy sauce
1/4 cup sugar
2 Tbsps. olive oil
1 1/2 lbs. large shrimp, shelled and deveined

This recipe is perfect for outdoor grilling! In saucepan, heat and stir together peanut butter, soy sauce, sugar, and olive oil. Place shrimp on skewers and brush with peanut butter sauce. Grill over medium-hot heat for 3 minutes, then turn and grill for another 2 minutes or so, basting if needed. Serves 4.

CARMELA'S CROCKPOT MEATLOAF

1/2 cup milk
2 slices white bread
1 1/2 lbs. ground beef
1 small onion, chopped
1 tsp. salt
1/2 tsp. pepper
1 tsp. dry mustard
2 eggs

1 (12-oz.) can whole tomatoes

Pour milk into mixing bowl and then add bread. Let stand for a few minutes until all the milk has been absorbed. Break bread into small pieces. Add ground beef, onion, salt, pepper, and dry mustard to bread mixture and mix until well combined. In separate bowl, beat eggs, then add to beef mixture. Shape beef mixture into a round loaf and place in crockpot. Drain tomatoes and pour over beef. Cover and cook on low heat for 5 to 6 hours. Before serving, uncover pot. Turn heat to high and reduce the sauce until it's nice and thick. Serves 4.

AVA'S JUJU VOODOO PEANUT BUTTER COOKIES

1 cup sugar
1 large egg
1 cup peanut butter (any kind)

Preheat oven to 350 degrees. Mix sugar and egg together, then add in peanut butter. Form dough into 1″ balls and press gently with a fork. Bake on greased baking sheet for 10 to 12 minutes. Yields 1 dozen cookies that are so easy to make, it's practically magic!

CAJUN HONEY-SPICED NUTS

1/4 cup honey
1 Tbsp. butter
2 Tbsps. Cajun spice mix
4 cups mixed nuts

Melt honey and butter together in large microwave dish on high for 1 minute. Stir in spice mix, then stir in nuts until all ingredients are well mixed. Cook on high for 6 minutes, stirring nuts every 2 minutes. Spread out to cool, then enjoy.

CARMELA'S QUICK SHRIMP ÉTOUFFÉE

3/4 cup butter
1 cup onions, minced
1 cup green pepper, diced
6 Tbsps. flour
4 tsps. paprika
salt and pepper to taste
4 cups water
2 lbs. shrimp, peeled

Melt butter in heavy saucepan. Add onions and green pepper and sauté for 2 to 3 minutes. Add flour and stir until well mixed. Add paprika, salt, pepper, and water and simmer for 12 minutes. Add shrimp and simmer for another 15 minutes. Serve over fresh-cooked rice.

BIG EASY BROWNIES

1 cup butter
3 squares unsweetened chocolate
2 cups sugar
4 eggs, slightly beaten
1 1/2 cups sifted flour
1 tsp. baking powder
2 tsps. vanilla
1 cup chopped walnuts

Preheat oven to 350 degrees. Melt butter and chocolate over low heat. Stir in sugar and eggs and mix well. Add sifted flour and baking powder and stir. Stir in vanilla and nuts. Pour batter into greased and floured 9-by-13-inch baking pan and bake for 35 to 40 minutes.

WORKING GIRL'S
QUICK BLUEBERRY SCONES

3 cups Bisquick
2 Tbsps. sugar
1 cup fresh or frozen blueberries
1/4 cup milk
2 eggs

Preheat oven to 400 degrees. In medium bowl, combine Bisquick, sugar, and blueberries. In separate bowl, beat milk and eggs together. Add liquid mixture to dry mixture and stir until moistened but still crumbly.

On lightly floured surface, pat dough into a 9-inch circle and cut into wedges. Place on ungreased baking sheet and bake for 10 to 12 minutes or until golden. Serve immediately with butter and jam.

LAZY MORNING
BREAKFAST CASSEROLE

8 slices of bread, cubed
1 lb. ground sausage, cooked
3/4 cup cheddar cheese
1/2 cup mushrooms, sliced and sautéed
5 eggs
1 3/4 cups milk

Preheat oven to 350 degrees. Place cubed bread in casserole dish, sprinkle cooked sausage on top. Add cheddar cheese and mushrooms. In separate bowl, beat eggs and milk, then pour over top. Let stand for 5 minutes, then bake for 35 minutes until bubbly.